ONLY THE NEGATIVES

ONLY YOU, # 3

ELLE THORPE

WWW.ELLETHORPE.COM

Only the Negatives by Elle Thorpe
(Only You, #3)
Copyright © 2018 by Elle Thorpe
All rights reserved
No part of this book may be reproduced in any form or by any electronic or mechanical means, including information storage and retrieval systems, without written permission from the author, except for the use of brief quotations in a book review.

❀ Created with Vellum

For Felicity and Heidi. May you be as strong and independent as Gemma is.

1

GEMMA

The open sores on my hands left a trail of bright red blood as I dabbed them gingerly on my jeans and cursed myself for not grabbing my gloves. A rookie mistake I hadn't made in years. But I also hadn't expected to have to push myself thirty kilometres along broken roads to the hospital where my father might be dying.

I ignored the stinging pain in my palms and pushed my wheels again. Sweat rolled into my eyes, and my shoulders ached, but I had to get to him. Had to tell him I was sorry, and that I loved him, because if I didn't get the chance again, I'd never forgive myself.

Dirt billowed around me like a cloud and the first car I'd seen in an hour ignored my stuck-up thumb. I normally loved country living but right now I despised it. I hated that I'd had no phone reception when my mother had been leaving frantic voicemail messages on my phone, trying to tell me that my father had collapsed in the middle of one of our riding rings. I hated that I hadn't seen or heard the ambulance from the back end of the property in time to get to them before they'd gone tearing down the main road with my father on a stretcher and my mother by his side. I hated that there was no bus, or Uber, and that my wheelchair was not made for navigating these potholed roads.

My mouth was bone dry, and I was desperate for water when the rumble of a car engine sounded in the distance. Oh lord, please. A car. Any car. I lifted my head and brought one hand up to shield my eyes from the slowly sinking sun.

My stomach dropped.

Any car but that one.

I put my head down, stubbornly refusing to stick my thumb out and reasoning that it was probably only another ten kilometres, though the thought made me want to weep. Mr Ryker's rusted ute slowed anyway, and I gritted my teeth to keep my focus on the road. I didn't want to deal with him. There was nothing but bad blood between our family and the Rykers, and the old man was probably drunk. He always was by this time of the day. I needed to get to the hospital, not die in a car crash along the way.

The window rattled as it wound down. "Gemma."

I froze.

I hadn't heard that voice in four years, but there was no mistaking it. I whipped my head up, and sure enough, my gaze collided with Adam Ryker's chocolate-brown eyes. He sat behind the wheel of his father's car, with a baseball cap shoved low on his brow. He was a little older, a little more filled out than the teenager who'd once made my life a living hell, but still him all the same.

For a long moment, neither of us spoke, while my heart thumped unevenly. Then I turned away and shoved my wheels so hard they sent dirt flying. What was he doing back? He'd been gone for years. To where, I didn't know and I didn't care. I'd just liked knowing he wasn't going to ambush me on the side of the road. He was entitled to visit his father, but that didn't mean I had to have anything to do with him. He could visit, then go back to wherever it was he'd come from. Go back to blissfully being out of my life.

Boots thumped when they hit the dusty road, and a car door slammed. I pushed my chair harder, the sting of my open blisters only spurring me on faster. I choked back the sob rising in my throat. Damn him. This day was already a nightmare—him being here was just adding salt to the wound. His footsteps increased to a jog, and then he was in front of me, and I had no choice but to stop or run him over. Though the idea of mowing him down did give me a sick sense of pleasure.

"Gemma," he said again.

I suddenly hated my name.

"Stop."

"Leave me alone, Ryker. I've got somewhere I need to be."

"I can see that. Let me drive you."

I shook my head and tried to go around him, but he stepped in front of me.

I glared up at him. "Get out of my way."

"You're going to the hospital, right? I heard in town that your dad had been taken in an ambulance."

Of course he had. The gossip grapevine around small towns moved surprisingly fast considering how far apart people lived.

"Your hand is bleeding."

"No shit, Sherlock," I mumbled rudely.

He ignored me. "Please, Gemma, just get in. You must have been out here for hours to get this far. And I owe you one."

I snorted. He owed me a hell of a lot more than one. With every ounce of my being, I hated that he thought I needed his help. I didn't. I'd already made it more than halfway on my own. Admittedly, I was the worse for wear, but I knew I could make it the rest of the way.

But Ryker didn't appear to be moving, and I *was* desperate to see my father. Time alone on the side of the road gave me entirely too much time to think, and all I could think about was what a shit daughter I was.

"Fine," I gritted out, turning around and moving to the passenger side of the ute.

"Here, let me—"

He froze at the look I shot him then slowly he withdrew his hand. I opened the passenger door, grateful the ute was low to the ground, which always made transferring that bit easier. Then I hoisted myself into the seat, leant out to take the wheels off my chair, and collapsed the seat. Pulling the pieces into the dual cab, I placed them on the floor behind me.

Ryker hovered around my door looking unsure, until I slammed it in his face. That, I guess, gave him the hint that I didn't need his help. The tiniest of smiles lifted the corner of his mouth as he slid into the driver's seat. I pointedly ignored it while he put the gearstick in first and completed a U-turn on the wide road. To his credit, he didn't try to make any further conversation with me, and I stared out the passenger-side window with unseeing eyes, all too aware of how close he was. I just wanted to get to the hospital. Both to see my dad and to get the hell away from him.

Even facing away from him, he was everywhere. His scent drifted around the cab, fresh and clean compared to my dirt and sweat. And I'd swear I could feel him looking at me. The heat of his gaze on my back warmed my already too hot skin, and I wished he'd stop. I didn't need the little trip down memory lane his presence brought on. I didn't have it in me to do that right now.

The roads became paved as we travelled closer to town, and after we'd passed the two pubs and a handful of local shops on Main Street, Ryker pulled into our tiny country hospital. He stopped right at the door, though this time, he didn't try to help me. I reassembled my chair and shifted into it, banging my elbow in my haste to get out.

"Thank you," I said stiffly before I slammed the door and rolled to the entrance. I'd managed to make it through the whole car trip without looking directly at him. I was oddly proud of myself.

"You're welcome," he said quietly through the open window as the automatic doors whooshed open and admitted me into the cool interior of the hospital. They closed behind me, and a sigh of relief escaped me. With a bit of luck, it would be another four years before I had to see Adam Ryker again. Even better if I never did.

2

GEMMA

The elevator *binged* and the doors opened into the critical care waiting area, but no one seemed to notice my arrival. In the middle of the room my mother stood, pale and trembling, holding hands with my older sister, Reese. Reese lived in the city, and it took her an hour on a plane to get here, but she'd still managed to beat me. Dammit. Had I seriously been out on the road that long? Reese's boyfriend, Low, stood just behind her, and all three faced a grim-looking doctor whose stony expression made my heart sink.

"We've confirmed your husband suffered a stroke, Mrs Lawson."

Panic crushed in on my chest like a vice, and my mother let out a sob. I hadn't made it in time. I wasn't going to get to speak to my father again. I'd never get the chance to tell him I was sorry, and his last thoughts of me would be anger and disappointment. I didn't think I could bear it.

I was supposed to be the one teaching that class. He shouldn't have even been in the ring in the first place. This couldn't happen. I'd never survive it.

Reese squeezed our mother's hand, but I couldn't move. I

wanted to go to them and support them, but I was so caught up in my own swirling emotions I could barely breathe.

"Is he…" Reese trailed off tearfully.

The doctor shook his head. "He's stable. He's not a well man, but we expect he'll make a good recovery, in time. He's going to need physiotherapy and long-term care, and he may never be as able-bodied as he once was…"

The doctor droned on, but his words were eclipsed by the sudden wave of relief that washed over me. I gulped in air as my mother stepped forward, clasping the doctor's fingers with both hands, thanking him over and over again while Reese cried silent, happy tears beside them.

He was going to be okay.

I tried to calm my racing heart as Low pulled Reese into his arms and held her tight, whispering words into her ear that I couldn't hear.

I couldn't help but watch them, a streak of jealousy shooting through me. They were so lucky to have each other. What I wouldn't give to have someone to hold me like that. I'd never had that sort of connection with someone, and in that moment, I realised how much I was missing. That knowledge that someone always had your back, and loved you, even when you were at your lowest. The feeling that someone was always there to catch you when you fell. It must have been nice.

When she quieted, he tilted her face up to his and kissed her sweetly on the lips. And then he dropped down on one knee.

My eyes widened. Holy shit, was he—

"Reese," he said solemnly, from his position on the linoleum floor. He took her hand and she stared down with wide eyes.

"I don't know why it's taken me ten years to do this. I don't know what I've been waiting for. Maybe until I felt like I was worthy of being your husband. I have a ring, back home in Sydney. I was planning to do this anyway, I was just waiting for the perfect moment. But today has made me realise that perfect moments don't exist and life is short. I want to spend mine with you. I don't want to go another minute without asking you to be my wife."

"Oh my god." Reese laughed.

I glanced over at my mother, who had fresh tears pouring down her face, but now they were eclipsed by a smile that spread ear to ear.

"Reese Lawson, will you please marry me?"

Happiness lifted a tiny part of the darkness cloaking my heart when Reese nodded vigorously and dropped down on her knees as well. She threw her arms around him and kissed him so hard he rocked back. His fingers threaded through her hair as he pulled her tight to him, holding her with a touch that showed the room exactly how much he loved her.

Blinking back tears, I finally found the ability to move again and navigated to my mother's side. She looked down with surprise and teary, but happy eyes.

"I don't know what's going on." She laughed and bent to hug me. "The doctor just told us your father is going to be okay. And then Low proposed. I probably need to sit down before I fall down. I'm too old for this much drama in one day."

I couldn't agree more. I mentally added running into Adam Ryker to today's list of surprising events and frowned. He was one drama I could do without.

3

GEMMA

My eyes were heavy when the four of us eventually decided to go home and get some rest. We'd been at the hospital for hours, each of us taking turns to sit with Dad while nurses and doctors bustled around, checking machines and charts. He hadn't woken while I was in with him, but I'd cried quietly while I'd held his hand and whispered how sorry I was for letting him down.

By midnight, the nurses convinced my mother they'd call if anything changed. I let Low push my chair back onto the elevator, completely exhausted without adrenaline fuelling me. I just wanted to sleep. Mum walked slowly beside me, her shoulders hunched in, her head drooped. I knew she was worried about leaving, but she was wrecked.

"Adam?" she asked as we rounded the corner into the waiting room.

My eyes widened. Ryker, who had been sprawling on a chair, probably asleep, leapt up to greet my mother.

"Hi, Mrs Lawson. How's your husband doing?" he asked politely.

I was pretty sure my mouth was hanging open. Had he been here this entire time? Surely not.

"He's stable, for now."

"That's real good to hear. You came in the ambulance, right? I have my car here. Can I drive you all home?"

"We can just go with Reese and Low," I interjected, still flabbergasted as to why he'd stayed but unwilling to get in a car with him for the second time today.

"Actually, we don't have a car either. We caught the shuttle from the airport."

Dammit, of course they didn't have a car. There had to be some other way home, though. "We could call someone," I protested weakly, already knowing there was no one. I would have called someone earlier if there had been.

Confusion flickered in my mother's eyes. "He's staying next door, Gemma." Then she turned back to Ryker. "Thank you, Adam. That's very kind of you. Were you visiting someone? Your father wasn't admitted, was he?"

Ryker's brown eyes flicked to mine for the briefest of moments. He let her questions go unanswered, though, and we moved to the exit as a pack. Mum didn't seem to notice.

We piled into the Ryker's ute, but unlike earlier in the day, this time I sat in the backseat of the dual cab, as far away from the driver's seat as possible. I couldn't understand why he'd spent his afternoon and evening hanging around the hospital. It made no sense.

I rested my head on the window and watched trees and fields flicker by in the bright moonlight. Low and Reese monopolised the conversation, with my mother chiming in occasionally. Ryker was as quiet as I was.

When he pulled up outside our house, the others opened their doors, calling their thanks to Adam as they filed inside. I reassembled my chair slowly, giving them the chance to go ahead.

Sleep was calling me, but questions burned my tongue until I couldn't ignore them any longer.

Now that we were alone, I had to ask. "Why did you wait?"

He shrugged. "Just trying to be nice."

"I didn't ask you to."

"I know."

Before today, if anyone had told me Adam Ryker would go so far out of his way to help me, I would have laughed in their face. There had to be an ulterior motive. But in that moment, I couldn't see it. "Well, thank you. For the lift." I made my way around the front and headed for the doorway.

"See you around."

I paused and looked back over my shoulder. Ryker leant on the steering wheel, watching me through the open window. It had sounded more like a question than a goodbye. But he'd be going back to wherever it was he lived soon, and I doubted we'd run into each other again. So I just nodded and went inside the house. A moment later, Ryker's engine cranked over with a groan, and the gravel driveway crunched under his tyres as he left the property.

I crashed hard once my head finally hit the pillow, but like every other morning of my life, I woke before the sun was fully up. Pinkish light was just beginning to crack the horizon, and it reflected over the ceiling. My stomach rumbled; the packet of potato chips I'd had for dinner last night, courtesy of a vending machine, was now a long-distant memory. When I'd laid there for as long as I could stand, I decided to go get breakfast started. Mum was never up as early as Dad and me, and Reese had lived in the city too long. She was more likely to stumble down around nine. I wondered if five a.m. was too early to call the hospital.

The murmur of soft voices from the kitchen greeted me before I saw Mum and Reese, sitting in their PJs at the small, scuffed wooden table. They had their hands wrapped around mugs, and the smell of fresh coffee filled the room. Both looked over when I entered, and Mum gave me a smile, but it looked strained. Black circles lined her eyes, and I wondered if she'd slept.

"Morning," I said. "You two are up early."

"Couldn't sleep," Reese answered before taking a sip of her drink.

I poured myself a cup and joined them at the table.

"It's good we're all up early. I wanted to talk to you both anyway. Especially you, Gemma." Mum sighed and pushed her cup away. "I don't know what we're going to do about the business. I've been up all night, thinking it through. We don't know how long your father will be out of action. It could be months before he's back at work. Or…"

"Or he may never be able to come back." I supplied.

She nodded.

Reese covered Mum's hand with her own. "You don't need to worry about this stuff right now. Low and I can help financially if you need it."

Mum smiled but shook her head. "I can't let you do that. You'll need your money for your wedding. And your father would be horrified."

Reese frowned, but I knew my mother was right. Reese and Low both worked at Low's grandparents' stables and horse racing facility, and I knew they made good money. Reese was a vet, and Low was a trainer, but we couldn't just rely on them for handouts. We had to find a way to make the business work without my father around if we were going to survive in the long run.

"I'll take over," I announced. "The kids like me better anyway, and I can manage the lessons by myself."

I forced the words to sound strong and determined. My parents had always done so much for me. My mother had been my full-time carer for years, giving up any sort of life she might have once had to look after my daily needs. I'd had my accident at ten years old—and it had taken me a long time to become independent enough that I didn't need her help on a regular basis. I owed it to them to step up and take on more responsibility. If I didn't do it, who would? Reese had her own life. Mum had never really learned to ride properly and hadn't ever gotten back in the saddle after my accident. It was me or no one. I couldn't let our business fail because I'd rather be taking photos.

I swallowed down my guilt. My camera and the new lens that had only arrived yesterday morning, still lay discarded on my bedroom floor. That's where I'd been, when I'd finally got my mother's frantic voicemail message. I'd missed her calls because I'd been too busy goofing off, taking photos on the far edges of our property, and lost track of the time. Instead of helping my father with our little kids' riding class, I'd been congratulating myself over a shot of some kangaroos drinking from our dam. In hindsight, it all seemed so frivolous. He'd depended on me, and I'd let him down.

It wouldn't happen again.

Mum inclined her head. "That helps, but there's still the problem of all your father's other responsibilities. There's a lot of manual labour you aren't going to be able to take on. And I doubt I'll be able to do it all either. Your father is going to need full-time care while he recovers. That, plus the bookkeeping…I just can't see any other way around it. We need to hire someone."

I frowned. I wanted to be able to do it all. We'd modified the teaching ring and the stables to suit my needs, but there were some tasks I found difficult, and others that just weren't possible. Even with the use of my legs, there would have been too much for just me to take on. Not when I was going to be teaching every class myself. Mum was right. We needed two people out there.

"Can you afford to pay another employee?" Reese asked, worry lining her forehead. "Maybe I could take leave."

"And live apart from Low?" I asked.

"I would if I had to."

I shook my head. "Not the greatest start to your marriage. And what if Dad never recovers fully? You can't live here forever and not get paid. Plus, your lives are in the city."

We all fell into silence. There had to be a way around this.

"What about the shearers' quarters?" I said slowly, mulling over the idea as it became clearer in my head. My parents had never had sheep, so although the previous owners had created a small place for shearers to sleep, we'd never used it for its intended purpose. My mother had done it up a little, to use as a guest room since our cottage was so small. We rarely had visitors, though.

"What about it?" Mum asked.

"What if we rented it out?"

"It's just a bed and a bathroom. We'd have to let the tenant use our kitchen and laundry. We wouldn't be able to charge much for it. Not enough to cover a farm hand's wage, that's for sure."

I racked my brain. There had to be something we could do with that room that would help. "What if we didn't rent it out, but instead let someone live there for free?"

"How does that help?"

"They'd work around the farm in exchange for free room and board," I said slowly.

Mum sat up a little straighter. "Actually, that's not a bad idea. Could you get by with just a part-time farm hand out there, Gemma? You know the workload better than I do."

I nodded, already tallying a mental list of jobs that would need doing. "I'll make it work."

"And Low and I can come back more on weekends and help pick up the slack," Reese chimed in. "If you can find someone that will take the position, that is."

Reese was right. It wasn't easy to hire reliable staff out here. Most people who lived this far out worked their own properties or had businesses in town. Finding someone to take an unpaid position was going to be a challenge. But the more I thought about it, the more it seemed like the only workable solution.

I met my mother's eyes, hating the stress I saw there. I pulled my shoulders back as I addressed my sister's concern. "We'll have to. It's the only way we'll keep our heads above water."

4

GEMMA

The next week was a blur of hospital visits and long hours at work. Our students, and the parents of the younger ones, were all worried about my father and sad to hear he wouldn't be back at work for a while. Mum tried to field questions when she was home so I could concentrate on each class, but they still slowed me down. My head was a constant to-do list, and just as I thought I saw the end of it, I'd mentally add another five things. Low and Reese got stuck with the more manual work, but with their flights booked for the end of the week, I knew their help was limited. Mum was spending most of her time at the hospital, and with another small surgery booked for my father next week, she'd be gone even more.

We needed that new employee. Stat.

Reese put an ad online, and Low drove into town and put a printed copy on the local noticeboard. People still did things the old-school way out here, so that notice was just as likely to get us an employee as posting online. Some of our riding students also promised to spread the word around. But by Saturday, one week after my father had collapsed, I was getting worried. We hadn't had a single applicant for the job, and despite me reassuring everyone I'd be just fine on my own until we found someone, I wasn't all that confident. I was tired, and my body ached. In my bedroom, I'd run my hand longingly over my camera body and wondered when I'd get time to pick it up again. If this past week's intense pace was anything to go by, it wouldn't be any time soon. I missed the weight of it around my neck. And I missed my quiet evenings in my darkroom and the smell of processing chemicals. The urge to create was an ever-present itch in the back of my mind that teaching riding just didn't scratch.

Then guilt had sneaked up on me as hard as a slap in the face, and I'd forced myself to push those thoughts aside. I didn't want to be some selfish brat who couldn't see beyond her own desires when someone I loved was lucky to be alive. I'd put the camera in a cupboard and closed the door.

Out in the ring, I waved to my last students of the day as they bundled into their car, and slowly wheeled myself towards the house. I pushed my chair up the ramp and nearly rolled straight back down it when I collided with Reese, who was coming out the door at breakneck speed.

"Ow!" she cried, rubbing the spot where my foot rests had met with her shins.

"Are you okay? What's going on?"

"I was coming to find you. Did you see we have an applicant for the job?"

Excitement mixed with relief flushed through me. "Really?"

She nodded, a hint of mischief in her smile. "Yep."

My eyes narrowed. "Why are you smiling like that? Are you pranking me?"

"Of course not. I sent him out to the barn to see you. I figured you should be the one to interview him. I'm surprised you didn't see him out there. You must have just missed him."

"He's here now?"

"He applied in person."

"Shit. Okay." My mind went into overdrive. I'd never interviewed anyone before. "What should I ask him? Come with me?"

She nodded, that mischievous look on her face again. "Sure."

Ignoring her weirdness, I rolled back down the ramp, Reese close behind me. "Do we know anything about this guy?" I asked when we reached the barn door.

There was no sign of anyone, so he must have been waiting inside. Reese pushed the heavy wood, the hinges squeaking as they always did, and I added oiling them to my mental to-do list.

"I don't really, but I think you do."

"What does that mean?" I asked, but then Ryker's dark gaze met mine, and Reese's mysteriousness suddenly made sense.

He stood amongst hay bales and horse-riding tack, with his hands shoved into his pockets. His short-sleeved shirt pulled tight across his chest and shoulders in a way it never had when we'd been in high school. I wanted to stare him down, but heat crept across my cheeks. "You're the applicant?"

I swallowed hard, hating the squeakiness of my voice. No, no, no. This had to be some sort of mistake. Maybe he hadn't read the job description properly. Maybe he was lost. On a neighbouring property he'd been to hundreds of times as a kid. It could happen.

"Hi again, Adam." Reese stepped around me and offered him her hand to shake. "You know my sister, Gemma, right?"

He nodded.

Reese waited a beat, most likely giving me the opportunity to say something, but my mind was blank. Before last weekend, I hadn't seen Ryker in four years, since he'd left school when I was sixteen. I'd been happy about that. But now I'd seen him twice in the space of seven days. It was entirely too much. My palms were sweating, and my stomach churned. No. Not happening.

"This isn't going to work," I announced, trying not to care how rude it sounded.

Reese whipped her head around. "What are you talking

about?" she hissed. She turned back to Ryker and gave him a tight smile. "Sorry, Adam. Let me just speak to my sister for a moment."

She shoved my chair backwards, and I grasped wildly at the wheels to avoid smacking into a wall. Ryker's gaze lingered on me for a long moment before he nodded and moved deeper into the barn to give us some privacy. Hopefully he'd wander far enough to find the exit on the other side and just let himself out.

"I'm not working with him, Reese!"

"What? Why not? What's wrong with him? I thought I detected some weird vibe between the two of you last weekend and I just assumed that maybe there were some old romantic feelings between the two of you."

My eyes widened, and I yanked her arm so she had to lean down closer to my face. "Will you please be quiet!" I hissed. "He probably heard that!" I glanced around Reese to where Ryker was disappearing into the shadows of the barn. He hadn't turned around. But just because he hadn't reacted didn't mean he hadn't heard. "There's nothing romantic between me and Adam Ryker. Do you remember the bullying I put up with through high school?"

"Yes." Confusion wrinkled her brow.

"That was because of him! He was the one who started it!" I whisper-shouted.

I was sure by now my face had to be bright red. Anger felt like it was about to spew from my ears and pores as well as my mouth. I had so much pent-up rage within me, it had nowhere else to go.

Reese pulled back sharply. "Seriously? Him?" Her eyes narrowed, maybe remembering me crying myself to sleep every night until I'd finally confided in her. "Fucking asshole. He's got some nerve."

I relaxed at my sister's words, happy she was on my side.

But when she looked back at me, her expression had softened. "What other option do we have, though?"

"We just wait!"

"What if no one else ever applies, Gem? We both know this isn't exactly a glamorous, well-paying job. And you're exhausted after just one week. So am I. It's only going to be worse once Low and I leave. I really had no idea how much work Dad did around here."

"I'll manage," I gritted out.

Reese twisted my chair, getting down on my level so I had nowhere else to look but right into her eyes. "This isn't high school anymore. Here, you're the boss. You run the show and give the orders. Let's just interview him and see if he's even qualified."

I crossed my arms over my chest, but she was right. I did need the help. And the idea of the power shifting to me diluted my anger. I wasn't the same little girl I'd once been.

"Fine. You interview. I'll listen. But I'm not promising anything."

She kissed my cheek quickly. "Let's do it."

"Adam, we're ready for you," she called loudly.

"His name is Ryker," I told her as Reese pulled up chairs.

Ryker sat in one, his palms resting on his denim-clad thighs, his face schooled into a blank mask.

Reese glanced over at me, then back at Ryker. "Do you prefer Adam or Ryker?" she asked him politely.

"Either is fine."

"Okay then, since Gemma calls you Ryker, we'll just go with that. So why don't you—"

"Why are you here?" I interrupted, unable to stop the words. So much for letting Reese take the lead. "First last weekend, and now again today? I want a proper answer this time. Not just, 'Oh, I'm such a nice guy'. You aren't."

Reese made a choking noise beside me, but Ryker took my

insult in stride. He sat back and ran a hand through his dark hair. All the Ryker brothers were good-looking. They favoured their mother and her Maltese heritage. Ryker's skin had that permanent, year-round tan, and his teeth were always shining white in contrast. He'd grown a beard over the years he'd been gone, but it was short and neat. Barely more than stubble, really. Sexy.

The word jolted me out of my head. Where had that come from? The guy was a grade A asshole. He might be nice to look at, but his personality ruined the illusion. Definitely not sexy.

"Your ad said you were offering room and board in exchange for some farm work. I need a room."

"You don't even live in Erraville anymore."

He cocked an eyebrow, and I cursed myself for letting him know I'd kept tabs on his living arrangements.

"I moved back a few weeks ago."

"What's wrong with your dad's place?"

"I can't keep living there."

"Why not?"

"Gemma!" Reese elbowed me hard in the arm.

"What?"

"Quit being rude. He doesn't have to tell your why he can't live at home anymore."

"No, it's fine," Ryker cut in, his attention never leaving my face, even when Reese had spoken. "I lived away from home for the past four years. I'm used to being on my own."

"Your dad cramping your style with the ladies?" I asked snidely.

Reese sighed. I knew I was acting like a brat but I couldn't seem to stop.

Ryker paused before blowing out a long breath. "Look, Gemma. I know there's bad blood between us. But I work hard, and you know I have the experience to do whatever needs doing around here. Just give me a chance."

Reese looked over at me as I sat back and folded my arms

across my chest.

"Your call," she said quietly.

Emotions warred within me. I didn't want to say yes. I didn't want to look at his beautiful, jerk face every day. He was a constant reminder of a time I'd been happy to forget.

"If it helps, I work two other jobs. So if I'm not working around here, it's unlikely you'll even see me."

It didn't help. I knew I'd still lie awake at night, knowing he was just metres away. I knew I'd be constantly stressing that I might bump into him.

"Where else are you working?" Reese asked. "Do you have time for this job if you're working elsewhere?"

He turned to her for the first time since we'd started the interview. "I do fifteen hours a week at Erraville Auto Repair, and I do a couple of nights a week at the Blue Gum Pub in town. But I like farm work and I need to keep busy. I'll have more than enough time to do a few hours a day here."

Reese seemed satisfied by that response, which irked me. But apart from the fact I knew he was a jerk, I had no reason not to hire him.

"Fine," I huffed. "But on a trial basis. Your room is down here, kitchen and laundry are both up in the main house. You're welcome to use them, just clean up after yourself."

A small smile lifted the corner of his mouth, and my breath caught. Damn him, he looked even more handsome when he smiled. Shame about his cold, black, backstabbing heart.

Not able to tolerate sitting there with him a moment longer, I pushed my chair backwards and spun it so I was facing the door. "You can move in tonight, or tomorrow. Whatever. I'll leave a list of things that need doing on the chalkboard in the office, so you'll be good to go on Monday morning. I'm sure you'll manage to find whatever you need." I hoped so anyway, because the less I saw of him, the better.

"Thank you," he said quietly.

Without bothering to wait for Reese, I wheeled to the door. I was annoyed with her for making me hire him in the first place. Lucky her. She got to go back to the city and didn't have to put up with Adam bloody Ryker.

"Gemma?"

I paused but didn't look back. He must have realised that was the best he was going to get, because he only waited a moment then continued. "I'm not the same kid I used to be, you know."

I shook my head. "Well, neither am I."

EIGHT YEARS EARLIER—LORRINGTON Public High School

Crowds of teenagers streamed past my wheelchair, chatting happily and yelling to each other across the large open foyer that doubled as a meeting spot for students. A football whizzed by my head, and I flinched before a guy across the room caught it with a cheer. Everybody seemed to know what they were doing and where they were going. Everyone but me. Some of the crowd looked younger and were probably in my grade, but it was the first day of high school—how did they already walk around with so much confidence?

I pushed my chair slowly, moving closer to the wall, when I found a quieter hallway to turn down. Then I pulled my school map out of my bag and unfolded it across my lap. Heat burned my cheeks, and I prayed no one would notice the new girl with no idea what she was doing. Not for the first time today, I wished Rach was here and not at that stupid boarding school in Sydney. Having my best friend beside me on my first day would have made this all so much better. We would have laughed over getting lost and not being able to read our timetables. Instead, I was lonely and embarrassed. Our primary school in Erraville was tiny compared to the endless maze of hallways and classrooms that was the high school.

A bell pierced the air, and panic made me breathless. I was going to be late. I *hated* being late. Everyone would stare at me. If I ever found my classroom, that was.

Chatter about summer holidays and parties washed over me as passing students caught up after a six-week break, and I frantically scoured my map for F block. I bit back a groan at the worst map ever. The labelling was so small and smudged I couldn't make out any of the words. Sighing, I turned back in the direction I'd come from. I'd have to be a complete loser and find a teacher to help. Exactly the thing I'd been hoping to avoid.

Back in the main hall, I stopped when I glimpsed our neighbour's sons, Adam and Logan, standing in the middle of a large group of boys. Logan and I had never really been friends, probably because he was a few years older, but he'd always been nice to me. He had kind eyes and a gentle nature, and he made people feel good just by being in his presence.

Adam was only a year older than I was. Relief at seeing a familiar face in the crowd allowed me to take my first deep breath all morning. I hadn't seen Adam much over the past year, since he'd started high school, leaving me behind, and I'd missed sitting with him on the bus home each afternoon. His dad always had him and his brothers working in their fields after school, leaving us no time to hang out, and we'd drifted apart. I wheeled over to them, trying to catch his eye so I wouldn't have to draw any further attention to myself by calling him. It was already bad enough being the new kid in a wheelchair.

As I neared the group, though, a sense of unease washed over me. Something was going on, but it was hard to see through the crowd with my lower vantage point. The air swirled with hyped-up testosterone and the boys jostled and yelled over the top of each other, an argument drifting back to me in broken sentences.

A gap in the wall of bodies emerged, and a tiny cry escaped my mouth, shock punching me in the gut. The biggest boy in the group had Logan by the jaw. No. He wasn't a boy. Boys weren't built like him. He was a man, even if he couldn't be any older than seventeen. I couldn't believe that Logan, of all people, was involved in a fight. It just didn't compute with his kind disposition. This had to be some sort of mistake.

Logan's face gave nothing away, but his eye was already blackened and swollen. The noise from the other boys rose as a low chant took hold. "Fight. Fight. Fight."

My heart thumped. I wasn't misreading the situation.

Adam's panicked gaze darted between his brother and the other guy, then landed on me just as I tried to back away. Our eyes locked, and for a moment, indecision flickered before his expression morphed to steel. He turned to the big guy who was right in Logan's face and shoved him hard in the shoulder. The big guy instantly lost interest in Logan, turning his glare on the younger brother. I shrank back from the aggressiveness rolling off him, but Adam just smirked.

Then he pointed directly at me.

"Looks like your date's here, York," he scoffed.

The older guy, York, pushed him back. "What the fuck did you say, Ryker?" he snarled, following Ryker's outstretched hand to where I was sitting. His gaze ran over me, freezing me to the spot. He took a few steps closer.

I looked helplessly at Adam, unable to comprehend what had just happened.

"I'm sorry," he mouthed before lowering his eyes.

"My date, huh? I suppose she is the perfect height to suck my dick." He jerked his hips back and forth, thrusting into the air.

The boys around him burst into laughter, a few of them mimicking his actions.

I couldn't help the gasp that escaped my lips at their crude language. Hot tears burned the backs of my eyes, and I searched for some smart comeback that would put them in their place. But nothing came, and worse, a sob crept up my throat.

York took another step toward me, but it was Adam who

spoke again, drawing York's attention back to him. He leant in to speak into York's ear. I couldn't make out every word he said, but the sob in my throat doubled in size at the one I did hear.

Lame.

He may as well have called me a cripple.

I knew I was probably staring at Adam with a pathetic, hurt, puppy-dog stare, but I couldn't help it. Why was he doing this? Had he forgotten all the times we'd sat on the bus together, sharing Doritos and listening to songs on his iPod? Shame and embarrassment roared through me like a wildfire, and I tried to make my hands coordinated enough to work my chair. But I was all thumbs, fumbling to keep my bag from slipping from my lap and get the wheels going. I was trapped by my own hurt and outrage. York's big body cast a shadow over me, and I found Ryker's eyes through the crowd that jeered and taunted me. Nothing about him had physically changed, but suddenly, he was a stranger I didn't recognise.

"Your name is Lawson, right? Maybe we'll call you Lame Lawson, then? You here to suck my dick, cripple?" He laughed, the cruelty of his words twisting his mouth.

Finally gaining control, I spun around and pushed my wheels hard. The lump in my throat was rising, and I had to get out of there before I cried in front of them.

To my relief, they let me go.

"See you around, Lame Lawson."

Taunts and laughter followed me, but I hightailed it down the hall and locked myself in a bathroom. My skin crawled, remembering the way York had looked at me, remembering his disgusting comments and his leers. And Adam Ryker was no better. We were supposed to be friends. Years of childhood memories, all of them with him by my side, flashed through my head. I finally gave in, letting the sob bubble up and burst from my chest.

5

RYKER

The barn door slammed behind Gemma, causing one of the horses to let out a startled neigh. I sensed Reese's gaze resting heavily on me, and I lifted my head to meet it. Her eyes narrowed as she took four steps to stand in front of me. I was taller than her, but the steel in her look made me feel small. Not that I didn't deserve it.

"You know if we had any other option right now, I'd never have encouraged her to give you the job. You're an asshole for what you did to her in high school. You made her life a living hell."

She was right. The names the kids had called Gemma over the years, the constant taunts and jabs every time we passed her in the hall, had all been my fault. I was worse than an asshole. I was a coward.

"I know."

Reese peered at me with big brown eyes that looked identical to Gemma's. "Is that all you have to say for yourself?"

I glanced down at my hands again. What was the point of explaining? It had been eight years since that day in the hallway, four since I'd last seen Gemma. Nothing I said or did now could take away that day or the days after it.

So I said nothing.

Reese waited in silence for a long moment then she huffed out a breath, the sound conveying every ounce of disgust she held for me. She dropped a key onto the chair she'd been sitting on and strode to the doorway where she paused. "Your room is back through those doors and to the right. There's the key."

I nodded and picked it up, but I could feel her gaze still on me.

"I really hope what you said about not being the same kid is true, Ryker. Don't make her regret giving you a chance, even though you don't deserve it."

"I just want somewhere to live. And your dad is a good man. I want to help."

Reese nodded curtly. "Don't mind me if I don't believe it until I see it. But know this. You hurt my sister again, and she won't need me sticking up for her. All the shit you put her through made her strong. She's plenty capable of holding her own."

She turned on her heel and left before I could say a word.

I picked up the key, turning the small piece of brassy metal over in my hand, and followed her out of the barn. I walked around to the front of the house where I'd left my Mustang and slid into the driver's seat. For a long time, I didn't move, letting the silence in the car's interior wash over me, staring with unseeing eyes through the windscreen. Then I slammed the heel of my hand into the steering wheel. "Fuck!"

I folded my arms and rested my head on them. The interview had not gone as I'd hoped. What had I been thinking? Of course she wouldn't want me here. I'd rather live with my father for the rest of my life than make her uncomfortable in her own home. The expression on her face when she'd seen it was me waiting to be interviewed… Yet another shining example of the bad choices I seemed to make over and over.

But I hadn't been lying when I'd said I wanted to help. The job offer had seemed too perfect to be true. It'd been years since the catastrophe with Gemma and me. I'd lived my life, but the things I'd done and said to her...they stuck with me. Every now and then, when my mind hadn't been occupied by friends or work, my guilt gnawed away at me like a fuckin' sewer rat. I'd spent four years pushing that guilt down, trying to pretend it was just stupid teenage stuff, that it didn't matter, but I always knew it was more than that. If it hadn't been a big deal, I could have forgotten about it. But I never did. I'd lie awake at night thinking about it. About her. About long, dark hair and soulful brown eyes, full of hurt and confusion. When I'd moved back to Erraville, the insomnia had gotten worse, knowing she was just a few kilometres away. And when I did sleep, her face and the things I'd said played over in my dreams, the memories weighing me down until I avoided sleeping at all.

I had to make things right with her. I needed to prove I wasn't that same, stupid, scared kid I'd once been. Applying for the job at her property seemed like the ideal way to get to spend more time with her, to make her see that I was truly sorry.

Shit. I should have found another way. I raked my fingers through my hair then shoved my baseball cap back on my head. I couldn't just quit. Not after Reese had said I was their only option. I'd give her space. That was all I could do now. I'd work my ass off, and maybe over time she'd let me explain.

I threaded the key onto my chain, then started the car. The roar of the engine rumbled through me, soothing and familiar, and a little of the tension slid off my shoulders.

I pulled out of the Lawsons' driveway and onto the potholed street, navigating through the tree-lined roads until I reached the Blue Gum. The large parking lot was still relatively empty, since it was barely five p.m., but working here the last few weeks had taught me that within an hour, the place would be bustling. I moved through the bar area and grabbed my apron from the kitchen before I found Mike behind the bar.

He glanced over from restocking the liquor shelf. "You're early."

I shrugged. "Had nothing better to do."

"I'm not payin' you for this, you know."

"Didn't ask you to."

Mike shook his head and grinned. "You work more than anyone I know."

"You must know some bloody lazy people then."

He chuckled as he passed me a case of beer to unpack. "If you aren't here or at the mechanics, you're working at your pop's place."

I picked up a cloth and started wiping water spots off glasses. "Yeah, well, I won't be doing that no more."

"What does that mean?"

"I'm moving out of my dad's place. Can't stand it there."

He nodded. "Don't blame ya, kid. Your old man isn't the easiest guy to get along with."

That was one way of putting it. But I didn't want to talk about my dad or my living arrangements. I just wanted to work.

Patrons started rolling in around six. Most still wore dirt-covered work clothes, despite the fact it was Saturday. Not too many folks round here had the luxury of weekends. Ninety percent of Erraville's population were self-employed farmers, so if they didn't work, their families didn't eat. But you wouldn't hear too many of them complaining. Most of them had been born into this life and knew no different.

From the kitchen, Jilly, our cook, was making short work of orders that came in, and Mike and I delivered plates of schnitzels and chips and steaks to tables every time she hit her little service bell. In between we poured drinks and spent time shooting the shit with the regulars over the jukebox playing eighties rock in the corner of the room.

I was nodding along, vaguely listening while Jim Daley, one of our regulars, groaned about his broken tractor when the door opened, letting in a gust of cold air. Mrs Lawson and Reese stood in the doorway, taking off their jackets as they looked around them. Reese's boyfriend entered behind them and pulled off his baseball cap. I held my breath, and when they moved aside to an empty table, my gaze landed on Gemma who had entered last. Our eyes met for a brief moment before she whipped her head around to follow her family. Damn Erraville for being so small. So much for giving her space. We were the only place around to eat, unless you wanted to risk a case of food poisoning at the only other pub in the area. The Cedar Tree Hotel was dirty and dingy compared to the Blue Gum, its clientele rough and rude. It wasn't the sort of place you took your family for a Saturday night meal.

"You gonna go take their order, kid?" Mike asked, nodding in the direction of the Lawson's table.

"Can you?"

Mike looked as if he were going to argue. As the owner, he'd earned the right to get out of the grunt jobs. I always took the orders, unless we were swamped.

"Please."

He gave me a shrewd look, then picked up an order pad and a pen and greeted the Lawsons with his booming voice. I went back to half listening to Jim's troubles. He was already on his way to drunk, though, and his woes didn't keep my attention long. As the night progressed, my gaze found Gemma's table more often than it should have. She'd ordered white wine, which I'd poured carefully but let Mike carry to their table. She ate steak with chips, and by the bottom of her second glass, she was talking animatedly with her sister. Her laugh floated across the room, despite the music, and her smile was wide, her shoulders relaxed. Long dark hair flowed over her shoulder, sleek and smooth, and her eyes were just a touch shiny from the alcohol.

It had been so long since I'd seen this Gemma, and I couldn't keep my eyes off her. Not since we were kids, when she'd run through the fields of our property, calling my name to come play.

Even after her fall, she'd still been that carefree girl who smiled and laughed all the time. It was that day at school that had changed her. I had stolen her smiles, her lightness, and her laughter. A life-changing accident hadn't broken her spirit. But my words had. She seemed happier now, though I doubted she would ever again be the free-spirited kid I remembered playing hide and seek with. But after watching her retreat into herself all through high school, seeing her laugh now made my chest swell with feelings I'd tried to forget. She was fucking beautiful when she smiled.

Her eyes met mine, as if she'd felt me watching her, and this time, neither of us looked away. The moment drew out, and I thought I saw beneath the old hurt and anger that lingered there. I saw the girl she used to be, mixed in with the teenager I'd studied all through high school and the woman I'd met on the side of the road last week. Something stirred in my chest.

A loud belch to my right broke the moment, and Gemma wrinkled her nose, turning back to her sister. I sighed and moved to stand in front of the offending customer who'd slumped himself at the bar.

"Whiskey," he slurred, his bloodshot eyes barely focussing on me.

"Why bother, Earl? Mike's going to boot you out the minute he sees you. You know you're barred."

His brow furrowed. "Fuck Mike. Get me a drink."

I rolled my eyes and poured a whiskey over ice and pushed it across the bar top, not caring that half of it sloshed over the edge of the glass. He'd had more than enough anyway. He tossed it back then slammed the glass down in front of me. "Another."

"Where's your keys?"

"Ain't none of your business, boy," he growled. "Another."

Like fuck. I wasn't giving him anymore and I sure as hell wasn't letting him drive anywhere in the state he was in. It'd take him a week to sleep off his efforts, judging by the alcohol fumes I could practically see radiating from him. I walked around the bar to stand behind him and patted down the sides of his body like a cop would, looking for his keys. The fact it took him a minute to react told me exactly how drunk he was.

"Get off," the drunk old bastard yelled, no doubt drawing the attention of the entire bar behind me.

I was grateful I didn't have to see their horrified stares. This was why Mike had barred him from the Blue Gum. Earl had made one scene too many. And here he was, back at it again.

I grasped the keys in his pocket, pulling them out triumphantly. "You can have them back tomorrow."

Earl fumbled on his bar stool, trying to turn around to stop me, but he was too uncoordinated. "You little prick!" he bellowed, trying to snatch them from my hand before giving up and throwing his elbow backwards.

It took me by surprise and caught me in the gut. I grunted, doubling over as the air whooshed out of me, leaving a sharp pain in its absence.

I coughed as I straightened, only to be met with a right hook that knocked my head back and made me see stars. *Fuck.*

I blinked rapidly, trying to clear my eyes and registered gasps from shocked onlookers around me. Rage simmered deep inside me, the same rage I'd been carrying around for years, never letting it free because I wasn't 'that sort of guy'. Pocketing the keys, I took two steps towards him and saw the moment when his cockiness turned to fear. He might have got a lucky punch in, but that was all it had been. He was too old, too slow, and too drunk for more. Even if he had been a prize-winning boxer once upon a time.

I stormed the space between us, fisting my fingers in his shirt and getting in his face. His putrid breath made me cringe as it filled the tiny space between us, but I refused to let him go. "Do you think I'm still that same little boy?" I hissed under my breath, my rage bubbling to the surface. "The same little boy you used to beat the crap out of?" I shoved him toward the exit before I did something I wouldn't be proud of tomorrow. "I'm not." I spat the words at him as if they tasted bad.

"Ryker! What the fuck?" Mike bellowed, storming back into the main room, his face like thunder. I was probably about to get fired. Then his gaze settled on Earl, and his eyes narrowed. "Ryker, get your fucking drunk old man out of here, then get back to work."

I nodded and stepped towards the man I'd once called Dad, but he held his hands up in surrender. "Yeah, yeah, I'm fuckin' goin', ain't I?" he swore, stumbling towards the exit.

I followed, just to make sure he really went.

I felt Gemma's shocked gaze and the pain in my eye as it began to swell shut. But there wasn't anything I could do about either one.

6

GEMMA

The morning after the Ryker family showdown dawned dark and dreary. The sky matched my mood, but rain out here was welcome, so I couldn't stay annoyed for long. Rain was life in Erraville. Quite literally for many people. Less so for us, because we didn't have crops or large stock numbers, but we still felt the effects of droughts. Extra feed had to be brought in for the horses, water had to be bought for the tanks. The expenses added up.

Through my bedroom window, movement on the path to the stables caught my eye. A white, long-sleeved shirt stretched firmly across broad shoulders, and a narrow waist led to denim-clad thighs. I fought hard not to focus on his ass as he walked away from a shiny blue car with white racing stripes along the bonnet. Though an older model, it looked out of place, sitting next to my father's mustard-coloured four-wheel drive which was covered in mud and probably hadn't been washed in six months. Ryker's car looked like he polished it nightly.

"Ugh," I huffed. Childishly, I yanked the blinds closed so I wouldn't have to see him. Dealing with Adam Ryker at six a.m. and before coffee would push even a saint's patience. I flopped back onto my mattress and pulled a pillow over my head, hoping I would fall back to sleep. But scenes from last night played over and over again in my head. Things I should have said. Things I still wanted to say. Something that felt an awful lot like sympathy trickled through my reserves, and I wasn't sure I liked it. The scene his dad had made had been hard to watch, but I didn't want to feel sorry for Ryker. I was still too hurt and confused over the scene he had caused years ago. I couldn't just see him and be 'over it' like he seemed to hope I was.

My door crashed open, and Reese came bounding in. She launched herself onto my bed, making the mattress bounce, and narrowly avoiding landing straight on top of me. She tugged the blanket off me and tucked it around herself.

"Hey!" I snatched it back when the chilly air met my warm skin. Autumn days here were mostly pleasant, but the mornings and evenings were cool, and our old farmhouse was drafty.

"We're leaving today."

"I know," I replied, trying to disguise my disappointment. Reese would probably ring me the minute she got back to Sydney, and we'd talk for an hour. But nothing was as good as having her here in person.

"Mum is driving us out to the airport soon. Are you going to come wave us off?"

I shook my head and pulled the blanket up closer to my chin. "I can't. I've got a class this morning."

Reese pouted. "Well, then I guess I have to ask you now."

I shifted on the mattress so we were facing each other.

She grinned at me, her big brown eyes shining. "Do you want to be my Maid of Honour?"

Happiness spread through me. I'd had an inkling she might ask, of course. But hearing the words from her mouth, and the thought of being by her side on one of the most important days of her life, made my heart swell. There might have been ten years between us, but ever since my accident, she'd been more than just my sister. She was my best friend. "Of course I do, you dope! As if you even had to ask." But then I frowned, a disturbing thought crossing my mind. "You aren't going to make me wear a hideous dress, are you?"

She pushed my shoulder. "Please. I'm not even sure *I* want to wear a dress. I'm hardly about to make you wear something you don't like. Get a nice dress, or a skirt and top. Or a pair of jeans for all I care."

Relief coursed through me. Both my sister and I were no fans of dresses, but I'd still put money on her choosing something traditional. And I was sure I could find a nice cocktail dress in Lorrington that wouldn't be too awful. "Who else are you having in your bridal party?"

"Just you and Bianca. You remember her?"

I nodded. Bianca had been my sister's best friend for years. She'd never visited the farm, but I'd met her a few times when I'd stayed with Reese and Low in the city. "Who is Low having?"

"Jamison and Riley. He'll ask Jamison to be his best man, so he will be your partner." She frowned. "Though that leaves Bianca and Riley together, which might be a problem."

"Why?"

"They used to date."

"It didn't end well, I'm assuming?"

Reese scoffed. "That's the understatement of the century. They can't stand each other. I can't even remember the last time they were in the same room without a screaming match breaking out."

I rolled onto my back, and Reese did the same thing.

"It's your wedding. I'm sure they'll manage."

"About as well as you're managing having the person you hate around?" Reese asked, her voice soft.

I glanced over at her. "Has he already moved in? I just looked through the window, and he's out there."

She tucked a strand of hair behind my ear. "I don't know. Don't let him get to you."

"He's not," I huffed.

Reese threw back the covers and jumped up. "Good. Get up then. Low's already got breakfast cooked."

She padded across the room in her bare feet, closing the door behind her. I transferred to my chair, put on some clothes, and chanced another glance out the window. Ryker had rolled his shirt sleeves to his elbows, exposing tanned forearms. His biceps bulged beneath his shirt as he hefted a box from his car.

Goddammit.

The kitchen was empty when I got there but smelled deliciously of bacon. I stole a crispy-looking piece from a plate while Mum, Reese, and Low thundered down the stairs. Low pulled their suitcases along behind him, placing them by the front door before he came to sit down.

"You're up," he said, snagging himself a piece of toast. "I thought you might have been sick when I beat you into the kitchen this morning."

"I'm fine." Fine as long as I didn't have to see Ryker, anyway.

Reese set her phone down on the kitchen table and piled a plate high with bacon, toast, and fried mushrooms. My sister was an awful cook, but Low had skills. We all chewed in appreciative silence, until Reese's email alert cut through the quiet. She picked the phone up, letting out an excited squeal when she read the message.

I raised an eyebrow. "What's got you all excited?"

She shrugged casually, but I could see she was bursting out of her skin with excitement. "Did I mention we're getting married in July?"

I dropped my fork, and it clattered on the porcelain plate. "What! That's two months from now!"

Low nudged her, laughing at my shock. "Did she tell you we also want to get married here?"

"No."

"It's short notice. I probably should have made it later in the year, but with everything happening with Dad's health, I just…"

I nodded. "I get it. You don't want to wait." Neither of us voiced what we were probably both thinking. What if Dad's health got worse instead of better? We just didn't know what was going to happen.

"Did you know about this?" I asked Mum. "It's so soon."

She shrugged. She didn't look bothered at all. In fact, she looked pleased. I could practically see the images of grandbabies floating in her eyes. Meanwhile, I'd already mentally added fifty new things to my ever-increasing to-do list.

"Don't stress. We're going to organise everything from Sydney. You won't have to do a thing," Reese said with a smile, most likely sensing my rising stress levels.

I frowned. "That's not what I meant. I want to help. I'm your bridesmaid, not to mention your sister. I was just surprised. That's all." I always thought of Reese as my friend, and equal, but sometimes I still had the sneaking suspicion she babied me. It was probably inevitable with such a big age gap between us, but I didn't like to encourage it. I knew she didn't mean anything by it, if she was even aware of it.

"That's good, because I realised yesterday I'm going to have to hire someone local to make a wedding cake for us. There's no way I can get one from Sydney to Erraville in one piece."

I imagined Reese driving the twelve hours with a fancy, three-tier wedding cake resting on Low's lap as he sat in the passenger seat. Yeah. That wasn't going to work. "You want me to find someone?"

"I already did. That was them on my email. They have a shop in Lorrington and they do some amazing work if their website is anything to go by. They're booked solid for months, but they had a cancellation this afternoon." She turned her puppy-dog eyes on me. "We'll already be back in Sydney. Could you go for me?

Please? I'll organise the design with them over email, but could you go do the taste test and pick a flavour?"

"No worries. Eating cake for the afternoon doesn't sound like much of a hardship, and I'm free after this morning's class." I conveniently ignored the equipment I'd planned to clean and the lesson plans that needed to be written and swivelled to look at Mum. "If you're free to drive?"

But Mum was shaking her head. "I've got to take these two to the airport, and then I need to go up to the hospital. There's a specialist from the city coming out to see your father, and I need to be there to speak to him."

"Oh," Reese said, her face falling. Then added quickly. "No, Mum. Of course you need to be there. We'll find someone else. I'll cancel."

Reese smiled, but I could tell she was disappointed.

Low rubbed her back between her shoulder blades, obviously picking up on it as well. "I promise, no one will even look at the cake once you're in the room," he whispered, but it was loud enough for me to hear.

Something inside me twisted as my envy grew. He knew her so well. He knew the second something bothered her, even small things like cake, and he knew just the right thing to say to make it better. I'd never had anything like that. She leant in and kissed him lightly on the mouth.

I wanted them to have their dream wedding, and that included a top-notch cake. But it wasn't like I had the luxury of calling an Uber. The only bus that ran back and forth was the school bus, but since it was Sunday, I couldn't hitch a ride with them. I mulled over my options and realised I only had one. Shit. "I'll ask Ryker to drive me," I declared before I could think the terrible idea through too thoroughly.

Three pairs of eyes turned to stare at me, and I immediately wondered if I could take it back. I wanted to help my sister, but even if Ryker agreed, that would mean sitting in a car for two hours at a time with him. The thought of being in a confined space with him did not make me jump for joy.

"Really?"

I swallowed hard. *No.* "Of course. I don't want to be eating dry sponge cake made by old Mrs Manning at your wedding. Do you?"

"No, but…"

"But what?"

"You spent all of last night pointedly ignoring him."

Mum smiled carefully at me. "We've all been too afraid to even speak about what happened with him. We didn't want to upset you."

"Why would it upset me?" As soon as I heard the words, I realised the ridiculousness in it. "Yeah, yeah. So I'm touchy about him."

"It's understandable," Mum said, rubbing my arm.

I knew she was trying to reassure me, but all it did was make me feel like she was making excuses for my bratty behaviour. I didn't like it.

"I'll ask him about Lorrington."

Reese leant over and kissed my cheek. "Best little sister ever."

"Yeah, yeah. Whatever," I grumbled. My heart was already thumping over asking Ryker to take me somewhere. Not for the first time, I cursed the fact I couldn't drive. Why did a modified vehicle have to be so damn expensive?

Reese glanced at the clock on the wall. "We need to go or we'll miss our flight."

Mum pushed her chair back and took one last gulp of her coffee. "If you do go into Lorrington this afternoon, Gem, grab yourself something for dinner. I'm going to eat at the hospital with your father, and there isn't much here in the way of groceries."

Reese shoved one last piece of bacon in her mouth and

hugged me. "Thank you again. I'll call you when we get back to Sydney."

"And I'll answer. If I'm not in a sugar coma." I trailed them to the front of the house, watching while they climbed into Mum's van.

They paused at the top of the driveway to allow Ryker, in his obnoxious shiny car, to pull in. He must have done another run to his dad's house to pick up more of his belongings. Through the now somewhat dusty windshield, I could see he had the passenger side seat filled with more boxes and a pile of clothes. So much for him never being around. It was barely eight a.m., and I'd already seen him twice this morning.

THE MORNING WAS NOT TURNING out to be a good one. Reese and Low leaving, then Ryker moving in had been distracting enough that I'd completely forgotten today's lesson was in the big training ring. All week, I'd managed to avoid it, moving all my classes into the smaller ring we usually only used for private lessons. But there was no avoiding it today. Today's class was a large one. I just wouldn't be able to fit them all into the smaller space safely.

Students led their horses in, and family members who had come to watch the lesson took seats on the bench chairs. In a moment, all of them would look to me. They'd wait for me to enter the ring and take my usual position in the centre of it. But this week, my father wouldn't be next to me. This was our regular Sunday morning class. The one we'd taught together for years, except last week, I'd lost track of time, messing around with my new camera lens and leaving him to teach it alone.

I forced myself into the fenced-off area, focusing on the dirt. Was that where he'd fallen? There, in the centre, near that tufty patch of grass? Had he lain there, in pain, scared and alone while someone called an ambulance? My throat tightened.

I lifted my gaze and looked around at the fifteen students and their horses surrounding me. They were all silent. Waiting. Watching. Someone closed the gate, and my breath hitched, the space suddenly becoming claustrophobic, silent judgement crushing in on me. I should have been here last week. I was the selfish, uncaring daughter who shirked her responsibilities. They all knew it. They knew I wasn't cut out to run this business. That my heart wasn't in it.

My gaze flashed from person to person, the silence lingering, only the soft noises of the horses breaking the stillness until I felt like screaming.

"Gemma, there's a call for you."

I spun around to watch Ryker walk across the ring. His gaze met mine, an unreadable expression on his face. "It's a supplier. I can take today's lesson for you, if you like?"

Relief fuelled me even as I wondered if he knew how to ride. He'd never been much good when we were kids, but this ring was the last place I wanted to be, and I was grateful for any excuse to leave it. He gave me a small nod then called out an introduction to the waiting students and began a warm-up exercise. I hurried to the gate, letting myself out and escaped to the safety of the darkened barn where I sucked in deep breaths, trying to calm my racing heart.

Shit. I'd been on the verge of a panic attack. My parents were depending on me to keep this business running. I needed to get it together.

I edged into the office I shared with my father and looked at the phone, confused by it still sitting on the receiver. We only had one land line, it wasn't like Ryker could have put the supplier on hold.

In that moment, I realised it was Sunday. Why would a

supplier be calling at nine a.m. on a Sunday morning? Like a light bulb going off, the answer was clear. They wouldn't.

I wheeled back to the edge of the barn door and watched from the shadows while Ryker ran the class. I tried to talk myself into going back out there, but my hands stubbornly refused to push the wheels. So instead, I hid in the office until I heard all the students leave.

"You okay?" Ryker asked from behind me, his voice quiet.

I turned around slowly to face him, straightening my shoulders. "I'm fine. You didn't need to do that."

He shoved his hands into his pockets and nodded once before he edged towards his room.

"Thank you, though," I called after him.

He stopped and looked back at me. "You might need to undo everything I taught today. I haven't ridden in years. If they have their saddles on backwards next week, that's on me."

A tiny smile pulled at the corner of my mouth. "I don't normally act that unprofessionally. I just…"

"I know. I get it."

Oddly, although it had been years since we'd really known each other, in that moment, I believed him. But then I reminded myself that I'd once before thought I knew him, and he'd turned out to be someone completely different. He went to leave again, and it killed me to stop him. But I'd promised Reese and I couldn't let her down. I'd already let my father down today, even if he didn't know it. "Ryker, wait. I…um, I need a favour," I forced the words through my lips, my jaw aching from tension.

He didn't say anything, just waited patiently for me to continue.

"Could you give me a ride into Lorrington this afternoon? Please."

His expression changed to one of surprise, but he tried to cover it quickly. "Lorrington?"

"Yeah, I know it's a bit of a drive, so don't feel oblig—"

He shook his head. "I can see it was hard for you to ask, so it must be important." He grabbed his jacket from the end of his neatly made bed and a set of keys from the top of the old dresser drawers. "Let's go."

Well, that was easier than expected. "Wait, wait, I need to get out of my riding gear. Give me fifteen minutes?"

He shrugged his jacket on and shoved his wallet in his pocket. "Take as long as you need. I'll meet you in the car."

I nodded. "Thank you."

Pushing my wheels hard, I raced back up to the house and got changed in record time. I might not have liked the man, but I wasn't so rude that I'd keep him waiting. He was doing me a favour, after all. It wasn't like we'd have to talk during the trip.

7

GEMMA

Ryker's flashy Mustang may not have been very practical for farm life, but it was easy to get into, and the leather seats were smooth and cool. He sat quietly, watching me, and once I was in, he started up the engine which gave an obnoxiously loud roar. It settled into a low drone, though, and we crunched over dry grass and the gravel of the driveway before turning onto the road. We cruised through the handful of streets that made up the Erraville town centre then took the single road that led out of town. Gum trees, kangaroos, and small towns flashed by my window as the uncomfortable tension and silence between Ryker and I drew out.

After half an hour with only the engine and Ryker's old Pearl Jam album for background noise, the silence between us got to me. I glanced over at him, my heart stopping for a brief moment when my gaze collided with his. We both whipped our heads forward and stared out the front windshield.

"Gemma." My name came out of his mouth sounding croaky, and he cleared his throat, starting again. "I know we're past the point of an apology meaning anything to you. But can I at least try to explain?"

My gut reaction was to tell him not to bother. He was right. His apologies meant nothing. But I was also beginning to despise the awkward silence between us and the way it made me feel. I wasn't this catty, childish person who seemed to come out when he was around. We still had a lot of time left, stuck together in this car. And I couldn't just ignore him forever if he was going to live on our property and work for us. Some sort of truce had to be called.

Beyond that, there was a little part of me that still really wanted to know why he'd done it. He'd tried apologising before, back when we were in school, but never had he offered to explain. We'd been friends as kids, then suddenly he'd thrown me to the wolves. The wolves being Sam York and his crew. Despite all the years that had passed, I still wanted to know why.

I shrugged, and I guess he took that as a yes, because from the corner of my eye, I saw him nod. He paused for a long moment, debating over his words.

"You know my old man is a drunk, right?"

I glanced over at him. "The whole town knows that, Ryker."

He grimaced, and I continued, "What has that got to do with you and me?"

"The night before that day at school, he gave my brother a black eye."

Old images flickered then sharpened in my memory. Logan's eye already blackened and swollen as York held him by the jaw. "Your dad did that?"

Ryker nodded, navigating with one hand on the steering wheel, the other resting on the gear stick. The road was long and straight, and we both knew it well from the years of bus trips into school.

He chewed on his bottom lip. "My dad and I have a lot in common. We both like being outside, working on the land. Messing around with cars and bikes. Neither of us are all that smart, or good at school stuff, but we get mechanics. I was always his favourite when we were growing up."

I still had no idea what this had to do with Ryker and me but I didn't want to interrupt him. I'd been expecting a half-assed explanation of how young and dumb he'd been. I hadn't anticipated him spilling family secrets.

"He and I were outside in the garage, working on an engine when he went inside to get another beer. I heard yelling and followed him to see what was going on. He was screaming at Logan. Something about how Logan thought he was better than the rest of us with his fancy school awards. I stood behind him and watched as he grabbed a trophy from Logan's shelf and smashed it right into the side of his face."

I gasped, my stomach rolling. Everyone in town knew Mr Ryker was a bit rough and drank too much, but I'd never heard a rumour about him abusing his family.

Ryker glanced over at me, his mouth set in a hard line. "Yeah, that was pretty much my reaction, too. I remember standing there, frozen, while Logan crumpled to the floor holding his face. Blood trickling down his cheek. Dad's moods got pretty bad, but as far as I knew, he'd never hit any of us before. Not like that anyway."

"What happened after that?"

"Dad stormed out, probably to the pub. And I cleaned up Logan's face while the younger boys sat there watching. I'd never heard Jared and Dallas that quiet. The next day, his eye was black and blue. I told him to stay home from school, but he refused. School was Logan's life—his thing. He's not like me or our dad. He's smart. And I couldn't blame him for wanting to go. I didn't want to be in that house a minute longer than I had to be either.

"But then we saw Sam York on the way to our first class."

With a sharp turn of his wrist, he pulled the car to the side of the road and killed the engine, silence settling around us. Then he twisted in his seat so he was facing me. "You need to know, I was never friends with him. I couldn't stand him. But for self-preservation, we never made a big thing out of our dislike for him. Going against Sam meant being the target of his attacks."

I knew all about being the target of his attacks.

"York asked if I'd given Logan the black eye, and I was so horrified by the thought I immediately said no. If my brain worked quicker, I would have said it was me. Made something up about it happening while we were playing football or something. But York put two and two together and knew it had to be our father."

Ryker shook his head, a look of pure anguish crossing his features before he tried to hide it by looking back out the front windshield. His fingers dug into the leather of the steering wheel. "You have no idea how mortifying that was."

Despite how the memories of the day twisted a knife in my gut, the fleshing out of the events had me leaning in. I opened my mouth, unsure of how it made me feel. But I was sure this part wasn't Ryker's fault. "You couldn't have done anything, though, Ryker. You were only fourteen."

He turned on me, his eyes blazing. "You think that matters? I stood by and did nothing while my father beat up my brother. I'd stood there and watched and didn't say a word. I wasn't going to let anyone touch him again. Not my dad. Not some overgrown meathead football player who thought he was a big man."

He frowned and raked his fingers through his hair. His shoulders had tensed, and his fingers clenched into fists. He forcefully straightened them. "York was getting more and more agitated with all his cronies surrounding us, but Logan just stared him down. I didn't know what to do. I shoved him, hoping to get his attention off Logan, but he just shoved me back and went straight back to needling him. I knew Logan wouldn't break. He wasn't a big kid, but mentally, he's always been stronger than anyone I know. York was talking smack about our mum leaving, our brothers, anything to get a reaction.

And Logan would have just taken another beating rather than give York what he wanted. But I just couldn't watch it. Not again."

He looked up at me with eyes that begged me to understand. "He's my brother."

"So you threw me under the bus instead," I said quietly.

He nodded, turning back to me again. "I saw you there, and the words just fell out of my mouth. I thought York would turn on me. I swear, I never thought he'd go after you. I only said it to distract him from Logan. I thought he'd punch me out for saying he was…" Ryker trailed off, embarrassed.

"For saying he was dating a cripple." The words came out bitter, and the pain from that day crashed down on me like a wave. The words might have been years old, but they still burned. "I wouldn't have cared so much. York was probably going to pick on me at some point because there was no way I was going to get through six years of high school without some loser picking on the kid in a wheelchair. I was prepared for that. But I wasn't prepared for it to be you. Did you have to call me lame? I never escaped that word. I was Lame Lawson for six years. And every time someone called me that, I remembered it was you who'd started it. You were supposed to be my friend, Adam, and you didn't give me a second thought."

"What?" he asked. "I didn't start the Lame Lawson thing. York did."

I whirled on him, my face burning. His expression was full of confusion. "Don't. I heard you say it to him."

"Gemma. I didn't. I—" Dawning washed over his features, and he paled.

"You remember now?"

He met my gaze with certainty, a fire blazing behind them. The intensity of it made me pause.

"I remember every word of that day. It's so ingrained in my memory from reliving it, day after day, year after year. I swear to you, I never called you lame. I called *him* lame. My exact words to York were *you're being lame, leave it alone."*

He scrubbed his hands over his face. "You have to know *I* don't think of you like that, Gemma. You aren't less than anyone else because you can't walk. I've never thought that. But I knew he would…"

I sucked in a long, deep breath, trying to control my emotions as Ryker dropped his gaze to his lap.

"I never meant for any of it to happen. I never meant a word of it. I was just trying to protect my brother, and I fucked up. I was young and dumb. I know it's no excuse. Over the years, I've thought up a million different scenarios that would have turned out better than what I did. I could have tripped a fire alarm. Or thrown something through a window. Created a diversion some other way. Nothing I say or do will change it. But I've always wanted to tell you I know I made a huge mistake, and I'm sorry."

I sat back in my chair and folded my arms across my chest, trying to calm the anger that had raged inside of me for years. The thing was, I believed him. Nothing in his demeanour told me he was lying. He and Logan had always been close, everyone knew that. They were barely ten months apart in age and were more like twins than regular brothers. I thought about how close Reese and I were, and how I'd been willing to get in a car with my arch nemesis for her. She was not only my sister, she was my best friend. How much closer would we have been if we'd been the same age?

"Was that the only time it happened? Your dad hitting your brother?"

He laughed, but it was cold and forced. "No. He took his moods out on all of us after that. It was like something snapped in him and he didn't care to hold himself in check anymore. Logan always copped the worst beatings, though."

A little of my anger seeped away as my heart broke for the boy he used to be. For the boy whose mother had abandoned them for a big city life, leaving them with a father who drank himself into oblivion and took his anger at the world out on his kids. I didn't want to hold on to my own anger forever. It was turning me into someone I didn't recognise and didn't want to be. I'd been bullied, but so had he, and by someone who was supposed to love him. His father's betrayals were worse than any high school bulling I'd ever had to endure.

Plus, I needed him right now, no matter how I looked at it.

I could either keep holding a grudge and make both our lives miserable. Or cut him some slack for something he'd done when he was barely older than a child. I hadn't exactly had it all figured out at fourteen either. And he had tried to apologise over the years. I just hadn't wanted to hear it. Maybe it was time to let that go. Not necessarily to forget, but to release some of the hurt and anger that was holding me back. Because it was holding him back, too.

"Okay."

Ryker studied me for a long moment before he turned the key in the ignition and started up the car again. He nodded. "Okay."

He steered the car back out onto the road, and I settled in my seat.

"This doesn't absolve you of all wrongdoing, you know. And I don't suddenly trust you. But at least now, I understand why you did it."

"I get it. And maybe I can't ever earn your trust back, but I'd like to try. I'd like to be friends."

"Don't push your luck," I replied, but my voice had softened. It was pretty damn lonely out here on the farm without Reese home. I made do with FaceTime and chatting with Rachel online—she'd never moved back home after her years at boarding school, though we talked regularly and caught up when she visited her parents. But I didn't have anything resembling a regular social life. Or friends. A friend sounded…nice. Even if I wasn't ready to tell him that yet.

8

RYKER

A weight lifted off my shoulders after apologising to Gemma. It was only a beginning, but it was more than she'd ever allowed me in the past, and I'd take it. For a few brief moments, I let myself bask in the weightless feeling apologising gave me.

It was short-lived. A sign on the side of the road announced we were entering Lorrington, and the skin at the back of my neck prickled. Of all the places for this damn cake shop to be, it had to be Lorrington. The one place I didn't want to be right now. Unaware of the unease this town evoked in me, Gemma pulled her phone out of her bag and fiddled with it. When I glanced over, I realised she had a map app out and was putting in the address of the cake store.

"You don't need to worry about the GPS. I know where the shop is."

Her fingers hovered in the air above her phone. "You do? I never come here anymore. Not since school finished. I don't even remember there being a cake store."

I nodded. "I lived here until a few weeks ago."

She tucked her phone back in her bag. "So that's where you disappeared to when you left."

The bush around us gave way to a main road lined with individual shop fronts. Lorrington was bigger than Erraville, but it still wasn't big enough for an actual shopping centre. The high school was the biggest building in the whole town. "A friend of a friend hooked me up with an apprenticeship at a motor mechanic. It's just down the end of this road, actually."

"I guess you liked it here then. Since you stayed for four years."

I flicked a blinker on and turned off the main street, heading for the patisserie I'd occasionally bought sausage rolls from during my lunch breaks. "Yeah, for the first few years. I flew through my apprenticeship and finished it a year early," I said, trying to force enthusiasm into my voice.

"But then everything went to shit," she supplied softly.

My breath caught in my chest, and I darted a glance at her. Had she somehow found out what had happened with Gerard? Panic swirled in my gut. Nobody but Danni knew what had happened. I hadn't even told my brothers.

Gemma was staring at me with open curiosity, and I realised with a start she was probably just using common sense. Something had obviously happened to force me back to my father's house. After confessing about the abuse, she would have realised I wouldn't go back there voluntarily. Relief coursed through me as I debated over how much to tell her. I didn't want to lie to her, even if I couldn't tell her the whole truth. "Yeah, something like that."

"So that's why you moved back home with your dad?"

"Worst mistake of my life," I mumbled, pulling the car to a stop in front of the café-style shop that boasted a sign declaring it to be LuLu's Patisserie.

Gemma didn't speak or move to get out of the car, though.

"Not because I've ended up working and living at your place, or anything," I rushed to clarify. Shit. I didn't want her thinking I was an ungrateful asshole after I'd just made a tiny bit of progress with her. "I just meant living with my dad is... my dad is still a giant jackass. As you probably realised from the little scene at the Blue Gum last night."

"Yeah, I noticed. And your mum?" she asked hesitantly. "Does she know any of it?"

I shrugged, trying to tamp down on the emotions that always tried to get the best of me whenever I thought of my mother. "She left for the city when I was a kid. Couldn't blame her. Drought is hard. Dad was drinking a lot. And they fought. About the drinking. About money. About moving. About everything really."

I stared out through the windshield. We never talked about Mum at home. We'd learnt pretty quickly that bringing up her name sent Dad into a spiral, so we'd stopped. We'd just stopped talking about her as if she'd ceased to exist. She'd called at first, then Logan had told her not to. So the calls had stopped.

"But she just left you boys with your dad?"

"She could only afford a tiny apartment in the city. One bedroom. Not exactly big enough for four boys." Through the windshield, I watched as a mother and her two young children stepped out of the patisserie, holding a tray with three meat pies sitting on white plates and settled at one of the outdoor tables. I turned away, focussing back on Gemma. "She didn't know he'd started hitting us. Her phone calls stopped before that."

Gemma frowned and looked like she wanted argue, but I cut her off before she could say anything. "It doesn't matter anyway. We'd all lay him out flat now we're adults. He's the definition of coward—he only picks on people smaller and weaker than he is. My brother Jared—do you remember him? He's a year younger than you, I think. He's a fighter. Pretty sure Dad is a bit scared of him. Even I am, and I'm in his good books."

"So your brothers moved out, too?"

"We were all out the door the minute we could legally and financially swing it. Logan moved away for university and then stayed. Jared moved to live closer to training facilities. He teaches fitness and boxing classes at the gym he trains at to make ends meet. And he's getting to the stage where he gets some sponsorship money for his fights. Dallas only moved out a few months back, but he changes jobs and locations every five minutes. He was down in Tasmania last I heard."

Talking to her was oddly easy after so many years of silence or stilted, forced conversation. For a little while, it was as if the years had fallen away and we were those two tiny kids, running through the veggie garden and stealing cherry tomatoes from the vine. I hadn't expected her to ask about my family, and even though I didn't like talking about old hurts, I liked talking to her. It was on the tip of my tongue to ask why she cared, but I was so grateful she was talking to me, I didn't want to jinx it.

"How come you chose to come back home instead of going to stay with one of them?"

I paused for a long moment, but no matter how I tried to frame the truth, it all resulted in information I couldn't tell her. So I gave her the reason I gave everyone. "They've all moved to cities. I'm a country kid. Cities and I don't get along." I did hate the city, so that much was the truth, at least. "Come on, it's nearly three, and these cakes aren't getting fresher while we sit out here."

I got out and rested one hip against the side of the car, letting my gaze wander along the street while Gemma put her chair back together. I still wanted to help her, but she'd made it more than obvious she didn't need it.

"You ready?" Gemma asked, startling me out of my thoughts. She sat in her chair, her expression full of curiosity.

I forced a smile. "Yeah. Let's go."

A bell tinkled as I pushed through the patisserie door, holding it open for Gemma behind me. From the outside, the patisserie looked like any other café, with wooden tables and large umbrellas to provide shade, but the inside had a cosier feel. The room was dim, but rows of clear glass display cabinets lined one wall, lit up by artificial lights. My mouth watered at the sight of the most decadent-looking chocolate cake I'd ever seen. Trying some of these out really wasn't going to be the worst way to spend my Sunday afternoon.

"Gemma and Ryker?" the lady behind the counter asked, directing her question to Gemma. "Your sister called a few hours ago and said you'd be coming in. I'll bring some choices out for you to try. Go take a seat." She waved us over towards the tables and disappeared through a door behind the counter.

I chose a table in the centre of the room and moved a chair aside, making a spot for Gemma. The same awkward tension from the beginning of our car ride rose, and I realised I'd created it by sitting opposite her. I had nowhere to look except into her eyes— sitting like this felt more intimate that sitting side by side in the car. I drummed my fingers on the tabletop, wishing for the distraction driving had provided.

"You don't have to stay. I have a few things I need to do after this, so you can go do your own thing, and we'll meet back at the car later."

Did she want me to leave? But something told me she didn't. She was just saying it because she thought I didn't want to be there. She was kind of right. Sitting opposite her meant noticing how glossy her hair was when she wore it down like she was right now. Or the golden smoothness of her skin.

She'd always been beautiful. Even as kids I remembered thinking how pretty she was. I'd often found excuses to wander over to their property to talk to her. I'd been fascinated by their horses, and her mum was always kind to me. And then an easy friendship had formed between Gemma and me, and I'd spent more time there than at my own place.

We'd drifted apart when I'd gone to high school. My mum had

been long gone, and my father had us all working out in our fields every day after school. We'd made it through a long drought, but he'd had to let go of our two farmhands and sell off some of our machinery. I hadn't seen Gemma for months before that day in the hallway. If things had been different, I would have been stoked to see her again. I would have given her a tour of the school and made sure she knew not to use the D block bathroom if she didn't want to end up reeking of cigarette smoke.

I'd fucked that up, but I never stopped watching out for her. Every lunchtime, no matter what I was doing, I found myself seeking her out. In the halls between classes, I'd catch a glimpse of her, then I'd be late to class because I stood there too long, watching her as she rightfully ignored me. I knew she hated my guts, so I tried to keep my distance, but something about her always drew me back in. Somewhere beneath the hard exterior I'd forced her to put up was the girl who had thrown stones into the dam with me, because it was the farthest point from my house when my parents were screaming at each other.

Watching the way she dealt with York only made me like her more, until one day, I'd realised those little-boy feelings I'd had for her had developed into a full-blown crush. I'd never dared do anything about it. She wouldn't let me apologise—she wouldn't even look at me willingly, so I knew there wasn't a chance of repairing what I'd wrecked, let alone seeing if it could develop into something more. Then I'd left school and moved to Lorrington. There'd been women in Lorrington, but I'd always lost interest quickly. Gemma had always been close to the forefront of my mind. At the time, I'd thought it was because I still hadn't apologised to her.

But now, sitting in front of her, those same old feelings stirred.

Was it more than just regret that had made me think of her so often over the years? Was it because I still harboured a crush on her?

That was a sobering thought. I'd be single forever if that was the case. We might have called some sort of truce today, but I'd be lucky if I ever got to call her my friend again. I could only imagine her reaction if I tried to ask her out. But still. I didn't want to leave.

"Can I stay?"

She shrugged and turned away, but not before a hint of a smile cross her lips.

I liked the idea that she wanted me to stay. It was a start.

The woman from the store brought out different cakes, and for the next hour, Gemma and I sampled everything from vanilla to pink champagne flavoured cakes. Finally, we both agreed on the Devil's food cake I'd admired when we'd walked into the store. It was the best by far. She gave the woman our verdict, and she said she'd take care of the actual design with Reese via email. We thanked her and left the store, a gust of cool but fresh wind greeting us when we opened the door.

"Where to, boss?" I asked.

She squinted around at the handful of shops. "Is there a fresh food market? I want to grab some stuff to make dinner. We're down to pantry staples at home."

I nodded and moved behind her to the back of her chair. "This way. It's just down the road."

"You don't need to push me," she said quietly.

"Right. Of course. Sorry." I moved back to her side, the tips of my ears burning. We moved in silence, and I tried to pretend I hadn't just made things between us uncomfortable again.

"It's kind of a personal thing, you know?"

"No, no, I get it. I wasn't thinking. I know how independent you are."

"Not nearly as independent as I'd like to be, but thank you."

When we got to the market, she cruised the aisles slowly, with seemingly no idea what she actually needed. I drifted behind her, picking out some organic strawberries for myself, studying each one for freshness before choosing a punnet.

"Why are you looking at those berries like you've never seen one before?" Gemma asked, throwing tomatoes into a bag.

I winced.

"What?" Her hand paused in midair with a tomato clutched in her fingers.

"Don't buy those."

She held up the bag of juicy red tomatoes with their green stems and inspected them. "Why? What's wrong with them?"

"Nothing. They're just—" I sighed and ripped off another plastic bag from the roll provided by the store. "Get these ones instead." I filled the bag with organic tomatoes and handed it to her.

"Apparently you think I won lotto." She raised her eyebrow as she nodded towards the price tag. Which admittedly, was about double what the other tomatoes cost.

"No, but honestly, have you ever tried the organic ones? They don't have that pesticide taste, and they're so much fresher. You won't ever go back, trust me."

She gave me a look that clearly said she didn't trust me, even when it came to something as mundane as tomatoes. Fair enough. I knew I had to earn that. But she also really needed to try some organic produce. I peered down into the bag she had sitting on her lap and frowned, which earnt me an eyeroll.

"You want to replace everything in here with organic, don't you?"

I couldn't help but give her a wry grin. "Maybe. It's up to you, but you should eat at least one meal using all organic produce. You can thank me later."

"I didn't pick you as some organic, earth-loving hippie," she grumbled, putting back the things she'd already selected and accepted the new, obviously superior, organic veggies I handed her.

"I'm not. But our farm went organic years ago. Dad was pretty passionate about it. It rubbed off, I guess. I promise, you won't know what hit you."

She looked at me doubtfully, and I laughed.

"Fine. It may not taste all that different, but it's definitely better for you."

"Fair call."

"What are you planning on making anyway?"

She shrugged. "No idea. I'm a pretty boring cook. I'll figure it out when I get home."

"You could do a nice Stuffat tal-Fenek if you had some rabbit."

Her nose wrinkled. "Some what now?"

Her outright disgust was hilarious.

"Rabbit stew. My mum used to make it all the time."

She faked gagging, and I held my hands up in surrender.

"Fine, you make what you like from your boring old beef or chicken. But I make an awesome Stuffat tal-Fenek. You should try it sometime."

Her head snapped back, her eyes sharpening.

Shit. That probably sounded like I was asking if I could cook for her. Always so good with words. "Uh, I didn't mean…"

She shook her head, waving it off. "Yeah, of course."

I found myself disappointed in her reaction. We'd gotten along surprisingly well today, considering our history. Would it really be so bad if I had asked her out? I pulled my head out of my ass and reminded myself it had only been a few hours since I'd apologised. She was barely tolerating me right now, and I didn't want to ruin the progress I'd made. Even if every time I was close to her, the scent of her shampoo wafted over me. Something citrusy. Orange? Maybe mandarin? It was driving me nuts, and I had to fight with myself to keep a respectable distance from her. Grapefruit?

"I'm going to grab these and wait out front for you. I need some air." And a lobotomy. Letting old feelings for Gemma spark up again was a very dumb idea, and a surefire way to lose my current accommodation and find myself back at Dad's place. And that was something I definitely didn't want to do.

I pushed through the door of the market, pulling my baseball cap on and tugging it down low. I stuck close to the window of the shop, watching through the clear glass front as Gemma grabbed a magazine and joined the checkout queue.

"Ryker?"

I whirled around at the voice, and a true grin stole across my face. "Danni!" I grabbed her by the shoulders and crushed her to my chest before releasing her.

"Oof, you nearly cracked my rib."

I stepped back and looked at her familiar face. I'd worked with Danni the entire four years I'd lived in Lorrington and had slept on her lounge for the first six months of my apprenticeship. "Not even. You're a tough nut."

She laughed, but her smile slipped, and my stomach sunk. We'd been best friends long enough that I knew when something was wrong, and something was definitely bothering her.

"What is it?"

She stepped closer. "What are you doing back here? You shouldn't have come."

"What? Why?"

"Gerard hasn't contacted you?"

Dread rose in my gut at the very mention of that name. "No? Why would he? I'm up to date with my payments."

"Tim at the pub said he's calling in all his loans. Forcing people to pay them out quicker than originally agreed. I figured you'd be at the top of his list, especially since you don't have the workshop as collateral anymore."

Ice crept through my veins despite the pleasant afternoon temperature. "You've got to be fucking kidding me. He can't do that."

She raised an eyebrow at me. "Can't he? Who's going to stop him?"

She had a point. It wasn't like loan sharks had a governing body. "I haven't seen Gerard around lately, but you never know who he has working for him. He'll call you in if he sees you here. Just lie low, and maybe he won't bother you."

"Shit." I clutched the back of my neck. "I still have thirty thousand left to pay back. Every cent I earn is going to him, but I'm royally screwed if he calls in the rest of it."

Danni bit her lip.

"What?" There was something she wasn't telling me.

"They broke into my house. I think it was them anyway. They trashed it but didn't take anything."

"Shit, why would they do that? We haven't lived together in years. Are you okay?"

She nodded, the silky blonde strands of her hair falling over her eyes. "It was weeks ago, and I'm fine."

"Fuck. You should have called me."

"I'm a big girl, Ryker. I can take care of myself."

"I know. Do you think they were looking for me?"

She shrugged. "Maybe it was just some random break-in."

That seemed like too much of a coincidence to hope for. Lorrington wasn't exactly a hot spot for burglaries. Most people didn't even lock their doors. I glanced back over my shoulder through the glass windows to where Gemma was still sitting in the checkout line. My eyes met hers, and she quickly turned away. I sighed and focussed on Danni. "Maybe you should go stay with your sister, though? Just in case?"

She shrugged, and the grease monkey she was, tough as nails, never one to take shit from the other mechanics, shone out from beneath her feminine dress and pretty makeup. "I doubt they'd come back. They obviously didn't find anything interesting. Plus, I went to the RSPCA and adopted a Rottweiler." She gave me a shit-eating grin. "He's a pussy cat, but he looks pretty damn scary."

I smiled. "You always wanted a dog,"

"Yeah. It was a good excuse to finally do it."

I pulled her in for another quick hug. There'd never been anything more than friendship between us. And I'd missed it, these last few weeks.

"Be careful. The rumours about Gerard's guys make me nervous. I still hate that you're involved with them."

They made me nervous, too, but there was nothing I could do that I wasn't already. I was working two jobs to pay back the loan I'd taken to buy the workshop. And I was sticking to our agreement. I just had to hope Gerard would stick to his end of the deal. Danni waved, and with a final worried look, she walked away.

I watched her round the corner, wishing Gemma's check-out clerk would hurry up. I was more than ready to get the hell out of Lorrington.

9

GEMMA

The car ride home from Lorrington was painfully silent. I pretended to be engrossed in the photography magazine I'd picked up at the market, and Ryker pretended he needed all his concentration to drive along a straight road. I didn't ask who the cute blonde he'd been talking to was, and it annoyed me that I even wanted to know. Was she an ex-girlfriend? A current girlfriend, even? He hadn't kissed her, but maybe he just wasn't into public displays of affection. He hadn't offered up an explanation for who she was or why he'd been hugging her, but he was curiously silent. Was he thinking about her? Why was I even considering this? His relationships were none of my business.

I needed to get a life.

I buried my head farther into the magazine, forcing myself to focus on each page and take in the articles. But it was hard going, keeping my tongue from blurting out my questions. We'd carried on this charade for an hour when a half-page ad in the magazine caught my eye. *Win your dream photography career*, the ad shouted at me in green block letters. I pored over the details, no longer just pretending to read. It was straightforward. Send your best four sports photography photos in via email. Semi-finalists would receive an all-expenses-paid trip to a Melbourne gallery showing of their printed works. The winner would be announced at the end of the week-long event and would receive an apprenticeship with the magazine. Everything I'd dreamed of was right there on the page in front of me.

My fingers shook—with nerves or excitement, I didn't know, but both feelings were ridiculous. Maybe if Dad had been well, I could have entered. Just for fun. But there wasn't any point with things the way they were right now. I couldn't even afford a weekend off for the gallery, let alone leave the farm for a year to do an internship in Melbourne. And that was if I even made the top ten. Which I undoubtedly wouldn't. Some of the photos I took could be classed as sports photography, but I did a lot that captured the feeling and emotion between riders and their horses. My stuff didn't quite fit the brief. Still. I wished the competition had come up before Dad had had his stroke. It might have been nice to pretend for a little while that I was good enough to make a splash in nationwide competition.

By the time we got home, I'd read the entire magazine cover to cover and was full of inspiration and itching to pick up my camera. But the sun had sunk behind the horizon, and I wasn't one for night photography. I thanked Ryker when he dropped me off at the front of the house, relieved the afternoon was over with. Despite the painfully quiet ride home, the trip hadn't been as bad as I'd been expecting. For a little while there, I might have even been enjoying myself. Before things had gotten weird, anyway.

The house was dark when I let myself in, and I didn't bother to call out, knowing Mum would have been bustling around the kitchen if she'd been home. Flicking on lights, I made my way through the house and stopped in the kitchen to dump my pricey but pesticide-free veggies on the table. My stomach was still full of the cake we'd eaten that afternoon, and chopping them up and putting together a healthy meal wasn't even close to as appealing as stealing an hour in my darkroom. I still had the roll of film I'd taken the day Dad had collapsed, and food could wait.

I grabbed my camera from the cupboard in my bedroom and made sure the film had wound off properly before I opened the back and pulled it out. Feeling lighter than I had all week, I went into the laundry that doubled as my darkroom. There were no windows, and we'd installed a heavier door to block the light from outside. Once it was dark, I reached under the laundry bench top and flicked on the red safety light that allowed me to see what I was doing without ruining my film.

I didn't always shoot film. I wasn't a complete purist like some of the photographers I encountered on the forums I frequented. But there was something soothing about coming in here to process my photos. Swishing the papers through developing chemicals and watching them come alive on the page made my heart happy. Each one was like opening a new present, and I was never exactly sure what was going to be inside. Sure, I knew I was developing landscape shots, plus some of a little girl in my riding class, but there was always something unknown. Had I nailed the focus? Would she have her eyes closed? Would she have that look of determination on her face that made me so damn proud to be her coach because I knew she'd go places with her riding one day?

I hummed quietly under my breath, the only other sound the whirring of an exhaust fan my mother had insisted on installing so the chemical smell wouldn't go right through the house. The tension of the week lifted, photo by photo, as my work appeared in the trays, and I moved them to the retractable drying lines. I couldn't have them up full time, since they blocked the washing machine and dryer, but we'd found a retractable clothes line at the hardware store that did the job perfectly.

I ran my fingers along the edge of the last photo of the roll, pride filling me. It was framed beautifully, crystal clear, sharp as a tack, and I'd gotten the exposure dead on perfect. I lived for photos like this. Sometimes you'd process five rolls of film, and you'd get only one perfect shot. Or sometimes, like today, you got it on roll one. I liked those days. It didn't matter that the rest were average. One perfect shot was all I needed.

The laundry door swung open, smacking into the handles of my chair with a crack. I yelped as the force behind it sent me straight through the drying lines and careening into the washing machine. I grabbed the bench to keep from falling straight off my chair.

"What the hell?" Ryker muttered, peering around the door. His eyes widened when he saw me, tangled in drying lines and half falling out of my seat. "Shit, Gemma! What are you doing in here in the dark?" He dropped the basket of laundry he was carrying and rushed into the room, pulling my chair away from the washing machine. "Are you okay?"

I rubbed my left knee that had taken the brunt of the hit. "It'll bruise, but I'll live."

"You can feel that?" he asked curiously.

I nodded, screwing my eyes shut to avoid seeing the wreckage of my work. "My injury is incomplete. I still have some feeling beneath the damaged spot in my spinal cord. Not enough to walk, but I'm luckier than most."

It was no good, I had to survey the damage. My prints were scattered on the laundry tiles, the last few, including the perfect shot, ruined. They hadn't been dry when they'd hit the deck. I wanted to cry. All that work destroyed. At least I had the negatives.

I leant down to gather the prints from the floor, but Ryker beat me to it, collecting them up quickly and shuffling them into a pile.

He straightened, his gaze drifting around the dim room. "You were developing these yourself? The old-school way?" He stepped forward to inspect a photo that still hung from the mangled lines before turning his attention to the pile in his hands, shifting one behind the other.

I fidgeted in my chair, my fingers itching to snatch the prints from his hands. But a weird desire to know what he thought of them won out. In an ideal world, he'd be the last person I showed my work to, but I never got to show anyone my prints. Not since my high school photography class anyway. My ego wanted to hear someone other than my family say they were good.

I waited, studying his face for any sign of what he was thinking. He had long eyelashes, I realised. Dark and thick. Lucky bastard. His expression remained neutral, but I couldn't look away as he took his time, considering each photo, then moving it to the back of the stack. Even the ruined ones were examined as if they were fine art, his tan fingers holding the edges of the paper gingerly before he handed them back.

"You've gotten even better than you were in high school. These—" He paused and pointed to the photo on top of the pile. It wasn't the one I thought was perfect. It was a close-up of little Meagan's face. "That one, in particular, is amazing."

"Thanks." I looked at the photo he'd chosen, and while I liked it, I wished he'd seen my favourite shot before it was ruined. Then his words filtered through my brain, piquing my curiosity. "How did you know I did photography in high school?"

He rested back on the doorframe and folded his arms across his chest. I ignored the way his shirt stretched across his pecs and lifted my gaze to his eyes because I didn't want to focus on his forearms either. I knew from earlier in the day how distracting they were.

"You won that competition, remember?"

"I didn't know you went to that." The school had held an art exhibition when I'd been sixteen. It had been right before Ryker left for good. But I didn't remember seeing him there.

"There's a lot about me you don't know, Gemma," he said in his quiet manner.

Had he always been this quiet? This serious? He'd been more relaxed today, after I'd allowed him to apologise, more like the boy I remembered from primary school. He'd even made me laugh a little. But during the car ride home, we'd both put our walls back up.

He'd changed during his high school years, I realised with a start. Maybe as much as I had. We were both different to the kids who had sat together on the school bus. And I was beginning to see that we were different again from our teenage selves. I'd spent most of my teen years actively avoiding him, but it wasn't a huge school, and sometimes it seemed that I'd run into him more than any other student. He had often been alone or with one of his brothers.

Was it that day in the foyer that had made him distance himself from the other kids, as I had? I hadn't realised it at the time, but Ryker's high school experience and my own probably weren't too different. Both filled with isolation and loneliness. For a moment, I almost felt sorry for him. But then I remembered the years of abuse I'd had to put up with. And that feeling disappeared. I might have forgiven him and maybe I understood him and his motivations a little better. But I hadn't forgotten. A truce was nothing more than that. It wasn't a friendship.

He hadn't moved from his spot against the wall, his attention focussed on me. I probably needed to admit, at least to myself, that I found him attractive. I'd spent the last twenty-four hours trying to deny the way my breath hitched at the sight of him, trying to blame it on the shock of seeing him again after so many years. But it was pretty pointless when everything about him was a complete turn-on. The scruff on his jaw. The deep brown of his eyes. The fact I'd wondered what those back muscles would look like if they weren't covered by a shirt. If things had been different between us, maybe I would have pursued something more. Tried my hand at flirting with him. It had been a long time since I'd done any of that. But no matter how hot he was, our past was always going to be sitting there, like the dirty big pot hole we all avoided on Tadmore Road.

"I almost didn't get to enter that competition, you know?" The memory of the exhibition day came back in a rush. It had been one of the worst experiences of my life, followed by one of the best. A complete roller coaster of emotions. "You know why?"

Ryker stilled and had the decency to look down at the floor. I wondered if he was suddenly wishing it would open and swallow him whole.

"You do remember, don't you?"

He sighed. "York and his friends were messing with you. They wouldn't let you get past them and into the hall where they were taking the exhibition entries."

"When they finally got sick of it, the cut-off time had passed, and the officials wouldn't accept my entry. Did you know that?"

He nodded. "I saw you throw your prints in the bin when you left the hall."

That surprised me. I didn't remember seeing him there that day, though I'd been blinded by tears by that point, so I doubted I would have seen through them anyway. I'd spent three months shooting for that exhibition.

"I was just lucky Ms Davies took pity on me and got the other judges to change their minds. I couldn't believe it when I saw my prints up on the wall that night."

"That isn't what happened," Ryker murmured.

I rubbed absently at my arm. "What do you mean?"

"Nothing."

"No, tell me."

He sighed. "Ms Davies didn't do shit. I heard her talking to the other judges after you left. She tried, but the other two wouldn't accept it. They said they couldn't favour you just because you were in a wheelchair."

"What? I didn't expect any favours because I can't walk!"

Ryker held his hands out in what was probably supposed to be a calming gesture, but just pissed me off further. "I know. You've never used it as an excuse for anything."

A little of the steam rising inside me dissipated, and I lowered my voice. "So how did my prints get into the show then? Since you seem to know everything."

"I pulled them out of the bin and waited until everyone left to go get ready for the gallery showing. Then I snuck in through a window in the back. You remember the one that never shut properly?"

My chest tightened. I did remember. Only because in winter, we'd all sit at assemblies and freeze half to death because the hall had no heating and a window that wouldn't close. "I'm supposed to believe *you* put my entry up."

He shrugged. "I knew you'd put a lot of work in, and it was my fault York was picking on you in the first place. It was the least I could do."

My head swirled, confusion clouding in. "How did you know they would even accept it?" I asked in disbelief.

Ryker had gone out of his way, potentially risking expulsion, or at least detention by breaking and entering school property? All these years I'd thought it was Ms Davies. I'd even hugged her after I'd won and thanked her for all her help. She'd never set me straight, though I guess maybe she thought I'd meant her help in the classroom.

"I didn't. But I figured if your work was there on the wall, and clearly the best in the room, they wouldn't be able to just overlook it."

My gaze drifted to the pinboard I kept in my darkroom for my favourite photos. A faded blue ribbon was tacked to the top of it.

"You kept it," Ryker said.

"It was the first time I won anything that really meant something to me." I didn't add that it was the first time I'd considered that I might want more than just living and working on our family farm for the rest of my life. That blue ribbon represented a dream I still hadn't fulfilled. And despite feeling more chained to the farm than ever, that dream wasn't something I was quite ready to give up on yet. "Thank you," I whispered.

He nodded. The air around us grew heavy, and it was hard to draw my gaze away from him. Confusing, conflicting feelings became a band across my chest, and the tiny darkroom laundry suddenly felt claustrophobic. Or maybe it was just the chemicals getting to my head.

"What are you doing up here anyway?" I asked.

He started as if he'd been affected by the weirdness between us like I was. He blinked twice, then pointed at the basket of washing, with a two-minute noodle package sitting on top. "I thought I'd throw some clothes in the washing machine while I borrowed some hot water for my dinner."

"You're having two-minute noodles for dinner? Why didn't you grab something while we were at the market?"

He ran his hand through his hair and let it rest at the back of his neck. "I'm on a tight budget."

I frowned, and as if my stomach knew what we were talking about, it let out a growl of protest.

"You haven't eaten either by the sounds of it."

"I got distracted. I tend to lose track of the time when I'm in here."

"How about we make a deal? I'll cook if you'll share with me." He pulled a face at his two-minute noodles. "I'm really sick of these if I'm honest, and I already miss having a proper kitchen."

I raised an eyebrow. The thought of someone cooking for me right now, or anytime really, was pretty appealing. And Ryker looked oddly excited about the idea. Weirdo. But who was I to discourage the man if he wanted to cook me dinner?

10

RYKER

Gemma rubbed a hand over her face as I backed out of her darkroom.

"Knock yourself out. There's no rabbit for your stew, but you can use anything you can find."

It was only eight-thirty, but she looked exhausted. Dark shadows were already appearing under her eyes as she followed me to the kitchen, my washing and two-minute noodles forgotten for the time being. That urge to help her, to take care of her had risen again, and I was grateful she was allowing me cook dinner for her.

I eyed the ingredients on the table and opened the fridge, surveying the contents while she pulled her chair up next to the kitchen table. "Beef stir-fry good with you?"

"You cook it, I'll eat it."

"Deal."

"Can I help?"

"I got it. You relax."

Once I'd searched through the cupboards and drawers for knives and chopping boards, I made short work of slicing the beef and preparing a mixture of the vegetables Gemma had bought earlier. The beef sizzled when it hit the hot pan, and I relaxed as I shook it, the task as familiar as tying my shoes. My mother had been big on cooking and making sure her boys knew how to as well. We'd all been expected to help in the kitchen from the time we were old enough to stand on a stool right up until she'd left. I'd always enjoyed it, and the skills I'd learned from a young age at her side had come in handy when I'd found myself cooking each night for my three brothers. It wasn't like my dad ever bothered, so the responsibility had fallen to me. I liked to think I'd gotten pretty good over the years, with my combo of mother-taught meals and internet recipes.

By the time I'd thrown the veggies in and poured some rice into boiling water, Gemma was engrossed in her photography magazine again. I glanced over her shoulder when I passed behind her on the way to look for ingredients for a stir-fry sauce. "Photography competition? What's that about?"

She glanced up, as if she'd forgotten I was in the room. "Oh, it's nothing. Winner gets a sports photography internship in Melbourne. All expenses paid for a year."

I pulled soy and oyster sauces from the fridge along with some minced garlic, and leant back on the kitchen bench, letting out a long low whistle. "That's a pretty decent prize. Which photo are you going to enter?"

She shook her head quickly, pink spots blooming on her cheeks. "I'm not entering."

I squinted at her. "Hey? Why not? The photos you take of the kids on horseback—that's sports photography. And you're good. Why wouldn't you go for it?"

She rubbed at her eyes, and I vowed to get up extra early in the morning to start the list of chores I'd already seen tacked up in the stables. She had too much on her plate. She looked like she needed to sleep for a week.

"I can't just leave. Who'd run this place? I have responsibilities."

I mulled that over and doubted I'd be able to convince her to put herself first. Her work ethic and her loyalty to her family were admirable, even if I couldn't relate to the loyalty she had to her father. Her father was a good, generous man who would give his life for his family. Mine liked to take his anger out on little boys who weren't big enough to fight back. They weren't in the same league of men.

"But wouldn't you just like to try? Just to see if you make the cut? For bragging rights, if nothing else."

"Who do I have to brag to? It's not like I have any friends, bar my parents and a sister who lives twelve hours away."

Her words were tough, but her expression cut me like a knife. I knew that look. It was the same one I'd glimpsed all through high school, when she thought no one was looking. The one that only happened when her façade slipped for a moment. She'd never given York the satisfaction of breaking her, which was why he never gave up trying. She'd suffered his harassment with her chin held high, and even through my guilt, I'd admired her for it. She was a strong woman. Strong physically from her disability and the work she did around the farm, but also within herself.

She was always alone, though. In high school she'd locked herself away in the art rooms, and now she was locked away on this farm. It wasn't right.

I leant over her and squinted at the smaller print beneath the title, the citrus scent and close proximity of her making me close my eyes for a brief moment so I could focus. "Even if you aren't the winner, the top ten get to showcase their work in a gallery in Melbourne. Where real-life fancy-pants men in suits can buy your work." I nudged her shoulder playfully, trying to lighten the mood, before I realised my mistake. My heartrate picked up at the brief contact, and I knew immediately I'd crossed an invisible line between us.

She flicked her gaze to mine, and I knew she was thinking the same thing. Her eyes were wide, and she was breathing faster than normal. It took me a second to realise I was, too. I'd felt something in that touch. That touch erased all of our past, if only for a moment. She was just a woman, and I was just a man.

"Sorry," I muttered and turned back to the stove top.

"I'm not breakable."

I flinched. "I didn't say you were." She couldn't be more off base. I glanced over my shoulder at her. "You're the least breakable person I know."

Surprise flickered across her face, but she shut it down quickly, folded the magazine, and moved it out of the way. She pulled plates from a low cupboard, obviously ignoring my statement. The tips of my ears burnt as she handed me one, and I ladled rice, meat, and vegetables onto her plate.

Our fingers brushed when I gave it back to her, and she stilled, which in turn made me freeze. I had no idea what was happening here. I couldn't read her. Did she want me to leave? But then she passed me another plate and took her own to the table. I dropped stir-fry onto my plate and slowly sat next to her, being careful not to touch her again. I was walking on eggshells, but I didn't want to ruin all the progress we'd made today by overstepping the mark.

We chewed in silence for a few minutes, and I wondered if we were both too hungry to think or if we were just using food as an excuse not to talk.

"That woman on the street today..." she asked, her voice so quiet I almost didn't hear her.

I stopped chewing and swallowed before answering her. "Danni? What about her?"

"Is she your girlfriend?" she blurted. Then bit her lip like she was annoyed she'd let the words out.

"No, she's not. We used to work together." I poked at some stray grains of rice that were dangerously close to falling off the edge of my plate, surprising even myself with my next words. "Then she worked for me."

"You were her employer? Doing what?"

"I bought the motor mechanic shop from our boss early last year. His wife got sick. Some sort of aggressive cancer. He needed to move his family into the city to be closer to the big hospitals with cancer specialists. So he sold it to me."

Her eyes were wide again, but this time I thought it might have been with respect. When I'd told other people, most were shocked that Adam, the Ryker family screwup, had managed to buy a business. They would have expected it from Logan. Maybe even from Jared. But I was just a grease monkey who could barely read.

"Don't look at me like that," I said more gruffly than I intended.

"Like what?"

"Like you're impressed I owned a business."

She didn't know the whole story yet. She wouldn't be impressed by the end of it.

"But it is impressive. What happened with it?"

I sighed. "There was an oil fire a few months back. It got out of control really quickly."

She covered her mouth with her hand. "Was anyone hurt?"

I shook my head. "No. But I lost the entire shop. The whole place was one big accelerant, and there's no fire station in Lorrington. By the time the truck from Wessel got there, it was way too late. We just stood there and watched it burn."

"Wow."

She shook her head sadly as images of that night flashed through my head. The acrid smell of smoke burning my nostrils, the heat from the inferno licking at my skin. It was the worst day of my life, watching everything I'd worked so hard for literally go up in flames.

"Your insurance covered it, though? Are they rebuilding it? Is that why you moved back home?"

I gave her a wry smile. If only that was what had happened. "I wasn't insured. I had to borrow a lot of money just to buy the joint in the first place. I didn't have a spare cent between loan repayments and making sure Danni's wages were always paid on time." I paused, wondering why the need to tell her the full truth burned my tongue. Maybe somewhere, deep inside me, I felt I owed it to her. Maybe I needed to let her know that karma had kicked my ass after the shitty way I'd treated her.

"When Sal said he was moving and closing down the shop, the first thing I said was, I'll buy it. I didn't even think about how, I just knew I had to. But that turned out to be harder than I'd thought. The bank laughed at me. I had no credit rating, an apprentice income, and no assets to secure the loan. I thought I was out of the running. But Sal knew a guy named Gerard who did loans as a side business. I knew it was dodgy, but without the banks taking a chance on me, who else would give me the hundred thousand I needed?"

"Jesus, Ryker. That's a lot of money."

"Yeah, I know. But Gerard set out reasonable terms, even if the interest rates were high. The business was doing well; I knew I could swing the repayments and still pay myself enough to live on. I was determined to keep Danni on, though it would have made better business sense to let her go. I just didn't take into consideration all the other things that came with running a business." I hated to admit that. Hated to admit that I'd gotten in over my head. "I was doing okay, though. Keeping the business afloat," I added lamely.

"But then the fire happened…"

I nodded. "Then the fire happened."

"And without insurance…"

"Without insurance, I still owe a boatload of money with no way of repaying it."

"Shit."

"Yeah."

"Explains why you're working two jobs." She glanced over at my discarded two-minute noodles, still sitting on the top of my dirty washing basket. "And why you're eating those."

"It's the real reason I had to move back here. Every cent I earn goes to making Gerard's repayments on time. This job with you came up at the best possible time. It's pretty much the only good thing that's happened recently, if I'm honest. Not just because I'm out of that house, but it gave me the chance to apologise. Even when I moved away, I never forgot." I let the words sink in for a moment then added, "I'm going to make it up to you."

Gemma lifted her fork to her mouth and blew lightly on it before taking another bite. I watched from the corner of my eye, not wanting to make her self-conscious. When she didn't respond, I changed the subject.

"How is it?" I motioned towards the fork she was piling with food.

"Good," she said, food disappearing into her mouth again.

I grinned to myself as I gathered up another fork load of my own. Gemma wasn't one to dole out compliments unnecessarily, so I'd take that.

"How come you don't see Danni anymore?" she asked, surprising me by picking up the conversation again. "The two of you looked like you were having a reunion on the street today."

"I've been working all the time, and fuel to get out there and back costs too much to do it regularly. She told me something today, though, that I should tell you."

Gemma waited patiently for me to continue, though telling her was the last thing I wanted to do.

"Gerard might want his money back earlier than we agreed on. He hasn't contacted me, but that doesn't mean he won't. He's not exactly known for being a good guy, and I don't want to bring all of this into your home."

"Should I be concerned about you living here?" Worry tinged her voice.

I shook my head slowly, then shrugged. "No. I don't know. I'm well ahead on my payment reschedule, and it should only be another year before I can pay him out entirely. He has no reason to come looking for me, but he's unpredictable." I took another bite before I let my fork clatter to the plate. "Shit. This is really depressing. Sorry."

She eyed me for a long moment, then sighed. "Look. Fact is, we need you here. We don't have an alternative, nobody else wanted the job. If you're telling me you're still in the guy's good books, then we're fine. If that changes, then I guess we'll reassess."

We lapsed into silence again. I suddenly found I didn't like it. I liked talking to her, and I didn't want it to stop. But I didn't want to talk about Gerard anymore either. "So, are you seeing anyone right now?"

She pulled a face. "No"

"What was the face for? Do you like anyone?"

"Like who? You?" Her cheeks flushed red.

"Well, I guess not by that reaction." I laughed loudly but was the tiniest bit hurt by her words. I'd been trying hard to prove I wasn't the same stupid kid I used to be. Obviously, I still had a long way to go. I didn't have a ton of experience with women, but I didn't think I was totally repulsive. Just repulsive to her, I guessed.

She put her fork down. "I haven't liked anyone like that for a long time. Not since your brother actually."

Well, that stung.

"You liked my brother?" I choked out. "Which one?" Like it mattered.

"Logan. He was always really kind to me."

Unlike you. Her unsaid words hung awkwardly in the air between us. Jealousy flared inside me. Logan was kind to everyone. That was just his nature, but I did remember him going out of his way to talk to Gemma. He'd felt guilty over the fallout of what I'd said, too, though I'd told him a million times it had been my decision and mine alone. I was willing to take the consequences.

"He was my first kiss, you know."

"What?" The words came out like a growl, taking me by surprise. I coughed but doubted I was fooling anyone.

She looked at me strangely, and I tried to school my features into something calm and collected. But on the inside, I was anything but. He'd never told me.

"Yeah, at the formal dance. It was a pity kiss, but it was still my first."

Anger simmered in my gut. "That was a shitty thing for him to do."

"Why? I was sixteen and had never been kissed. He did me a favour."

"No."

She frowned. "No, what?"

"He didn't do you a favour. He used you. Your first kiss should have been special." I clenched my fingers.

"He didn't use me. I wanted him to kiss me."

"But if he didn't have feelings for you—"

Red spots bloomed on her cheeks as her brows drew together in annoyance. "Just drop it, Ryker." She pushed away from the table and put her bowl in the dishwasher with more force than necessary. She shoved her fork into the cutlery basket and moved for the door.

Before I could even consider the consequences, I shot my hand out and grabbed the back of her chair.

"Gemma, wait." I let go, giving her the option to leave if she really wanted to.

She didn't turn around, but she didn't try to leave again either.

"I would have kissed you. And meant it."

She spun around, and when her gaze landed on me, it was so full of fire I could feel the heat. "Stop. Don't be a jackass."

I held my hands up in surrender. "I'm not, I swear."

"Then why say that?" she spat.

"Because it's true. I wanted to kiss you that night." The words fell effortlessly from my lips, because they were the simple truth.

Her gaze lost some of its fire. "If this is a 'get Gemma to like me' ploy, it's a really sick one."

The barb stung, but what did I expect? I did remember that night, and I had wanted to kiss her. I'd wanted to kiss her many times, both before and since, but that night more than ever because I knew I was leaving school and wouldn't see her again. "You wore a red dress. It had thin straps and sparkles on the body. The skirt was long enough it touched your shoes. I'm not sure what colour they were, because it was pretty dark in the school hall, but I remember you'd painted your toenails red to match your dress."

Gemma's mouth dropped open, but I wasn't done.

"You had your hair down, but you'd curled it. It was pretty, but I thought it looked nicer straight—the way you usually wore it. I remember you got there late, because I was watching the door for you to come in. After everything York had put you through during the year, I wasn't sure whether you'd come or not. But then you were there, and I realised how stupid I'd been to think you'd let some meathead hold you back."

Gemma sat stiff in her chair, her fingers clutched tightly together. "How do you remember all of that? It was years ago."

I shrugged. "I told you. I wanted to kiss you. You pay attention to girls when you want to kiss them."

She relaxed in her chair again. "I don't know what to do with that. Why?"

"Why? Because you were beautiful. But you also intrigued the hell out of me. You were strong in all the times I was weak."

She seemed to mull that over. Then she asked curiously, "Why didn't you ever say anything?"

"Would you have listened? I'd tried apologising, and you mowed me down with your chair," I said, remembering the time she'd run right over my foot.

Gemma laughed quietly, which encouraged me to keep talking.

"I was going to try again during the formal dance, because I didn't think I'd see you again. But I waited too long, you went off with Logan and…" I shrugged. "I just let it go. I thought it was better to not ruin your night. I didn't know he was out there kissing you, though." I doubted I would have sat by and done nothing while my brother kissed the girl I liked. I'd always thought they were just friends.

I scooted my chair over so we were eye to eye. She looked bewildered and overwhelmed by my little sharing session. But her anger had dissipated.

"I'm really sorry, Gemma."

"You already apologised."

"But I didn't apologise for not telling you how I felt. Maybe it wouldn't have made a difference. Maybe you would have still gone off with Logan and your first kiss would have still been with him. But I'm sorry I didn't try."

I leant in slowly, and she stilled but didn't move away. Our mouths hovered inches apart, our breath mingling as lust swirled through me, threatening to ruin everything I'd worked to fix today. Gemma gazed up at me through hooded eyes, and for a second, I nearly gave in to the temptation to claim her mouth in the way I'd wanted to for years.

I wondered what it would be like, to feel her soft lips on mine, to feel her breasts against my chest, to have her fingers in my hair. It was all so close I could practically taste it. Her eyes fluttered closed, and my heart beat wildly. Fuck. I wanted to kiss her.

I wanted to kiss her more than any woman I'd ever kissed before. It should have been me. I should have been her first kiss. But I couldn't rush this. I forced myself away from her mouth, brushing my lips across her cheek before I stood and staggered my way back to my room in the barn.

11

GEMMA

Avoiding Ryker after his strange confession of a high school crush turned out to be easier than I thought. Dad was released from hospital the day after Ryker and I had had dinner together in the kitchen, so I focussed on spending time with him. He was walking with a cane, some paralysis still evident in one leg, but he managed if he rested regularly. His speech still wasn't great, and Mum took him back to the hospital most days for physio and speech therapy. The rest of the time, Dad sat out by the training rings while I taught from the centre. We were approaching winter, but even the cooling temperatures couldn't keep him inside. And now that he was home, I'd managed to get back into the main ring, without completely freezing up.

I saw nothing more than the occasional glimpse of Ryker for the next week. Most days he seemed to disappear around nine, with check marks already next to the list of jobs I left for him each day. And his car was absent from its parking spot by the barn most evenings, so I assumed the Blue Gum Pub was keeping him occupied. In fact, we saw each other so rarely I wondered if he was deliberately avoiding me as well.

So it took me by surprise one afternoon when I found him digging up the single veggie plot we had near the back of the house. He had headphones over his ears and gave no indication of noticing me. I couldn't help but stop and watch. He had his shirt off, the ends of the material shoved in his back pocket, the rest hanging down the back of his jeans.

The muscles of his toned torso and shoulders rippled beneath brown skin, covered in a fine layer of sweat and dirt.

I watched his abs flex, and thanked the lord for the warm Australian climate that meant even this close to winter, I could watch this great spectacle of human form. I quirked an eyebrow when he dropped to the ground, did a bunch of push ups, then picked up his shovel again. His muscles bunched and rolled as he dug a shovel into the soft dirt and turned it over for a few minutes before he dropped back to the ground to do sit-ups. I stifled a laugh. It was the strangest combination of work and workout. When he began doing sprints down one side of the veggie plot, I grabbed my camera from where it hung on the back of my chair and fired off a few shots. He stopped and picked up the shovel again, and I focussed in on the sweat droplet rolling down his neck. Through the viewfinder, I watched in distracted fascination as it travelled over a dirt smear on his pecs then I raised the camera to the relaxed concentration on his handsome face.

His eyes caught the light perfectly, and I snapped off a shot, before lowering the camera slightly to focus on his mouth. Full, pink lips that were wide in a laugh... I dropped the camera and fought the urge to put my hands on my hips. For once, I was grateful I couldn't move my legs because I probably would have stomped my foot like a two-year-old. He pulled his headphones off one ear, his laughter filling the air between us.

"You knew I was shooting you the whole time, didn't you?" I asked crossly.

He abandoned his shovel and smirked at me. "I might have."

I rolled my eyes. "Show-off."

"How'd your classes go this morning? I haven't seen you around much lately."

"Yeah, it's been busy," I said awkwardly, trying to pretend I hadn't deliberately avoided him because I'd thought he was going to kiss me. But then he hadn't.

"That's good, though."

"Yep."

He motioned to the shovel he'd stuck in the dirt. "I know the garden wasn't on your to-do list, but it looked like it needed some work."

I sighed as I surveyed the shameful veggie plot. "So you noticed none of us are much good in the garden then, huh?" I edged closer to examine his progress. He'd made a very small pile of pathetic, stunted-looking vegetables before he'd started digging up the rest of the plot. I picked up a short, fat, twisted carrot. "These are ridiculous."

He snickered, taking it from my hand and brushing dirt off it. "It'll still taste okay. But I can fix the plot for you. Get you going for next season."

I shrugged. "If you really want to. No one else is going to do it. I doubt we have money for seedlings. There might be some seed packets in the tool shed, though."

He shook his head and waved his hand around. "I'll take care of that, don't worry."

He leant on the shovel handle and wiped sweat from his eyes like he was a damn male model, and to my irritation, my stomach flipped. He was hotter than any model I'd seen, especially covered in dirt. He did things to my libido, even if I tried to pretend he didn't. I wasn't blind.

"You know, we tried vegetable farming once," I said, trying to keep my attention off his abs.

Ryker picked up a water bottle from the ground and twisted

the lid. He took a long swallow and I tried not to pant. My god. I needed to get a grip on my hormones.

"Where? You don't have the room."

I pointed to the thick grove of trees beyond the back of the barn. "We own another few acres on the other side of those trees."

Ryker's eyebrow inched up. "I had no idea. What's down there now?"

"Nothing much. Weeds and junk we don't use anymore but can't be bothered taking to the dump. Dad takes a slasher down there in the early summer in case of a bushfire, but other than that, no one goes down there."

The ground was rocky and uneven in parts beyond the trees, so I hadn't been down there in all the time since we'd given up on veggies and stuck to our strengths.

"Shame to waste the space," Ryker said thoughtfully, pulling his shovel from the ground and returning to the digging.

Despite my hormones telling me to stay and enjoy the free show, I headed for the house. But before I reached the door, I stopped and turned back.

"Ryker?"

He shielded his eyes from the sun as he acknowledged me. "Yeah?"

"Thanks for what you said the other day. You know. For apologising." I took a deep breath. "It meant a lot to hear you say that."

He studied me with his usual quiet intensity, his steady gaze pinning me in place, even from across the yard. "I wish I'd apologised sooner. I wish I'd never said it in the first place."

I nodded. "I know."

He gave me a tentative smile, and this time, I returned it with a genuine smile. Possibly the first one he'd received from me since we were ten years old.

Winter temperatures finally arrived more than halfway through the season. Until then, the weather had been pleasant. But mid-July brought a cold wind that whipped around the training ring, picking up dust and leaves as it went. I tucked my scarf closer around my neck and fought to keep a shiver at bay.

"I think we need to push Meagan up to the more advanced class," I said to the little girl's mother, then pressed my teeth together to keep them from chattering. I'd been talking to the woman for the past ten minutes, and I was really regretting not moving into the barn to discuss her daughter's progress. I'd forgotten how much she liked a chat.

"She'll be so excited. She's been asking for her own pony, and we said not until she advanced. We just wanted to make sure she likes horse riding first, you—"

The email alert on my phone *binged* loudly, and I gave Mrs Wilson an apologetic smile while I listened to the rest of her questions and concerns before Meagan whined she was hungry.

Her mother shushed her, but I piped up, taking the chance to end the conversation. "That's okay, I'll let you guys go. We can talk more about it next lesson."

Mrs Wilson nodded, and Meagan dragged her off to their parked car. I waved as they disappeared onto the road. Shivering when the wind whipped again, I hightailed it for the safety of the barn, pulling the wooden doors closed behind me and dropping the crossbar so they wouldn't fly open. Ryker looked up from putting a horse in its stall and raised a hand in greeting. I waved back, then rubbed my hands together, trying to force some feeling into them.

Remembering the email I'd gotten, I pulled the phone from my pocket and tapped the email notification. The preview told me the sender was Inside Photography. That was weird. I didn't remember signing up for their newsletter since I religiously bought their magazine. When it opened, I read the first line, and my heart stopped. Scanning the rest of the email, I then went back to the top and read it over again, shaking my head in confusion.

Yep. It still said the same thing the second time around.

Adrenaline rushed my system, my heart rate kicking over and thumping a hundred miles a minute to make up for the way it had stalled out earlier. It had to be a mistake. They must have meant for this to go to someone else. I hadn't even entered their competition. But when I checked, my name was at the top of the email. I glanced helplessly around the room, wondering what the hell I was supposed to do with this, wondering who to call to get it straightened out, when my gaze landed on Ryker's broad shoulders. And suddenly, with complete certainty, I knew exactly how this had happened.

"Ryker!" I snapped, making the horse closest to me skitter in her stall.

Ryker gave me a sharp look that said I should know better than to yell around horses, which just pissed me off all the more, because of course I bloody well knew that. I shoved my wheels hard in his direction and wondered if he could see the steam coming from my ears. Because it had to be there. How. Dare. He.

"What?" he asked, a frown pulling at his eyebrows. "You scared the crap out of Sabrina."

I narrowed my eyes. "Well, I wouldn't have had to if you hadn't gone behind my back and entered me in the photography competition! You know, the one I explicitly said I *wasn't* entering?"

"Oh," Ryker said with a wince. "That."

I closed my fingers into fists. I swear if I'd been able to stand, I would have thrown a punch at his face. As it was, I was considering throwing one anyway. It'd still hurt plenty, considering I wasn't too far from his junk.

"Wow. I thought you'd at least deny it for a few minutes. What gave you the right to do that? How did you even get your hands on my photographs anyway?"

He shrugged, as if my seething anger didn't faze him in the least. Which, of course, angered me all the more. A horrifying thought occurred to me, and I gasped. "Did you go into my room to get them?"

"What? No! Of course not. I sent them the ones you threw out after I walked into your darkroom that day."

The blood drained from my face. "Please tell me you aren't serious right now. You sent my *throwaway* photos to a national competition?" I wanted the earth to swallow me right then and there.

"You shouldn't have thrown them out. They were good!"

I rubbed my hands over my face and groaned. "Ryker, with all due respect, what would you know?"

His shoulders fell, and for a moment, I felt bad. I knew deep down he'd only been trying to help, but he'd overstepped the line.

"So, you didn't get in then? Look, Gemma, I'm really sorry. I was trying to help. You're so good; your talent shouldn't be hidden away out here on this farm. I really thought you had a shot."

My cheeks burned.

"I'll make it up to you. I promise," he said quietly.

Guilt swirled in my belly at the sadness in his voice.

"I got in."

Ryker's head snapped up. "What?"

"I got in," I repeated.

"You got in."

"Yeah. Just got the email."

His face split into a smile so wide I was sure it'd crack his cheeks.

"You got in! I knew you would!" His smile turned smug. Then confused. "Why are you angry at me then?"

"Because now I have to ring them and decline. It's embarrassing, Ryker." And not only that, he'd made me want it. I'd dismissed entering because of everything happening here with my dad and the wedding. And I'd been okay with that, telling myself I wasn't good enough to get a spot anyway. But now, it was there in front of me, and I still couldn't have it. And that hurt so much worse than not trying in the first place.

He looked at me like I'd grown another head. "Why would you decline?"

"I already told you all this. I have responsibilities here. I can't just up and leave. I have a full weekend of classes, and they want me there on Saturday morning. As in, *this* Saturday morning!" It was only Monday, but still. That was way too soon.

"So cancel them."

He didn't get it. "We need the money. I can't just cancel. I'm needed here."

"It's one weekend. I'm sure your parents would be happy to let you off the hook for such a big opportunity."

His words rang true, but I stubbornly shook my head. "No."

"Yes."

My blood boiled all over again. "What makes you think you have any say in this?"

He blew out a breath, his frustration with me evident in every movement he made. He dragged a chair over and sank into it so we were level. His dark gaze met mine, and he visibly calmed himself while I fought not to get lost in his eyes. Just because we hadn't been this close in weeks, didn't mean I had to lose myself in my stupid attraction to him.

"Tell me the real reason you don't want to do it."

"I did!"

His voice turned hard. "Don't bullshit me, Gemma. You live for photography. Teaching horse riding is just something you do to pass the time and help your parents."

My mouth gaped open. "That's not true. I love the kids I teach."

"You can keep lying to yourself if you want, but I know there's something more behind you not wanting to go to Melbourne. Have you ever been before?"

"No," I said stiffly before turning away. For all I claimed to be an independent woman, it was embarrassing to admit to him I'd barely left my little hometown.

To my surprise, he leant in and lifted my chin so I had no choice but to meet his eyes.

"Me neither. But I've heard it's amazing. Full of funky restaurants, and there's shopping and street art, and you can catch trams everywhere."

The chance to go to an art gallery alone was tempting. A little of the fight went out of me. "It does look beautiful."

"So, tell me again why you don't want to go."

I felt sick. Something in me wanted to trust him. Wanted to confide in him, but fear gnawed at me. This Ryker was so different from the old Ryker I thought I knew, and it was hard to reconcile the changes. Hard to trust someone who had let me down so badly in the past. But fear had always held me back. Maybe trusting him again was the first step beyond that. "Because I never go anywhere."

Ryker sat back in his chair, and when he said nothing, I sighed and continued. "I've never travelled alone. Around here, people are used to me. They don't automatically just see the wheelchair. They know I'm not some invalid who can't take care of herself."

"And the people in Melbourne will see that, too." He crossed his arms over his chest.

"But…what if I can't take care of myself?" I said quietly. "What if there's no disabled access and people have to carry me upstairs? I'd die of embarrassment. What if I get there and they think I can't do the job? What if they're right? It's sports photography, for Christ sake! I can't run after athletes."

"I have two working legs, and I can't either," he said calmly. He pulled out his phone, typed something in, then turned it around to show it to me. It was a photo of about fifty men, squished together in stadium seating, each one with a camera lens as long as a small child. "That's the media pit at the last Olympic games. No mere mortal can keep up with those guys. The photographers sit in a pen with their telephoto lenses."

He tucked his phone back in his pocket. "But you're getting ahead of yourself anyway. Just go to Melbourne and do the gallery. Melbourne is a big city, and you won't be the first disabled person to go there. You'll do just fine. And if there's a problem, you ask for help. There's no shame in that, and it doesn't make you weak. Being able to admit when you need help is what makes you strong."

His words hung in the air around me, and I huffed out an annoyed breath. "I really hate when you make sense."

He quirked an eyebrow. "So, does that mean you're going to go?"

"I don't know. Maybe? I'll have to clear my schedule, but…"

He was right. I couldn't give up a free trip, or the chance to see my work displayed in a gallery. I knew there was a good chance they'd take one look at my chair and rule me out of winning the position, but was I really going to let the opportunity pass me by? I knew there was no chance of my parents coming with me, we didn't have the extra funds for the flight, and although my sister did, I knew she had a dress fitting this weekend. If I was doing this, I was doing it alone. Maybe I needed that.

I nodded.

"Yes!" He rocked forward on his chair, grabbing me by the shoulders, and pulled me into a hug.

For a moment, I froze, taken aback by the sudden physical contact. But his arms around me felt strong and powerful, and I slowly relaxed into his embrace. The moment drew out, and he made no move to let go. His breathing increased in pace, matching my own, and I slowly slid my hands up his back. Muscles tensed and bunched beneath my fingertips. His masculine, outdoorsy scent, mixed with just the faintest trace of cologne or deodorant, swirled around me, and despite knowing I shouldn't, I let my eyes close.

I'd never been held like this by a man. I'd had exactly two kisses in my entire life. My first being Ryker's brother. The second, a drunken party kiss on graduation night with some random. But neither of those kisses had been more than a brief brush of lips with a bit of sloppy tongue thrown in for good measure. Neither of those guys had held me the way Ryker did now. And I was surprised to find how much I liked it.

We held the embrace for what could have been a minute or an hour before I realised how long it was going on. I pulled away, embarrassed that I'd held on to him like a desperate koala. But he caught my hand and tugged me back to him tilting my chin so I couldn't stare at the ground. His face was inches from mine, his warm breath coasting my lips. My gaze dropped to his mouth, and heat pooled low in my belly, and I wondered what it would be like to kiss him. Wondered what it would feel like to be in his arms as a woman he desired, not just because he was happy I'd won some competition. I dragged my gaze back to him and waited for him to move out of my personal space. But he didn't.

Butterflies rioted in my stomach. "What are you doing?" I whispered.

"I don't know," he murmured and inched closer so his lips hovered over mine.

A tremble coursed through him, as if he were fighting to keep himself back, and in that moment, realisation dawned on me. He was as confused as I was. I'd spent the last ten minutes yelling at him but now I was looking at him with bedroom eyes.

"I don't know either," I whispered. My head shouted warnings, but my body screamed at me to lean in. To not let the moment slip away like it had in the kitchen.

"I'm nervous. I want to kiss you so bad."

His words melted any reserve I had left. I let my eyes drift closed and talked my head into doing what the rest of me already knew was right. I closed the distance between us and kissed him.

Ryker's lips were soft and warm, moving against mine, opening as his fingers snaked into my hair. He deepened the kiss, and I allowed him in, sending heat and awareness across my skin. Suddenly, I wasn't cold anymore. In Ryker's arms, with his body heat engulfing me and his warm, wet mouth on mine, it felt like a glorious sunny day.

I don't know how long we sat there for, just kissing. Long enough for his fingertips to move from my hair, to my face and trace along my jaw. Long enough for my hands to roam his back and shoulders, until I moved onto his biceps. Long enough for me to marvel at how complete I felt, kissing this man who had once been a friend, then an enemy, and now something entirely new.

When we finally broke apart we were both out of breath, and Ryker's lips were swollen from our kiss. I didn't need a mirror to know mine looked the same. I probably had a nice rash around my mouth as well from his stubble. But I didn't care. I could have sworn I felt that kiss in my toes, even though I knew that was impossible. But his kisses made my whole body feel alive.

"I...um..." I stammered, not really sure what to do now we'd stopped kissing.

"That was..." he murmured, his cheeks blushing pink. Then he smiled.

A laugh escaped me. "I'm sorry, I'm making this super awkward, aren't I? I don't know what to say."

"Me neither. I feel like I should thank you. Because that was a phenomenal kiss. Would that be weird?"

I shrugged. "Yeah, probably."

He chuckled. "I won't then. I'll just say I really liked it."

My heart squeezed with a happiness I hadn't felt before. "I did, too," I whispered.

He stood and took a few steps back. "I should get on with it. I still have most of your to-do list left." He stepped back again and knocked over a stainless-steel bucket, which he quickly picked up and righted.

I snorted. "I'm going, too. See you later?"

He nodded. "You will." He bit his lip like he wanted to say more but was holding back, then he shook his head slightly before giving me a final grin. He turned and disappeared into his room at the end of the barn.

I let out a slow, shaky breath. I wheeled myself out of the barn and back into the blustery wind, but this time, I barely felt it. That kiss had been nothing like when I'd kissed his brother. Ryker's kiss sent my heart racing, and I knew I was grinning from ear to ear. Fumbling through the bag hanging on the back of my wheelchair, I grabbed my phone and dialled Reese's number.

"Gemma! Hey, I was going to call you—"

"I kissed Ryker."

"—later when— What? I thought I heard you say you just kissed Ryker?"

"I did."

"But you hate him."

I laughed. "I guess I don't anymore."

Reese went quiet. "Are you sure that was a good idea? He treated you so badly…"

I shook my head, and my enthusiasm died a little. Reese was still in that place I'd been a few weeks ago. She didn't know about how different Ryker was from the kid I'd known in high school. She didn't know about his family, or the tentative friendship we'd formed. We'd talked on the phone, but I'd been keeping all of that to myself until I worked out how I felt. She had the right to not be excited about this.

"He's grown up, Reese. You said it yourself. We aren't in high school anymore. Things are different. He isn't what I thought."

I could practically hear her pasting on a smile.

"Then tell me all the details!"

There was hesitation in her voice, and fake enthusiasm, but I let it go because I knew she was trying. She was my sister, and she was worried. But she was also my best friend, and I was busting to talk to someone about it. The need to spill my guts won out.

"Argh, Reese, it was amazing. I didn't know kissing someone could make me feel like that. What do I do now? Do we talk about it? Do I kiss him next time I see him? I have no idea what I'm doing here." I didn't even care. That kiss had made me giddy.

There was another long pause. Long enough I worried I'd done the wrong thing in telling her. I didn't even know what this thing between Ryker and me was. Maybe it was nothing.

But that kiss hadn't felt like nothing. And I was excited. I wanted someone to be excited for me.

"What, Reese?"

"You just sound… You just sound really into him."

I frowned. "Why do you say that like it's a bad thing?"

"It's not. I just want you to be careful."

"I am."

"Don't let him push you into anything…"

My cheeks heated. I had an inkling of where she was going with this, but I asked anyway. "Like what?"

"Like sex."

I was suddenly regretting calling her. She had apparently morphed into our mother while I wasn't looking. "We didn't have sex. It was just one kiss."

"I know but… Have you had sex before?"

I was glad I was alone on the path back to the house, because now I knew my cheeks were red. "No," I admitted. Then, my defence mechanisms rising, I added, "Is that really so bad?"

"No! Of course not! It's just… Do you want to have sex with him?"

"I don't know! Maybe?"

Huh. Where had that thought come from? Did I really want to lose my virginity to him? I let the thought marinate in my mind for a moment, and when heat rushed through me at the thought of getting naked with him, I decided that yes, I was definitely interested in losing my virginity with him.

"Have you…tested the waters, so to speak? I mean, I know you can have sex obviously. But will it be enjoyable for you? I don't want you to feel pressured into doing something you might not enjoy. Not that anyone really enjoys their first time, but you should get something out of it."

I rolled my eyes. "Are you asking if I masturbate, Reese?"

She made a weird noise on the other end of the phone. "God, I made this awkward, didn't I? I just don't want you going in unprepared…"

I laughed, happy that I wasn't the only one finding this conversation highly uncomfortable. "Let's just say he wouldn't be sailing uncharted waters."

Reese laughed, and I shook my head.

"Can we please stop talking about this now? Remind me never to ring you again about guy stuff, by the way. You're worse at this than Mum is."

"Don't you dare. You'd better ring me as soon as you and Ryker are done doing the nasty."

"Oh my god. I'm hanging up. I'll see you next weekend?"

"Bye, lover girl."

"Jesus. Bye."

THE LIVING ROOM was a warm cocoon compared to outside. I found Mum and Dad sitting together on the overstuffed green lounge we'd had for as long as I could remember. Dad's cane rested against the wall next to him as they watched a movie.

"Gemmmmmaaa," Dad called with a smile. His words were still

a little slurred, but he'd improved a lot in the few weeks since the stroke.

"Hey, honey, did your classes finish?" Mum asked, turning away from the TV.

I nodded. "Yeah, they're done. Listen, I want to talk to you guys about something."

Mum paused the movie and shifted in her seat. "Is anything wrong? You look very serious."

I forced a smile. "It's fine. I just need this weekend off."

"Oh." Mum frowned. "Any reason why?"

"I'm going to Melbourne," I said, forcing my voice to sound cheerful instead of desperate. I was overcompensating, the nerves in my belly at complete odds with the determination in my voice.

Mum's frown deepened, and I rushed to continue before she started with the objections I knew were coming.

"I got a place in a photography competition. I get to have some of my work displayed in a gallery."

"Well, that's lovely, but we just can't afford the plane tickets right now. With all of your father's medical bills…"

"I'm twenty, Mum. I didn't mean that you had to come with me."

Mum's eyebrows shot up in surprise. "You want to go by yourself?"

"Yes." I squared my shoulders, determined to make her believe it, even if I wasn't one hundred percent sure of it myself. "I'll be fine."

"Okayyy," Dad said.

Mum's face relaxed into a smile. "You'll have a great time. I just wish we could afford to see your work in your very first gallery show. We'll see the next one, though, I promise."

My mouth dropped open. "I'm sorry, what?" My gaze bounced back and forth between them, and I was sure my eyes were hanging out of my head. Who were these people, and what had they done with my parents?

"I'm not sure why you seem so surprised, Gemma. You're an adult, you're more than capable of taking yourself to Melbourne," Mum stated.

"I thought you'd be too worried and would fight me on going."

"I think it's great. You never want to go anywhere. You spend all your time here on the farm, it's not good for you. You're so isolated. There's no doubt in my mind you'll be just fine on your own for a weekend."

Mum was basically repeating everything Ryker had just said out in the barn. Apparently, I was the only one with doubts and fears about getting around on my own. A warm feeling spread through me.

"Thank you," I said quietly. "The weekend lessons, though…" I looked to my dad.

"Pppass me the phone. I'll ring Jjjimmmy from Oakly Rrrridge."

Mum clapped her hands before she got up to grab a phone. "If Jimmy's daughter can come lend a hand, we'll be fine for the weekend, Gem. We'll sort it out."

A slow smile spread across my face. "So I guess that means I'm going to Melbourne this weekend?"

"I guess you are," Mum said.

"Bbbbring me back a pressssent," Dad added.

I grinned. I was going to Melbourne.

12

RYKER

Friday arrived cold and clear, and I was up at the ass crack of dawn to get a start on Gemma's to-do list. She'd written out the next three days' worth of chores since she wouldn't be here on the weekend, and I had a lot to do. I got Sabrina out of her stall and led her out to the warm-up paddocks, checking her blanket was still firmly tied around her.

She nuzzled at my pockets, knowing I always kept treats there, and I pushed her away gently, chuckling at her nerve. My back pocket vibrated, and I stopped in the doorway to pull out my phone. A familiar name flashed on the screen, and my stomach dropped. Fuck. He was the last person I wanted to speak to, but I knew better than to not answer it. Not answering would only piss him off. And a pissed-off Gerard was not something I wanted.

"Ryker! Long time, no see, my friend."

I ground my teeth together at the word 'friend'. We were anything but friends. He was a shark of a man who had taken advantage of a dumb, naïve kid. But I'd made my bed and now I was lying in it. "What can I do for you, Gerard?"

"I'm just wondering where you've been, kid. Haven't seen you much lately."

"I've been around," I said, deliberately vague, though I was under no illusion that Gerard would buy it.

"We paid a visit to your girlfriend's house, but looks like you don't live there anymore. Got a new bird, do you?"

Rage built in my chest, and I gripped the phone so hard I was surprised it didn't crack. "You didn't need to do that. I'm not in breach of our agreement."

Gerard chuckled, the sound somehow menacing even through the phone. "I'm sure you've heard through the grapevine. Terms have changed."

My blood ran cold. "I don't have all the money. You know that."

He paused, and for a long moment, all I could hear was his breathing. "Well, that's a problem, isn't it?"

"I've got the five thousand we agreed on for today's payment. You can have that now, and I'll get you the rest as soon as I can."

"Yeah, that's not going to work for me. You owe another twenty-five, and I need my money back."

There was a long silence as I looked helplessly around the warm-up ring.

"Maybe we can come to some sort of agreement, though."

I cringed. Gerard's idea of an agreement probably involved a literal pound of flesh.

"What sort of agreement?" I was a fly caught in a spider's web. A very big, very dangerous spider who could eat me alive if he wanted but would most likely play with me first.

"Did I ever tell you how much I like cars, kid?"

I glanced over at my Mustang parked next to the barn, still covered in melting frost from the cold night. "No."

"Well, I do. And I saw you driving around Lorrington with your crippled friend the other day in a very nice little ride."

My blood boiled over. "Fuck you, Gerard. She's not a cripple. And you aren't having my car."

"Oooh! Touchy, touchy! Maybe she's not just your friend, huh, Ryker boy? Maybe she's the reason you ain't living with your little grease monkey girlfriend no more. Is that it?"

I bit my lip until I tasted blood, tightening my fist around the lead rope attached to Sabrina's halter. The damn spider had me cornered.

"I'll take your silence as a sign I'm on the right track. So, here's what's going to happen. You'll bring the cash and the car to my office, and we'll talk. You have an hour."

"An hour! I—"

The call cut out when he hung up on me. Sabrina sniffed my hair and pulled at the lead, impatient to go out.

"Fuck," I said to the horse, staring blankly at her. "I'm literally fucked."

THE MAIN HOUSE was quiet when I let myself in through the back door, in search of Gemma. Mr Lawson looked up from his chair at the little kitchen table as I entered. He sipped at a mug of coffee, the slight tremor in his hand and his cane next to him the only indication he wasn't quite the same man he'd been a few weeks ago.

"Mr Lawson," I said, nodding at him. "Is Gemma up?"

He glanced at his watch. "It's eaaarly, even for her. Sssshe's still in beeed, I think."

I nodded. "Right."

"You okay, kkkid?"

I cringed at the word kid. The same word Gerard used to make me feel ten inches tall. But coming from Mr Lawson, it felt entirely different. His voice was gruff, but there was affection behind it. Which was kind, considering we barely knew each other.

I nodded distractedly. "I need to head out to Lorrington. Could you let Gemma know? I wanted to say goodbye and wish her luck for her competition, but she'll probably be gone by the time I get back."

Fuck Gerard and his shit timing. I wanted to be here today to see Gemma off. Nothing else physical had happened between the two of us since our kiss, but I'd spent all week thinking about her and making excuses to talk to her. She seemed to be doing the same with me, showing up where I was working, bringing me lunch. One night when I'd gotten home from the Blue Gum, she'd still been out in her office in the barn, and despite it being past midnight, we'd sat there talking until three a.m. We seemed to be on the same page, happy to take things slowly and get to know each other again, and I'd felt light all week at the possibility of a new beginning with her. But Gerard's phone call had sent me crashing down from my Gemma high to the cold, hard earth.

Mr Lawson nodded. "Will dooo."

I grabbed my wallet from my room and the thick envelope of cash I'd withdrawn from the bank yesterday in preparation for today's drop-off. I threw them on the passenger seat as I slid behind the wheel and gunned the engine.

I'd known this day was likely to come. I'd already considered selling the Mustang to pay off Gerard, of course, but something had always stopped me. It wasn't so much that I loved cars. I liked them as much as any other guy, but this one was special. My dad had bought the shell when I was too young to even remember, and he'd slowly done it up over the years. One of my earliest memories was working on it with him, sliding underneath and listening in fascination while he'd pointed out each part and explained what it did. Logan had never been interested in cars, and Jared and Dallas were too young to do anything but get in the way, so it became something special. Something just for the two of us.

But then my old man had started drinking. And that had been the end of any father-son bonding we might have been doing out there. For a long time, it sat, partially done, until I'd realised he was never going to finish it. He'd lost interest in it. And in me. I finished it myself, and he hadn't said a word when I'd announced I was taking it.

I should have just sold it a long time ago, but the only good memories I had of my father were wrapped up in that car. But what Gerard wanted, Gerard got. Or his guys would find you and take it from you. No way was I risking them coming out here to find me. They could take the bloody car.

The sun was still oranges and pinks from its early morning rise, but I barely noticed. I tried to keep my mind blank when I drove away from the Lawsons' property, but the various ways this meeting could go down played in my head. Gemma was a distraction, and losing the car was a punch to the gut. I couldn't let my mind wander off down those tracks. I'd never been much good at thinking quickly but I needed to be sharp and focussed when I saw Gerard.

When the bush scrub roads gave way to the little town of Lorrington, I drove to the fish and chip shop that doubled as a front for Gerard's business, waited at the security gate for them to ID me, then pulled into the basement car park. The fish and chip shop ran legally, as far as I could tell, but all Gerard's shady business took place in the damp basement office. Out of sight and out of mind from the employees and the general public.

I reverse parked the car and sighed as I killed the engine. I ran a hand over the leather seat one last time, nostalgia and disappointment ripping through me. This was fucking bullshit. But keeping Gerard away from Gemma outweighed everything else. I grabbed my wallet from the passenger seat but didn't bother picking up the cash. Let him get it himself.

I forced myself across the otherwise empty parking lot to rap on the door of Gerard's office, my knuckles white from clenching my fingers so tightly. I concentrated on relaxing them as Gerard called me in, voice smarmy.

"You're late."

I tossed the keys on his desk. "I had to stop to get the cash," I lied. "It's on the passenger seat."

"All of it?"

"Every last cent."

He pushed his chair back and stood. He wasn't a particularly tall man, no taller than myself, but he was intimidating nonetheless. His eyes were sharp, and I knew from experience he missed nothing.

"So we're square now. The cash, and the car, and my debt is clear. Agreed?"

Gerard strolled to my side of the desk and leant back on it, crossing his arms over his chest and studying me like I was a piece in an art museum. Blood pounded in my ears.

"You know, Ryker. I do sincerely apologise for this."

I nearly snorted. He wasn't sorry in the least. He was a shark through and through, preying on people's weaknesses. He probably went home at night and jacked off over the sick power trip his 'job' gave him. "It's terribly unprofessional of me to call in your loan early, but you know how things go in the business world…"

He meant the criminal world, but whatever. He looked like he honestly believed himself to be a businessman. "There are deals to be made, and those deals require money. And you did owe me."

"And now I've paid you. Right?"

He plucked the keys from the desk and shook them at me. My anger threatened to bubble over. It would be so easy to punch him in his ugly face. Break his long nose, or knock out one of his impossibly straight, impossibly white teeth. Make him feel as small as he was trying to make me feel. I wasn't a particularly smart man, that was my brother's domain, but I was smart enough to know punching Gerard would be a very bad move. Despite sparring with Jared over the years, I was no fighter. Gerard's bodyguards would be all over me in a heartbeat, and who knew what they were capable of.

"Let's go have a look at your car." He glanced over his shoulder at me as he passed, a cruel laugh twisting his mouth. "I mean, my car. I've got to admit, just watching you driving it around Lorrington the other week made my dick hard."

Bile rose in my throat, and I glanced at the daylight spilling in through the garage door. Freedom was on the other side of that door. So close, yet right now, it might as well have been a million miles away. I was Gerard's play thing until he said otherwise.

He opened the driver's-side door and slid behind the wheel. I shoved my hands into my pockets, until the passenger side window rolled down.

"Get in," he ordered.

Fuck.

I lifted the door handle and sank down into the leather seat. The leather seat I'd recovered myself with the help of one of the guys I'd gone to school with.

"Gotta say, Ryker my boy, this is a real nice car. Who would have thought a pauper like you would have such a little beauty tucked away." He sat back, folding his hands behind his head. "Seriously, this car does things to me, Ryker. Look."

I made the mistake of doing as he said. His suit pants tented over his erection. My heart thumped, and I quickly turned away.

"This car gets you hard too, doesn't it?" He ran his hand over the custom-made steering wheel my dad had installed about ten years earlier. "You ever fuck your pretty little crippled friend in this back seat, Ryker?"

I dug my fingers into the leather, fighting to keep myself from launching at him and ripping his tongue out. "Are we done here?"

I seethed, barely keeping myself in check. "I've got somewhere to be."

He laughed, but his eyes darkened. "For now." He waved his hand dismissively.

Thank. Fuck.

I got out of the car, slammed the door, and forced myself to walk calmly to the exit that opened automatically when I approached. As soon as I rounded the corner, out of sight of my car and the piece of filth sitting in the driver's seat, I stopped. Doubling over, I vomited into the gutter.

13

GEMMA

"You have all your stuff, sweetheart?"

I'd somehow managed to sleep late, which had resulted in the world's quickest shower and a frantic few minutes of throwing things into an overnight bag. It was all Ryker's fault. I'd lain awake last night, replaying our kiss in my head, just like I had every night since it happened. But last night, my imagination had gone way beyond reality and morphed into thoughts of what it would be like to do more than kiss. It had been late when I'd finally talked myself out of going down to the barn and seeing if he was up for finding out. My dreams had been full of brown eyes, kind smiles, and wandering hands.

I patted the bag sitting on my lap and felt the hard cylinder tube that held the four prints I'd be displaying at the gallery the next night. A mixture of excitement and nerves swirled in my stomach.

"Let's go, then," Mum said.

"Yeah, just…"

"Just what? We need to get a move on. Your flight leaves soon."

"I know, I just wanted to say goodbye to Ryker." There was

nothing official between us, but we'd been spending time together when we could. I couldn't just leave the state without at least saying goodbye to him. I pushed my chair towards the door.

"He'ssss not here, Ggggemma. He came looking for you early thissss morning. You were still asleep butttt he asked me to tell you he'd be ggggone for a while."

I frowned. "Gone where?"

"Not sssure."

"Oh." The crashing wave of disappointment that broke over me took me by surprise. Some silly little part of me thought he would be here to see me off on my big adventure, but of course, there was no reason he would be.

I smiled more brightly than I really felt. "Probably a good thing, because we really would be late if I went to find him." I planted a kiss on my father's cheek before Mum and I got into her van, stashing my chair and bag behind us.

Mum chattered the whole way to the airport, and somewhere in the middle of her relentless questions about whether I had my emergency catheters, my phone charger, my prints, and a million other things, my disappointment over not seeing Ryker morphed into nerves. Nerves over leaving the farm. Nerves over travelling alone. Nerves that maybe, just maybe, I'd win and then I'd have to explain to my parents why I didn't want to work in the family business they'd built from the ground up. The thought sent a ball of guilt straight to my gut.

"Just drop me out the front, Mum," I said, as we navigated into the maze of airport roads. "Parking here costs a fortune." The quicker I got out of the car, the better. Before I chickened out of going to Melbourne, where I didn't know a single soul. Or drowned in my own guilt over not telling her the full truth about the competition prize.

"Are you sure? I don't mind coming in."

I almost let the panic take over. But I forced myself to answer. "I'll be fine. I'll call you when I get there."

Mum pulled into the drop-off zone and put the car in park. She leant across, and I wrapped my arms around her, inhaling her familiar scent, letting it calm my breathless lungs.

"I'm proud of you, you know? You've taken on a lot since your father has been out of action. You've really stepped up, and it's been good for you. Dragged you out of your shell a little bit."

Oh lord. She had no idea how her words twisted the knife I'd already stabbed myself with. "I wasn't in a shell," I complained weakly.

Mum tilted her head. "I'm glad you have this opportunity. I want you to get out and explore the world. It makes me nervous, of course. You're my baby. And sometimes when I look at you, I still see you as a little girl. But lately, you've come into your own. Being the boss suits you, honey. I don't think you're going to be happy being your father's underling for much longer. If you ever were."

My breath caught in my throat. "That's not true. I love Dad. And the farm."

"Of course you do. But that doesn't mean you have to stay forever."

"Are you kicking me out?" I squeaked, my face burning.

"Never. But look me in the eye and tell me teaching horse riding is really what you want to spend the rest of your life doing."

"I..." I turned away, wondering when my mother had gotten so perceptive. Or maybe I was just doing a bad job of hiding it. I winced.

"Didn't think so."

"But Dad—"

"Dad will be fine. He'll be back on his feet soon. This whole thing has made me realise we need to put contingency plans in place. He can't do this sort of work forever, and we need to think of the future. But none of that is your problem, Gemma. Your biggest problem right now is beating the rest of the competition and getting that job."

My mouth dropped open as a car parked in front of us, releasing excited passengers who pulled their suitcases from the boot. "How did you even know about that?"

Mum rolled her eyes. "Contrary to popular belief, I do know about this thing called the internet. You never even mentioned you could win a pretty amazing job from all of this."

"Because odds are I won't. And I couldn't leave everything on Dad right now."

"If you win, you will take it, Gemma. I won't have you sacrificing your own happiness for the sake of ours. That's my job as a parent, not the other way around." She laughed, squeezing me hard. "Don't look so surprised. Mothers always know more than their children think they do. Now go. Take a ton of photos and call me at least three times a day."

I was still trying to process her blessing, but I groaned good-naturedly and hugged her one last time. "Got it."

"Now go, before I get a ticket from the parking police that always hover around here."

I lifted my chair out, clicked on the wheels, and transferred into it before placing my bag back on my lap.

"Love you," I called. The guilt of leaving them still sat in my stomach, but it didn't feel so overwhelmingly permanent anymore. More like something that would resolve, given time.

She blew me a kiss as she pulled the van away from the curb, leaving me alone in front of the little country airport terminal.

I waved until I couldn't see the van anymore, then turned and wheeled myself into the airport, ready for the biggest weekend of my life. I was alone, but it felt pretty damn good.

GETTING through the airport and onto the plane went without incident. The flight wasn't long enough for a meal, but I enjoyed some complimentary peanuts and flicked through a photography magazine distractedly as the plane began its descent only an hour after we'd taken off. I sucked in a deep breath and got my first glimpse of Melbourne.

The competition had booked transfers from the airport for contestants, and a man holding a sign with my name on it was standing in the crowd when I arrived in the public waiting area.

"I'm Gemma Lawson," I said when I reached him.

I waited for the inevitable double take when he realised I was in a chair, but it didn't come. He simply stuck his hand out, and I shook it with a smile. Step one, make it to Melbourne without causing a scene: complete.

"I'm Gus. I'm yours for the three days you're here, so just let me know where you'd like to go. Perhaps the hotel first, so you can settle in?" he asked, strolling towards the parking lot.

Electric doors opened when we approached, and the cool, but fresh Melbourne air smacked me right in the face.

A multi-level parking tower loomed, and I followed behind Gus in his preppy button-down shirt and tailored pants. "Actually, can we just go straight to the gallery? I'm going to be too nervous to do anything until I've handed my prints in."

"Of course." He nodded, showing me to a white sedan.

Then we were on our way. The city streets bustled even in the middle of a workday, and I peered through the window, taking in the swarms of people and cars. We stopped at an intersection, and I grinned as a tram rumbled past. Tall buildings rose up on either side of us, but it was different to Sydney. Sydney felt like a crazy rabbit's warren, while Melbourne felt streamlined and organised with its wide, straight roads. After a few minutes of driving, Gus stopped the car in front of a squat, square building with glass windows lining the front façade. Multicoloured spears of light reflected off the glass, and 'Whiskey Street Art' was scrawled in elegant script on the sign above.

I eyed the front door and was relieved to see there were no stairs to get inside, just a small lip I'd be able to get over without a problem. So far, so good. No stairs was always a bonus. With Gus's card tucked firmly in my wallet so I could arrange my pickup, I waved goodbye before pushing open the glass door.

The light wasn't as bright on the inside of the building, and the ceilings were higher than I'd expected from the front. Exposed beams, and brick and glass on all the walls gave the room an industrial feel that was foreign to me, but I loved it all the same. A grin spread across my face. Holy shit. Was I really here, in an art gallery that was going to display my work tomorrow? How had this happened? I pulled my shoulders back and tried to look professional, like I did this sort of thing every day. But I was pretty sure the dopey grin was going to give me away as a country kid whose big-city dreams were all coming true. I pictured myself handing over my photographs and watching as someone framed them and hung them with care on a gallery wall. Pride and excitement took over any remaining nerves. I'd been dreaming of this moment for years, never daring to hope it may actually come true.

A tall reception desk sat in front of me, made of wood and metal. The woman behind it peered over the top, her bright red lips pulled into a taut smile that looked stiff and phony. "Sorry, we're closed right now. The first showing for the weekend is tomorrow night, or I can make you an appointment for a private tour if you prefer." She tapped a pen on the top of the desk.

"I'm Gemma Lawson. I'm one of the competition winners for the show tomorrow. I spoke to someone over email this week, and they said I'd need to come here before the show so I could get my work hung."

She huffed out a sigh that froze me to the spot.

"Nobody told me you were in a wheelchair. We haven't made any special arrangements for you."

Well, it was nice to get this far without a drama. I steeled my spine and sat up straighter. I'd known I'd get this sort of response from someone. It was inevitable. I tried to remind myself that the indignant annoyance rolling off her in waves might not have anything to do with me personally. But all the same, it stung. I bit back my smart-ass remark and instead spoke calmly. "I don't need any special arrangements. I just need to know what I'm supposed to do with my photos."

I forced a smile I didn't feel, and she pointed behind her.

"Fine. A couple of the other photographers are here as well. Just go through the doorway behind me and to your left."

On the other side of the door, mess and chaos greeted me, at complete odds with the sparse feel and the extreme quiet of the reception area. Papers, cardboard boxes, packing crates, Styrofoam packaging, and drop cloths had been left haphazardly on every available surface. The walls were bare except for picture frame hooks at regular intervals. And in the middle of it all, a group of five people talked across a high white table. My skin flushed hot, and I groaned internally. What was with all the high tables? The kind people in fancy offices loved because standing was more ergonomic than sitting. Also, the bane of my existence. I refused to let them know that, though. I plastered my fake smile on and approached the group, hoping I'd be able to hand my stuff in and get out of the way.

There were two guys, perhaps only a few years older than me, two women, and a man who clutched a clipboard to his chest and seemed to be directing the others. His black t-shirt was splattered with paint—whether he'd been painting or that was just the shirt design, I didn't know. He was the first to notice me and pulled off his reading glasses when I edged closer.

"I'm Gemma," I said, reaching the group, but since he was the only one paying me any attention, I directed my words to him.

He glanced down at a green clipboard in front of him. "Lawson? Great." He waved towards an unidentifiable pile at the far end of the table. "I hope you brought your submissions. You need to frame them, hang them, then get the hell out of here so I can work my magic with this place. Fuck knows, I have enough work to do without you lot underfoot."

I blinked. Well, that was blunt. I didn't dare ask questions or point out that hanging my work on hooks well above sitting height wasn't going to work. Instead I went to the end of the table and wondered how the hell I was going to do this. The other competitors looked up as I passed them to get my materials, one girl with long, auburn hair and freckles across her nose smiled kindly at me, but then she quickly went back to working on her entry. No one spoke, so I didn't either. I was dying to see what sort of photos the other competitors were entering, but with the table a good few inches over my line of sight, there wasn't any hope of that. I found my pile of frames instead and pulled them down, praying something wouldn't fall on my head. I managed to stay concussion free and settled the four frames on my lap.

They were large, and while I didn't have trouble with their weight, their size and shape and the fact there were four of them made them awkward. I put two of the frames down on the floor, leaning them against my chair and got to work, prying open the back of the first frame. I struggled with it for a few moments, but I needed both hands to get each side open, which left nothing to stop the frame sliding right off my lap and smashing on the polished concrete floor. That was not a scene I wanted to create. The nerves were threatening to morph into panic, and I took a deep breath. There was a simple solution for this. And it was to just work on the floor. They'd all stare at me, and the thought of being the centre of attention was embarrassing. But I didn't have much choice.

Shifting my legs to one side, I put the frames down and

lowered myself onto the floor. Then got to work. I had the first frame open in less than thirty seconds. I could feel the eyes of the others on me, and I told myself it was because I was about to pull my entry from my bag and they would all want to check out the competition as much as I did.

Lifting my first photo from its travelling cylinder, I smiled as Ryker's face unfurled in front of me. It was a black and white from the day I'd found him working in the garden. Sweat dripped from his temple, and veins popped in his biceps. My favourite part of it was the tiniest of smirks, the sign that had given away he'd known I was shooting him. It may not have been participating in an actual sport, but the shot had showed off how fit he was, the light was good, and I'd loved the grain of the black and white film I'd used. Plus, the odd location, surrounded by dirt and ripped up veggies, made it interesting and could be a talking point. At least I hoped so. It tucked neatly into the frame and I sat back and admired my handiwork for a second, letting his handsome face reassure me. The photo was good. And the gorgeous man in it had kissed me.

Around me, the other contestants were hanging their work on hooks attached to the walls. One of the guys had a four series sequence of water polo players, determination and strength radiating from their expressions and water droplets frozen in midair. A middle-aged woman with short brown hair hung a series of shots, each one a different sport but all with a stunning sunset or sunrise as the backdrop. The colour she'd achieved was phenomenal.

Someone walked behind me, looking over my shoulder, but from her neutral expression, I couldn't tell whether or not she thought my work was any good. I shrugged it off and focussed on getting my other shots into their frames. I was the last to finish, so every other contestant was milling around waiting while I brought my first piece to a blank space on a wall. Feeling self-conscious, I hung it on the lowest of the four hooks, straightened it until I was satisfied, and moved back a few inches to examine it again. I collected my next frame, tucking it between my thighs and chin, and hung it on the hook next to my first one.

A sense of pride nearly overcame me when I looked at them. They were both shots taken on our farm, one of Meagan jumping a log with her horse, the next of her nose to nose with him as she combed him down afterwards. One was an example of sports photography in its fullest form—action and movement flowing through a crisp, clear shot. The other showed what I was more about. I loved the technical challenge of sports photography, but so much about it was people, too. People and their emotions. I wanted to demonstrate I could be good at both.

The woman with the sunset photos appeared beside me, my last two prints in her hands. I'd been so caught up in seeing my work on the walls of a real, live gallery, that I hadn't even seen her move from her spot.

"May I?" she asked, motioning to the two higher hooks we both knew I didn't have a hope in hell of reaching.

I smiled at her, grateful she'd seen my dilemma and offered her help, saving me from having to ask. "Thank you."

She nodded and hung the last two prints, the ones of Ryker in the garden. Someone cleared their throat behind me, and I turned to see it was the young receptionist from out the front. She took her glasses off and stepped closer, studying each photo intently. She paused for an extra-long time on the photo of Ryker, and when she turned around, she focussed on me. "These are yours?"

I nodded, holding my breath. She may not have been the one choosing the winner, but for some reason, I wanted her to like them. She'd made a snap judgement when I'd first arrived, and I wanted her to eat her words.

She put her glasses back on. "Hmm."

My heart sunk as she strolled past to the next competitors work. What did that mean?

I straightened my shoulders. Rejection was part of being an artist. Not everyone was going to like my work. I knew that.

With all my prints up on the walls, I was done for the day, and it was still early enough for me to call Gus and ask him to take me sightseeing for the afternoon. Reese had told me about a restaurant she'd eaten pancakes at every day for a week the last time she'd been to Melbourne, and sugar seemed like a great idea right now. I rolled away towards the receptionist desk but paused in the doorway to take one last look at my entry, up on the gallery wall. The receptionist may or may not like them, but whether she did or not, my work was still hanging on the walls of a prestigious Melbourne art gallery. And that was something to be celebrated.

The two young guys had shifted to stand in front of my photographs. I tried to convince myself to just keep moving but there was that damn incessant need to know what other people thought again. They obviously both had talent, and I was past the point of being objective about my own abilities. I couldn't tell any longer if it was good or if I was deluded, so the opinions of others was all I had to go on.

"Great," one muttered to the other. "We haven't got a chance against her."

My face flushed with pleasure as an embarrassed smile stretched across my face. I was glad they hadn't noticed me behind them. The guys calling me a threat took a little of the sting off the receptionist's dismissal. I pushed my wheels quietly, praying they wouldn't squeak on the polished concrete floor and give away the fact I'd been eavesdropping on their conversation.

"Agreed," the other guy said. "As if anyone is going to beat a chick in a wheelchair. She'll sit next to her photos and every judge will give her the sympathy vote. Or they'll pick her just to look good to the public. Her work isn't even proper sports photography. This is unfair."

The smile fell straight off my face, my mouth dropping open

in confusion and surprise. A lethal mix of shame and anger swirled within me, stealing my breath. Worse, hot tears pricked the backs of my eyes. I racked my brain for something to say, for the strength to put them in their place, but the pure shock of such a malicious and unfair comment, even if it hadn't been meant for me to hear, rocked me to my core.

Not once in my life had I used my disability as an excuse for anything.

Not once had I asked for special treatment. But I couldn't control how other people treated me. I'd had teachers at school who had marked my work higher than I deserved. I'd had people at riding events pull me into photos I had nothing to do with just for the publicity a disabled rider would bring them.

If by some miracle I did win, all I'd hear was those two guys saying I didn't deserve it. With two comments, they'd cursed me to forever wonder if I'd only won because the judges and the magazine wanted to be politically correct, or worse, they wanted to use my disability as an advertisement for how inclusive they were. Disabled girl wins sports photography internship. Yeah, wouldn't that get them some good press.

A fire within me burned to take the two guys down a peg. But what was the point of telling them off? They were probably two privileged white men, used to getting everything they'd ever wanted on a silver platter. My anger would mean nothing to them. They hadn't even had the decency to check I'd left the room before they'd started slagging me off. There was no hope for people like them. I straightened my shoulders and left the room without a word.

My head might have been held high, but my soul was crushed.

14

GEMMA

No longer in the mood for any sort of company, I didn't call Gus. Instead, I made my way out onto the street and wandered around, looking at the multitude of coffee shops and graffiti-filled alleyways until I found myself at a tram station. I'd already researched them and knew they were wheelchair-friendly, with lowered platforms. As I sat waiting, I pulled my phone out, scrolling through the contacts list until I found Ryker's name.

I hovered my finger over the connect button and tried to come up with a plausible reason to call him. I could ask about the farm. Or ask where he'd been this morning. But I was worried I might blurt out the fact I just wanted to hear his voice. I wanted to unload my shitty day on someone. Not just anyone. Him. I'd almost convinced myself when the tram trundled up. I put my phone away and got on.

A big part of me had been disappointed when he hadn't been there to say goodbye this morning. I'd missed him. How could I have missed someone I only saw yesterday? The same someone I'd hated just a couple of weeks ago? Somewhere along the way, I seemed to have developed a case of feelings.

I found the hotel without a hitch, and the sun was beginning to sink outside the floor-to-ceiling window by the time I made it to my room. I briefly noted the interior was on the fancy side with a huge bed and modern-looking bathroom, but I couldn't bring myself to care or get excited about the luxury.

Instead, I stayed in the spacious shower for an obnoxiously long time, shaving my legs and soaping my hair and generally trying to clean away the grime of the day. It didn't make much difference, though. My grey mood didn't lift, nor could I wash away the insults that seemed to follow me from the gallery.

Once dry, I bundled myself into bed, called room service, and picked a movie from the pay-per-view menu. The magazine could pay for that one.

Food came, I ate. The movie rolled, and I watched. None of it made any sort of impact. All I could think about was talking to Ryker. I grabbed my phone, and before I could chicken out, I called him. It went to voicemail, and not caring if it looked desperate, I hung up and rang again, rationalising that the farm was a big place and he may not have been close enough to his phone to answer the first time.

"Come on," I whispered. "Please answer." I needed to hear his voice. But it rang out again, and I dropped the phone on my bed. Exhaustion and disappointment threatened to drag me under. This day just needed to end. I was out minutes after my head hit the pillow.

Thumping noises from the hallway woke me from a deep sleep. My eyes were heavy, my arms uncoordinated as I sat up and tried to work out where the hell I was.

Hotel. Right.

When silence greeted me, I strained my ears in the darkness, wondering if I'd dreamt someone knocking on the door. There were a lot of rooms on this floor, maybe the knock had been for someone else.

But then it came again, and this time there was no mistaking it. "Yes?" I called to the closed door, but there was no response. Damn thick fancy hotel walls. I flicked on the bedside lamp and pulled my chair over, transferring into it before wheeling across the room. The knock came again. It had to be a staff member, or someone drunk with the wrong room number, which made getting out of the warm bed even less appealing. I was too low for the peephole, so I made sure the safety chain was on, then scanned my key to pop open the lock.

The bright light of the hallway, the stark comparison to my dim room blinded me for a moment, but when my vision cleared, I found myself staring up at a dishevelled-looking Ryker.

"Hey, Gem."

My mouth dropped open and I gaped at him through the gap.

He gave me a tired smile, his eyes crinkling at the corners. "Can I come in?"

I closed the door with my heart thumping out of my chest, praying I didn't look like a swamp creature, and slipped off the safety chain to open it wide. His jeans and hoodie were wrinkled, his hair mussed up in every imaginable angle.

"What are you doing here?" I asked, rolling back to let him in. "What time is it?"

He moved through the darkness to perch on the edge of my bed while I found the panel that controlled the lights. I blinked in the glare, shocked when Ryker was still sitting there, seemingly not an illusion. Because let's face it. Him turning up at my hotel room when I was disheartened and lonely was a pretty good dream.

"A bit after one a.m."

"What are you doing here?" I asked again, dumbly.

His head dropped as he leant forward, resting his elbows on his knees. He scrubbed his hands across his face and through his hair, not that it made an ounce of difference to the way it stuck up at odd angles. I wheeled over to him, so we sat opposite each other. He was like a different man to the one I'd seen just over twenty-four hours earlier. There was no trace of the smiles I'd seen from him more and more since the day we'd kissed in the barn. He looked haggard, and I didn't need the set of his shoulders to tell me how tense he was. It rolled off him in waves.

"I..." He glanced around the room before focussing on me again. The pain in his eyes made me want to cry. "Honestly? I don't know. I had a really shitty morning, and when I thought about what would make me feel better, all I could think about was talking to you."

A smile lifted the corner of my mouth when I remembered how I'd called him. "I tried calling you earlier, but it went to voicemail..."

"You did? My phone died hours ago." He tucked his hands into the pockets of his hoodie. "I wanted to say goodbye to you this morning. I'm sorry I wasn't there. Gerard called me in. He took my car as payment for my debt."

"What?" My head jerked back. "Shit, Ryker. I'm sorry. You have to go to the police."

"I know. I did. I made a report."

I breathed a sigh of relief. Thank god. Knowing the police were dealing with it made the situation a little less terrifying.

"So...you flew here?"

He shook his head. "I also gave him all my cash. Well, almost all. I hitched a ride here to save what I have left for the flight home."

"You hitched the fifteen hours from Erraville to Melbourne."

"Well, from Lorrington. But yeah. I would have been here earlier otherwise."

An astonished but delighted laugh escaped me. "You're insane. You could have been killed by some psycho who picks up hitch hikers and scoops out their eyeballs with spoons."

A small smile tugged at his lips. "He was okay. Didn't smell the greatest but he didn't rob me when I fell asleep, so there's that."

He fluttered his long, dark eyelashes at me. "And my eyes are still intact."

He pushed to his feet and strolled to the window, pressing his hands against the glass. I let myself drink in the sight of him. Even dishevelled as he was, just the sight of him did things to my libido. All the nights I'd lain awake this week, thinking about him, were still at the forefront of my mind. Now here he was. And we were alone. In a hotel room.

He turned and glanced down at me as I parked myself next to him. "So, this is awkward."

I started, and the smile slipped from my face. "Is it?" It didn't feel awkward to me. It felt great. Knowing he'd travelled fifteen hours just to see me melted my insides. No one had ever gone so out of their way to see me before, and I kind of liked how it felt.

"I thought you'd have a lounge I could crash on for the night."

We both glanced over at the bed.

"But it's okay," he said hastily. "I'll get my own room."

"Was this your ploy all along?" I asked with a laugh, raising one eyebrow. "Show up here in the middle of the night and crawl into bed with me?"

Ryker held his hands up in surrender. "I swear, I just came to talk. I'm not going to try anything. Unless…"

My heartrate picked up again. I'd been joking but suddenly I really wanted to know what he meant. "Unless what?"

His eyes turned hot, melting through me like lava. "Unless you *want* me to try something."

My heart stopped. We'd had that one kiss earlier in the week, and I'd wanted more to happen between us, but this was the first concrete sign I'd had from him that maybe he wanted the same thing.

"Like what?" I whispered.

He knelt in front of me, his knees sinking into the plush carpet, making our eyes level. He grasped my chair and tugged it close so my feet brushed his thighs. His fingers crept slowly along the metal rails, until he reached my hand resting on my wheel. I watched in fascination as he linked his fingers between mine. "I can't stop thinking about that kiss," he said, his voice sounding husky.

My heart kicked again, thumping so loudly I was sure he'd hear it. "Really?"

"Yes, really." His thumb rubbed at my skin, and I tried to focus on that rather than the heat that was spreading from his touch. "It was a good kiss."

"I haven't got much to compare it to," I admitted.

He pulled back an inch. "You haven't?"

I shook my head, embarrassed, wanting to punch myself for saying anything in the first place. He didn't need to know exactly how inexperienced I was.

His gaze lowered to my lips. "I don't know why. You could have any man you wanted, Gemma."

And just like that, the warm fuzzy feelings he'd been giving me turned ice-cold. I pulled my hand away and laughed, but the sound was hard. "Don't say things like that."

"Why not?"

"You know why not. People don't see me. They see the chair. It happened today at the art gallery."

"What did? A guy didn't want to hook up with you because of your chair?" Ryker asked in a strangely strangled voice.

Was that a hint of jealousy I heard? That flash in his eyes told me I might not have been the only one harbouring a case of feelings. The idea softened my mood so quickly I almost laughed.

"No, dumbass. A couple of other contestants made some comments, and I let them get to me. They see me as the token disabled chick. Same thing happens with guys. They see the chair first. They don't bother trying to get to know me. Or maybe they just assume I'd be too much work for too little pay off. Or maybe they're just weird about getting with a girl who can't feel her legs.

I don't know. But whichever way you look at it, people see the chair first."

"I don't."

My breath caught.

His fingers circled my wrist, and he tugged it gently until I looked back into his eyes. "Listen to me when I say this. I think you're incredible. And not just because you were strong enough to put up with years of torture in high school and still come out the other side a nice person. And not just because you gave me a second chance when I didn't deserve one. You're hot as fuck, Gemma."

He ran a hand up my arm, stopping at the side of my face so his fingertips brushed my pulse and his thumb coasted over my lips. Sparks went off in my body like it was New Year's Eve on Sydney Harbour. I'd always suspected the extreme sensitivity in my upper body was a by-product of having only fleeting feeling in parts of my legs, but his fingers touching the delicate skin of my neck and lips in unison sent my pulse into overdrive.

"No one's ever called me hot as fuck before," I whispered against his thumb. I couldn't help the smile spreading across my face. Just like that, my shitty night did a one-eighty.

"Then they're all dumb or blind," he said with conviction.

I expected him to move back, maybe get up off the floor and find somewhere more comfortable to sit, but when he didn't, my gaze found his, his eyes burning bright.

"Can I kiss you again? Please?" he asked quietly.

"I—"

He closed the gap between us, his lips meeting mine, hot and demanding and melting me on the spot. I inched forward on my chair, and his arms came around me, pulling me to his chest. I skated my fingers up his arms, over the top of his hoodie and around his neck. We found our rhythm quicker this time, more familiar with each other, and it was only a few moments before I opened my mouth to deepen the kiss. He responded instantly, his tongue meeting mine, and we moved together in slow, languid touches.

Despite my lack of experience, part of me knew that kissing didn't normally feel like this. There was more to this than just the physical. I couldn't imagine anyone else kissing me the way Ryker did now. Holding me so gently, yet with so much strength. Replacing the hate I'd once felt with something so warm and tender.

I snaked my fingers into his hair, combing through the tussled ends, tugging him closer so our lips crushed together. What would it be like to be skin to skin with him? To feel his hard chest against me? To touch every inch of him, to explore his body and find out where and how he liked to be touched? Heat rushed through me at the idea of finding out.

"Fuck, Gemma," he mumbled around my lips. His hands roamed my back, his fingers sliding over the skin where my shirt had ridden up.

It was all I could do to stop myself from begging him to take it off.

"What?" I gasped, my skin rising into goosebumps everywhere he touched.

"I…" He shook his head and pulled back and stared at me. His dark eyes like laser beams, his chest heaving as we both fought to catch our breath. "Tell me to stop. Because my self-control is down to negative figures right now."

He didn't even wait for me to respond. His lips crashed back to mine like he couldn't stand to be away from them a second longer. His tongue dove into my mouth, dominant and possessive, a side of him I hadn't seen before but wanted more of. My nipples tightened, and I moaned, trying to increase the friction against him.

"Don't stop," I breathed. "Not yet."

He groaned against my lips and tightened his arm around my back. Without missing a beat, he scooped me from my chair, pushed to his feet, and carried me across the room to the bed. He laid me down like I was made of porcelain, never once lifting his mouth from mine. Then he was on top of me, a delicious weight that felt oh so right. My skin was on fire beneath the long-sleeved, winter sleep shirt. Ryker's lips moved off the edge of my lips, along my jaw to my neck, and I closed my eyes, relishing the hot wetness of his mouth on one of my most sensitive places. He kissed his way up and down my neck, his breath misting across my skin until I couldn't stand it anymore. I fisted the back of his hoodie and yanked it up, making it obvious what I wanted. He sat up, his legs straddled either side of my hips, his abs appearing when he pulled the material over his head. As he untangled himself, my gaze traced the ridges of his toned stomach, then lower to the noticeable bulge in his jeans. When I looked back up, he was watching me quietly, but unashamed.

"You good?"

I smiled. "Better now your shirt's off."

He grinned, his fingers finding the edge of my sleep shirt and slipping underneath. He ran a flattened palm across my stomach. I wasn't wearing a bra, and his fingertips were centimetres from the swell of my breasts. Breasts that ached for him to move his damn hand an inch north. I wriggled restlessly on the bed.

"Can I—"

"Yes," I interrupted. I didn't even know exactly what he wanted to do, but I liked the direction we were heading in. And right now, with his hands so close to my breasts, I only wanted to do more of it.

He leant down and kissed the space just below my navel, making me jerk, more because I anticipated what was to come than because I had a lot of sensation there. His lips brushed over my abdomen, inching my shirt up as he went. The material slipped over my breasts, my nipples hardening in the cool air, and Ryker continued his path of kisses, right through the centre of my chest, stopping at the base of my neck. I lifted my shoulders so he could free the back of my shirt, then waited while he threw it on the floor. His gaze travelled over my skin, and I was surprised to find his eyes on me didn't make me self-conscious. He was the only man to ever see me bare, but all his gaze did was heat my blood.

"You're so beautiful." His voice was husky.

"Kiss me," I whispered.

Ryker obliged, but it wasn't my mouth he kissed. His lips closed over my nipple, and I hissed in pleasure, my back arching at the foreign feeling, then melting into the silky softness of the sheets. I hadn't noticed earlier how nice they were, but now it was as if every nerve ending came alive under Ryker's touch, the grey cloud that had been hovering all day lifting to reveal a bright-blue sky.

His tongue swirled around my tip, and he sucked gently before letting his teeth graze the sensitive skin. I groaned when his fingers joined in and stroked the swell.

"You're so responsive," he murmured, letting his fingers trail across my other nipple, squeezing it gently.

"By-product of a spinal cord injury. Everything above the injury is super sensitive."

He shifted to the side to lean on one elbow, fingers trailing across my breasts. "So, you like this?"

"Yes." The way I writhed under his touch and my hardened nipples surely told him everything he needed to know.

"How about here?" He slid a flattened palm down my stomach, heading south.

My heartrate picked up. "Yes."

I propped myself up, watching as he tucked his fingers below the elastic of the yoga pants I'd worn to bed. He looked at me questioningly.

"I don't have full feeling beneath my belly button. I can feel more in my left leg than my right."

"Do you have enough feeling to orgasm?"

When I'd thought of getting naked with someone for the first time, I'd always thought I'd die of embarrassment. My body didn't work the same as other women's. I'd thought it would be awkward to have to explain the ins and outs of sex with a paraplegic—even more awkward because I didn't really know what I was doing either. But in that moment with Ryker, I wasn't embarrassed at all. Annoyed because the kissing and touching had come to a halt while I explained to him, but not embarrassed. And maybe that told me all I needed to know. I felt comfortable enough with Ryker to speak about my body without fear of judgement. That told me he was the right person to be doing this with.

I nodded. "I have before. But not easily. Or quickly." It had taken me years and a vibrator to work out how and where I had the most sensation, and how to get myself off. I could do it easier now, after realising a lot of it came from my head. I needed visual stimulation, and my brain had to be on board. If my brain was horny, the rest of me responded accordingly. I didn't know if I felt orgasms the way other women did, but I did feel enough to enjoy it.

Ryker ran his fingers back and forth along my waistband as he nodded. "But if I learnt how to touch you the right way, and found your sensitive spots, you could?"

I nodded, heat flushing through me at the thought.

"I'll make it my mission then." Then his eyes widened. "Only when you're ready, though. It doesn't have to be tonight. I didn't come for sex. You know that, right?"

Jesus. He was saying all the right things. I knew he was telling the truth. Nobody hitchhiked fifteen hours for a booty call. A big part of me wanted to do more. I was dying to see what he looked like beneath his bulging fly. Dying to run my hands over it and feel the hard length of him. I wanted to make him feel as good as I felt right now. But we didn't need to rush into this. We'd only shared one kiss before this, and for tonight, maybe second base was enough.

"I want to," I whispered. "But not tonight. Just keep kissing me."

He leant down and kissed me sweetly. "You got it. I'll be here, whenever you're ready, Gem. Just say the word."

15

RYKER

For a couple of country kids, the two of us managed to do a pretty good job of sleeping in. When I woke up on the silky hotel bedsheets, light was already streaming in the large windows. Beneath the warm blankets, I found Gemma's still topless form and tucked myself in behind her, letting my fingers graze her bare skin, refamiliarizing myself with the shape of her that I'd discovered last night. I rolled her nipple between my fingertips, making her moan as she fully woke up, and I leant in to kiss her neck.

"You need to stop that, or we won't be getting out of this bed today."

I chuckled, squeezing her nipple again. "Is that a promise?"

My morning erection was pressing against her ass, and her moaning wasn't helping matters. She turned her head, capturing my lips in a kiss.

"I'm already regretting stopping us last night. Don't make it worse."

I made a little room, and she rolled over so we were facing each other. My gaze couldn't help drifting to her pink nipples showing just above the blanket.

"Do you need a date for the gallery tonight?"

She sighed. "I'm not sure I even want to go."

I frowned. "Yes, you do. Because if you don't, those dickheads will know they got to you. And you deserve to be there every bit as much as any of them do. Not everyone thinks like them."

"Did you bring a suit by any chance?"

"I didn't even bring underwear."

"Ew!"

"Don't worry, I'll rent a suit. And go commando."

She cracked up laughing. "That's disgusting."

I kissed her forehead. "I know. You'll get used to me."

"Will I?"

"I hope so. Because I want to stick around."

She paused, then her smile lit her eyes. "I think that can be arranged. I know your landlord."

I went in for a kiss, but she playfully pushed me away. "Stop. We need to go get some food and find you a suit. We can kiss later."

Gemma locked herself in the bathroom for a while before letting me in for a shower. When we were both dressed, we took the elevator to the ground floor, bypassing the hotel's buffet breakfast in favour of a Melbourne City café. Down an alley, covered in beautiful, artistic graffiti we found a place that looked promising. The delicious aroma of fresh brewed coffee and pancakes led us in by our noses, and we ate in a companionable silence that felt as comfortable as breathing.

After, we wandered the main streets in search of somewhere to buy a suit that didn't cost me the last few hundred dollars I had to my name. Gemma paused in front of an Op Shop. In the window, a mannequin wore a dark-brown suit that was probably from some poor sod's eighties wedding. "It's a suit, and it's probably cheap?"

"There's a reason for that."

"Just try it on, you snob."

"Only if you try on that." I pointed to a bright-pink formal-style dress that wasn't much newer than the suit was.

She wrinkled her nose.

"Now who's the snob?" I chuckled.

She tilted her head to one side, considering the ruffles and fluoro pink taffeta. "At least it doesn't have shoulder pads, I suppose."

I pushed her up the ramp and into the store before either of us could change our minds. A middle-aged woman behind a desk smiled at us when we asked to try on the clothes in the window and enthusiastically undressed the mannequins for us. We were the only people in the large shop that was filled with racks and racks of secondhand clothes. You could easily lose a small child in the maze.

In the spacious changerooms, with nothing more than a thick curtain made from a cheap scratchy material to separate us, I tried not to think about Gemma stripping off just inches away from me. Instead I eyed the suit. It really wasn't so bad, apart from the colour. The jacket was double-breasted with gold buttons, and the collared shirt beneath it looked to be decades newer than the suit itself. I shucked my clothes, slipping on the pants and the shirt. I opened the curtain to the main room, shrugged on the jacket, and went to stand in front of the full-length mirror. I was surprised to find it fitted well. Even the gold buttons were growing on me. I picked up the price tag hanging from my sleeve. Forty bucks. Sold.

I grinned into the mirror as Gemma appeared in the reflection, holding her blindingly bright dress across her chest. She pulled a face at me.

"I hate that you look hot in that while I look like I'm going to a fancy-dress party. Can you do me up?" She leant forward and motioned to the zip at the back.

I did her up before stepping behind her so she could see her reflection in the mirror.

"I like it," I said as seriously as possible, while fighting back a laugh. The dress was ridiculous. It had so many ruffles you could barely see any of her actual shape. "You should get it."

"No chance in Hell."

I laughed and pulled out my phone. "Fine. But we're taking a selfie at the very least."

I knelt next to her, and we moved in close to take the shot. We both stuck out our tongues at the last second.

Gemma laughed when we inspected the photo. "We used to do that as kids, too, remember?"

I did. Neither of us had ever much liked having photos taken.

She shoved the strap of her dress off her shoulder and scratched at the skin beneath it. "I don't know how they managed to wear these dresses in the eighties. This material is awful."

I grabbed her hand and kissed the bare shoulder she'd been scratching. Her skin was so soft under my lips I couldn't help kissing her again. She stilled. I inched the strap a little farther down her arm and ran my lips from her shoulder up the side of her neck.

"Agreed. The awful material needs to go."

The store around us was still empty, with no sign of the woman who worked there. The only noise was the golden oldies station that played through crackling speakers and Gemma's slightly accelerated breathing. I moved back, and she gave me a smile as I pushed her backwards into her changeroom, pulling the curtain closed behind us.

"This definitely needs to go," I whispered, leaning in to kiss her mouth.

My fingers found the zipper I'd done up just moments earlier and tugged it down so I could roam her back with my hands while we kissed. Our tongues tangled together and the front of her dress dropped, exposing her perfect creamy breasts. I palmed one, flicking my thumb over the nipple, and she gasped into my mouth. My cock came to attention as her fingers snaked into my hair and she crushed her mouth to mine, both of us desperately pulling each other closer.

"How are you two doing back there?" the woman called loudly.

Gemma broke away, her eyes wide with panic and gave me a hard shove, catching me off guard. I toppled back through the curtain, landing in the main room on my ass.

I found myself looking up at the woman who ran the store with what was probably a very noticeable boner. The woman's eyes crinkled at the corners, and I could tell she was fighting back a laugh.

"Did you get lost, love? Your changeroom is that one right there."

I winked at her as I leapt up. "Of course. Thank you. We'll take the suit."

She patted me on the shoulder and nodded. "Lovely choice. I'll be at the desk when you're ready, then."

She walked away quietly, and Gemma stuck her head through the curtains. Her eyes met mine before we both burst into laughter.

16

GEMMA

When we got back to the hotel, we grabbed a late room service lunch then Ryker sprawled across the bed to watch football, giving me free rein in the bathroom. Gus had called to say he'd be waiting in the lobby for us at five, but Ryker seemed wholly unconcerned, despite only having ninety minutes to get ready. I was a low-maintenance sort of woman, but this was a big night, and I did want to look nice. I didn't have much experience with makeup and hair, so I figured I might need the extra time.

I took a long shower, even though I didn't really need one, soaping myself with the body wash I'd brought from home. The familiar citrus scent helped calm the rioting butterflies in my belly. When I'd turned the taps off, I wrapped myself in a fluffy white hotel towel, dried and straightened my hair, because that's about as much skill as I possessed in the hair department. Then put on some light makeup. It was a simple look, but I was pleased with my reflection when I glanced in the mirror. I dressed slowly, pulling on the ivory dress I'd brought with me. The bodice was tight, the material gathering to the side to form a single strap while the skirt fell around my legs in soft waves, stopping at mid-calf. A pair of heels that sparkled in the bathroom light were strapped to my feet, and I was glad I'd gone for a pedicure when I'd been out dress shopping with Mum during the week. I added a bracelet and a pair of drop earrings with twenty minutes to spare.

When I emerged from the bathroom, Ryker was yelling at the TV. He stopped and lifted his head as I came into the room, though, the words dying on his lips. Something flashed in his eyes that made my breath hitch. His gaze travelled over me, slowly, leisurely, burning a path of heat through my body as it went. I was panting by the time he spoke, and slightly shaken that just a single look from him could have such an effect on me.

"That dress…" he said, getting off the bed and coming across the room. He stopped in front of me, lifted my chin, and claimed my mouth as his.

He kissed me long and hot—lust ignited within me, demanding I rip his clothes off then and there, gallery be damned. How had I ever thought I'd been kissed before him? I hadn't. His kisses were life. They were like air, and sunshine and passion all rolled into one. Those same lips that had once blackened my heart now made it beat again.

He moved away reluctantly, too soon for my liking. "I'm glad you didn't get the pink one now."

I laughed and shoved him towards the bathroom before I did something stupid like pull him into bed. "Go get ready. Our ride will be here any minute."

With one last, lingering stare he disappeared into the bathroom, the sound of the shower filtering through the walls a minute later. I tried to catch my breath while my heart rate slowed.

Being a typical guy, Ryker emerged from the bathroom ten minutes later in that ugly brown suit that somehow looked like it had been made just for him. It was tight across his broad shoulders, and the pants fit his narrowed waist to perfection. He left the top two buttons of his shirt undone, and his hair was wet and slicked artfully to the side. The suit complemented his dark-brown eyes and tanned skin and I pushed myself to the door before my hormones got carried away and had me panting all over him. Again. The thought of licking him was appealing, though. He was damn lickable in that suit.

The ride to the gallery was short, and when Ryker held the door open for me, the receptionist from yesterday looked up from her computer, peering at us over the top of her thick, red-framed glasses. Her gaze lingered on Ryker, probably checking him out, not that I could blame her, before she motioned for us to go through to the back where the showing would begin in an hour.

I stopped dead on the other side. Yesterday, when I'd come through this doorway, I'd been greeted by chaos and a mess of packaging and piles of junk. Tonight, the polished concrete floor shone under the gallery spotlights, not a scrap of paper or Styrofoam to be seen. The photographs we'd hung yesterday were lit up on the walls, and fairy lights twinkled across the ceiling. A man in a black suit immediately approached us and offered us glasses of champagne, which we both accepted, then moved into the space. The other contestants all seemed to be there, as well as a few other people I assumed to be their dates. The two young guys from yesterday were deep in conversation about something, but they all turned to watch when we approached. Ryker placed his palm lightly but reassuringly between my shoulder blades. He followed me as the woman who'd helped me yesterday disentangled herself from the group and came over to greet us, a tall blonde trailing her. I smiled at them both, happy to not be completely ostracised from the group.

"You made it! And you look sensational," she said with a smile. "I'm sorry, I realised I didn't even introduce myself yesterday. I'm Rose. This is my partner, Laura."

I smiled and took her outstretched hand. "Nice to officially meet you both. I'm Gemma. This is Ryker."

"Ah, the man of the hour," Laura said with a wink.

"Excuse me?" Ryker asked, his eyebrows pulling together in confusion.

"Your photos are getting quite a bit of buzz already." Rose pointed to the two black-and-white photographs of him working out in the garden.

Shit. My cheeks burned. I'd completely forgotten that two of my four entries were photos of Ryker. He knew I'd taken them, of course, but I hadn't told him I was using them for the showing. I hadn't expected him to be here to see them. I bit my lip. I probably should have had him sign a model release. Or at the very least, asked his permission.

"Ryker, I—" I started, but he held up his hand, cutting me off as he left our little group of three and walked to where my photos were displayed, my name as the photographer in letters below.

He studied them for a long moment, and I found myself back in the darkroom at home, desperately wanting to hear what he thought of them. But this time was somehow more important. *He* was more important.

He spun around and crossed the space between us in four long strides. A gnawing pit of worry opened up inside me. I couldn't read the expression on his face at all.

"Ryker," I tried again, "I'm sorry, I—" He leant down and kissed me so hard my head tipped back.

When he pulled away, he was grinning. Over his shoulder, Rose and Laura smiled at us.

"You're amazing. I can't believe you managed to make me look that good."

I laughed, knowing full well that how good he looked had nothing to do with my photographic abilities. "So, you don't mind? I really should have asked first."

He winked at me. "Don't worry, when I'm a rich and famous model, I'll credit you with giving me my big break."

I rolled my eyes. "Great. I've given you an ego."

He smiled, but then his features sobered. "Seriously, Gem, your photos are amazing. I think you have a real shot at winning this."

A flush of warm pleasure coursed through me at his words, and I reached for his hand, linking my fingers through his. He squeezed them lightly.

People were trickling through the door, and soon after that, the trickle turned into a stream. The music was turned up, and more waiters circled the room, carrying trays of drinks and canapes. Ryker ate copious amounts of whatever was offered, but I was too nervous to eat. The competition winner wouldn't be announced until later in the week when the exhibition closed, but that was my work up there on the wall that people were talking about. Snippets of conversations floated in the air around me—critiques on the lighting, praises on composition… We made our way around the room, looking at the other competitors' work, but my gaze consistently strayed back to my photos, wondering if the people standing around them were enjoying them.

"Stop stressing," Ryker said, planting a kiss on top of my head. "Nobody hates them."

Easy for him to be cavalier. It wasn't all his hopes and dreams pinned on this night. I grabbed another drink from a passing waiter and took a hefty gulp, enjoying the cool fizz as I swallowed.

The music dimmed, and a microphone buzz took its place. The dull drone of low conversations around the room settled to silence when the receptionist stepped onto a small wooden dais, microphone in one hand, glass of champagne in the other. I realised her red glasses matched the her long, flowered dress nicely.

"Good evening, everyone. I'm Sally Thorborne, owner and operator of the Whiskey Street Gallery."

I quirked an eyebrow. She'd never given any indication she was more than just an employee. Shame on me for assuming. Didn't I hate when people did that to me?

"I want to welcome you all to Inside Photography's first ever gallery showing. The work you see on the wall belongs to a select group of up-and-coming photographers that the magazine, and us here at Whiskey Street, think have extreme talent. They come from all walks of life, from all around the country. And I'd like to take a moment to introduce you to each of them."

I was suddenly glad I'd worn makeup because I was sure the blood had just drained from my face, probably leaving me as pale as a ghost. Ryker squeezed my fingers, and I looked up at him gratefully. It was a nice feeling to know someone had your back when you were about to be dragged up in front of a room of strangers.

Sally stepped down from the dais and moved to the closest competitor's work, introducing the artist and asking a question or two about their pieces. I tried to listen, but my nerves made it difficult to focus. Of course, I was the last one she introduced. When Sally finally stood in front of my photos and called my name, I thought I might vomit. Ryker leant down and kissed my cheek as heads turned to look in my direction. I rolled slowly across the room to stop in front of my work.

"Hi, Gemma," Sally said with the first smile I'd seen from her in two days. "Do you want to tell us a little about your work?"

I steeled my spine and pulled my shoulders back, trying to appear confident, even if I didn't feel it. I took a deep breath and then told the crowd that I lived in a rural part of New South Wales, and that I'd begun photographing the kids my father taught when I was in high school. I told them how I preferred film to digital, and that due to my location, I'd had to create an old-school dark room in my laundry.

The more I talked, the more comfortable I felt. There were probably one hundred people in the room, so one hundred pairs of eyes were focussed on me, and I didn't mind. My nerves melted away, and I found myself enjoying the moment. Everyone smiled and nodded, and a sense of pure pride came over me, my grin stretching ear to ear. I'd put up a lot of barriers before getting here, but with a little push from Ryker, I was doing it. And loving it.

"And what inspired these photos, Gemma? Besides your very attractive boyfriend over there," Sally asked with a smile in Ryker's direction as the room turned to stare at him.

The word boyfriend jolted me for a moment, but Ryker's mouth was turned up at one corner and he gave a little wave to the room before they focussed their attention back on me.

I thought about it for a moment and asked myself why I'd picked up the camera at each of those moments in time. "I like seeing people succeed," I said slowly, giving my jumbled ideas time to transform into some sort of coherent thought. "I guess that's my favourite thing about sports photography. Athletes put in so much time and dedication, and watching them succeed makes me remember that it's all worth it. It's always worth chasing your dreams and working hard and pushing yourself out of your comfort zone in order to get there." My eyes met Ryker's through the crowd. "And even if you get knocked down once or twice, you get back up and try again. It might be as simple as a little girl jumping her horse for the first time. Or it might be some guy working on his abs in your garden." Ryker laughed along with the rest of the audience. "But either way, we all have goals. And I enjoy capturing them."

The room broke out into polite applause, and Sally thanked me, while I scooted out of the way to get back to Ryker. I'd barely moved, though, when a middle-aged couple stopped me to tell me how much they liked my photos. As I was talking to them, a young hipster-looking guy with a long beard joined us, complimenting me enthusiastically. He seemed to have a list of questions about the farm and my portfolio. More and more people joined, and I was bombarded with questions and praise all while my heart thumped out of my chest. I answered their questions in amazement. I was at a gallery showing of my work with people stopping to tell me they loved it. Unbelievable.

Ryker stood alone, leaning on the wall, watching me with a prideful smile. He held his glass up in a 'cheers' motion, and I grinned, my stomach flip-flopping at having that million-dollar smile directed at me. I turned back to the people around me, but for the rest of the night, I continually sought him out, always finding he was watching me in that quiet way he had, always making me feel like he could see straight through me. Straight through all the bullshit walls I'd put up and the excuses I made.

By the time Sally got back to the microphone to close the exhibition, I felt as if I'd had conversations with every person in the room. The people began to empty out, but I let them go, content to be the last to leave. There'd been no mention of me being in a wheelchair. Not one person had made me feel anything less than equal tonight, and I was positively giddy at all the praise and attention my work had received. My work. Not that disabled woman's work. To this crowd, it was all about the art. And I was already craving more.

I started as a warm hand touched the bare skin of my back. Ryker looked down at me with shining eyes before he swept me into a bear hug, crushing me to his chest.

"You killed it tonight," he whispered in my ear.

"Thank you. I'm sorry I neglected you, though. We barely got to speak."

He shook his head. "I was happy to just sit back and watch you shine. Because you did, Gem. Every person in this room saw that tonight, and I'm just really glad I got to be one of them."

A blush heated my cheeks, but I was saved by Sally making her way over to us. "Gemma! I'm glad I caught you. I just wanted to tell you in person what a phenomenal job you did tonight. You worked the crowd like a pro."

"I did?" I hadn't been deliberately working anything.

"I've already had an offer on one of your photos."

My mouth dropped open. None of the work in here was actually for sale. It was just a showing for the magazine.

Sally nodded. "The one with the little girl and the horse in the sunset. Are you interested in selling it?"

I nodded dumbly.

"Fantastic! I'll set it all up and email you the details."

I was so shocked I didn't know what to say.

"Did anything else sell tonight?" Ryker asked.

Oh. Good question. I was suddenly dying to know the answer, too.

Sally nodded. "Two other competitors had offers as well."

I wondered which ones.

"Anyway, it's getting late, and I think all of the drivers are here to take the competitors back to the hotel. So, I'll let the two of you go. The magazine said they'd be emailing you all with the winner's announcement by the end of next week." She reached out to shake my hand. "It was lovely to meet you Gemma. I hope we'll get the chance to work together again in future."

She walked away, her heels clicking on the cement floors, and I stared up at Ryker in amazement. "Did that really happen?"

He chuckled and nodded, taking the handles of my chair and steering me towards the door. Halfway there though, he stopped dead. "Shit. Sorry. I know you don't like people pushing you. I wasn't thinking."

He stepped to the side, but I grabbed his hand and smiled up into his gentle eyes. "I don't like just anyone pushing me, but for some people I make an exception."

"Am I one of them?"

"You are now."

He smiled and stood behind me again, and I let him push me

out to the car Gus had waiting for us. I was still wired from the adrenaline of the night as Ryker and I sat together in the back seat of the luxury car. He draped an arm around my shoulders, and I nestled my head into the crook of his neck. His fingers wandered over my palm, tracing patterns, and I closed my eyes, enjoying the sensation of having a warm, male body so close to me. We were silent, the Melbourne streets flashing by outside the window, but every stroke of his fingers across my bare skin sent tingles deep within me. The memory of the looks Ryker had been giving me all night only fuelled the fire inside me.

Rose and Laura had invited us for drinks in the hotel bar, but the ache inside me was so strong, it was all I could do to stop myself from jumping Ryker right there in the lobby. I made a beeline for the elevators instead.

Ryker trailed a finger down my spine while we waited for the elevator doors to open, and I shivered. "We could have gone for that drink if you'd wanted, you know."

I gazed up at him and registered the pure lust in his eyes as he stared back at me. "I don't want a drink."

The elevator pinged, signalling its arrival, and Ryker pushed me inside. "Thank fuck. Neither do I," he gritted out, his voice hoarse.

Then the doors closed, and his lips were on mine. I moaned and opened for him, fisting my fingers in his shirt and pulling him closer. All the pent-up sexual energy that had been building between us all night exploded now that we were alone. We pulled away, breathless, when the elevator doors opened on the eighth floor.

"I've wanted to do that all night," he confessed.

"Me, too." I remembered his eyes on me every time I'd turned in his direction during the exhibition. I remembered the look he'd given me when I'd left the bathroom in my dress, and I remembered the way he'd touched me last night, eliciting pleasure I'd never felt with a man before.

I swiped my room key, and we hurried inside, letting the door slam behind us. Within seconds he had me out of my chair, my arms wrapped around his neck, our mouths fused together like we needed each other to breathe. His fingers worked the zipper on my dress, the silky ivory material falling off my shoulder as he sat me on the bed. His palms skated my body, pushing the material down until it pooled around my waist. My fingers found the buttons of his shirt and I frantically fumbled to get them undone. He hissed when I ran my palms up his abs and over his chest to push the shirt from his shoulders. Then he was looming over me, pressing me back into the softness of the mattress with the force of his kiss. We shuffled up the bed, our lips never breaking apart, our kisses becoming more and more heated as our hands roamed each other's bodies.

My skin came alive under his touch, and within moments, he'd freed my breasts from my strapless bra and I'd wriggled out of my now crushed dress, leaving me bare except for a tiny piece of lace.

Ryker sat back, straddled across my legs, and let his gaze run over me. And I basked in it. The way he looked at me with so much desire left no room for self-consciousness. I felt sexy and confident and wanted. It was a heady feeling.

His mouth found my nipple, and I arched into him, gasping at the sensation. We were right back where we'd left off last night just a few minutes after walking in the door. But tonight was different. Tonight, I wasn't stopping him. I reached for his belt buckle, but he covered my fingers.

"We don't have to go any further if you aren't ready. This doesn't have to happen tonight."

I almost laughed at him. I was so ready for this to happen.

Sure, I had some nerves about having sex for the first time, but I liked him—more than I'd ever liked anyone. There was something between us, I knew I wasn't the only one who felt it. This wasn't just a random hookup. Plus, losing my virginity here in a fancy hotel seemed a whole lot more romantic than losing it out in Ryker's room in the barn when we got home. Because I couldn't keep fighting my attraction to him, or the feelings I was developing. Sooner or later, this was going to happen. "What if I want it to be tonight?"

He dropped his face to my neck, kissing the sensitive spot behind my ear. "You sure?"

"Yes."

"Then it will be."

I closed my eyes, letting sensation roll through me. Holy shit. I was finally going to lose my virginity.

17

RYKER

I licked along the length of Gemma's neck while a multitude of emotion ran through me. The darkness that had plagued me since I'd answered Gerard's call yesterday had disappeared the minute I'd seen her again. Spending the day with her today and watching her shine tonight at the gallery felt like bursts of light that erased the gloom and left me standing in the sun.

Lying here next to her, touching her, felt so damn right.

I buried my face in Gemma's neck and inhaled the smell of her, while my hand drifted back to the perky swell of her breast.

"There's something else you need to know, though," she said quietly.

"What's that?"

"I'm a virgin."

I pulled back and looked at her, surprised. She'd sounded so sexually aware when she'd explained her body to me last night. "You are?"

She nodded.

A wicked realisation came over me, and a grin split my face. "So that means—"

She rolled her eyes. "That means I know all about my body because I create my own orgasms. Is that where you were going?"

My brain abruptly conjured up images of her naked apart from underwear, her fingers working hard beneath the fabric, her head thrown back in pleasure. My dick had already been hard, but now it throbbed in my pants. "Fuck. That's hot."

She laughed. "Don't be a guy."

I returned to kissing a path down her body, pausing between kisses to speak. "Just tell me…if you…need to stop." I circled my tongue around her navel, finding the tiny scrap of underwear with my fingers and pulling them down her legs.

I let my gaze roam over her, taking in the neat triangle of hair at the junction of her thighs before deciding on a plan of attack. She'd said yesterday that it was possible for her to enjoy this, and I was determined to make sure she did, first time and spinal cord injury be damned. I ran my palms along her thighs, then parted them so I could nestle in between. Gemma propped herself up on her elbows, watching as I opened her up to me. Her pretty pink folds just begged for my mouth. But all in good time.

I experimentally placed open-mouthed kisses along her inner thigh, keeping eye contact with her the whole time so I would know if anything I was doing was working. She didn't react, so I didn't hover there long, switching to the other leg and doing the same thing. Her breath hitched, and I raised an eyebrow.

"That's the leg I have more feeling in," she confessed.

Good to know.

I grazed her skin with my teeth, and kissed my way back up to her centre, swiping through her with my tongue. I knew from a Google search some paraplegic women had trouble with lubrication, so even though I wasn't getting a lot from her right now, I was determined to stay there until her body was ready. Slowly, I licked her up and down, flicking my tongue over her clit and dipping it into her opening. Her breathing changed the more pushed my tongue inside her, so I concentrated on that. Focusing less on the external and more on the internal.

"Do you like what you see?" I asked against her clit, hoping the vibrations of my voice would help stimulate it.

She was still propped up on her elbows, watching while I licked her.

"Maybe," she said with a small smile.

I slicked a finger through her folds, testing her. When it met no resistance, I slid it up inside her and watched in triumph as her eyes fluttered closed and her head lolled back. She was still up on her elbows, which gave me a great view of her tits. It had been way too long since I'd touched one.

Keeping a steady rhythm, teasing my finger in and out of her, I crawled up her body and took her nipple in my mouth.

She let out a throaty murmur, the noise going straight to my dick, which demanded to be released from my suit pants. Switching to her other breast, I lavished attention on that side until her hands snaked through my hair, holding me to her. I slid my fingers through her wetness with ease and knew she had to be close. I claimed her mouth when she clutched me tighter, thrusting my tongue against hers and relishing the pressure on the back of my head from her hands. We kissed like we'd done this a million times, moving perfectly in time with each other. I increased the pace, loving the tiny sounds that fell from her lips and the way her breaths came in rapid succession. And then she cried out, finding her release, her fingernails digging into my back, her body trembling beneath mine.

There was silence for a long moment, nothing more than her breaths in the air between us as she came down from her high. Then the crinkle of a foil packet by my ear startled me away from her lips.

"Where did you get that from?" I asked, taking the condom from her fingers.

"Complimentary from the hotel. There's another one in the drawer."

"Remind me to tip them."

I sat up and unzipped my fly, tugging my pants and boxer briefs down my thighs. My cock sprang free, still hard and proud, and when I glanced at Gemma, she had her bottom lip caught between her teeth, staring at me. I rolled the condom on and kissed her until she settled back on the bed. Finding her breast with my fingers, I slid myself deep inside her, groaning when her warmth surrounded me. I stilled as she moaned.

"You okay?"

She nodded. "I have more feeling internally than externally."

"I noticed."

She grinned, and I slid out then back in again. I fused my lips to hers, kissing her deeply, thrusting slowly. I pinched her nipple, making her gasp, and rolled it between my fingers, while I grazed the skin of her neck with my teeth. Her fingernails scratched up and down my back until they reached my ass. She dug her fingers into my flesh, urging me on.

"Oh god, there."

"Could you come again?" I gasped and thrust into her, harder and faster, finding her lips again as my balls tightened. I sought out her eyes and loved what I saw there. Passion but something more. Trust. Respect. There were feelings between us I'd never felt, and the sheer intensity of that moment was enough to do me in.

She shook her head slightly and moaned. "I want to watch you."

Her words were like liquid heat, stroking the pressure I'd been trying desperately to keep a hold on. I let go. A groan ripped from me as I came, and she silenced me with her mouth until my movements slowed. I pressed my fingers into her soft flesh, aftershocks ricocheting through me. My arms shook with the effort of holding my weight before I collapsed down on top of her.

Holy shit. That had been so much more than I'd thought it would be. I'd known there was something between us, but now my heart thumped with a knowledge that hadn't been there earlier.

This thing between us was more than friendship and a mutual attraction. It was more than years of pent-up frustration.

I could fall in love with this woman.

18

GEMMA

The next week was a whirlwind. With only days left to prepare for Reese and Low's wedding, everything around the farm went into hyperdrive. We'd cancelled the weekend lessons, but we couldn't do much about the weekday ones. We needed the money too badly, and most of the weekend crew rescheduled their lessons for the days before.

So while Dad and I managed the extra lessons, Ryker worked both his jobs and did an insane number of hours around the farm, clearing space for the wedding. This left Mum to run around gathering fairy lights for Ryker to put up and filling mason jars with candles.

In the evenings, Ryker and I fell into his narrow bed in the barn in an exhausted heap. But somehow, our clothes always ended up on the floor, and we were never too tired to explore each other and learn what the other liked. Mum and Dad didn't comment on the fact my bed hadn't been slept in all week, and I didn't explain. It was pretty obvious to all what was going on. The way Ryker touched me, even when it was completely innocent, made it obvious we were together.

Making love with him each night was new and exciting, and

waking up with him each morning, in a tangle of arms and legs from sleeping in such a cramped space, was comforting and quickly became familiar. I was almost dreading Reese and Low's arrival because it would mean less time for Ryker and me to spend in our little bubble. Every day, my feelings for him grew in intensity. I was head over heels. Maybe not in love, but heading down that track. It was only a matter of time.

I was high all week, my smile too big to be wiped off. And it wasn't entirely because of Ryker. The afterglow of selling a photo kept me in a permanent state of happiness. On Thursday, Sally from the gallery emailed me and asked if I had a website. I wrote back, confused, and said I didn't. She was disappointed. The person who had bought my photograph had asked to see more. After I picked my jaw up off the floor, I emailed her back and asked her to give me a few days. It was crappy timing, but she was right. If I wanted to work as a photographer, the first thing I needed was a website.

It was time to get serious. Photography might never be my full-time job, but coaching riders was never going to completely fulfil me either. I needed more, and the weekend in Melbourne had made me think that maybe I could have both. So that night, after I'd scarfed down some dinner, I took my laptop to the barn, sat on Ryker's bed with him, and began building myself a website while he kissed my neck and palmed my boobs and tried everything in his power to distract me.

"You're hot when you're being all nerdy, you know that?" he said in my ear as his tongue traced patterns down the side of my neck.

I grinned and shoved him hard enough he landed on the floor with a *thunk*, making us both laugh. He climbed back on the bed and gave an overexaggerated sigh.

"Fine. What can I do to help then?"

I smiled and kissed him quickly on the cheek. "Nothing. You've done enough for me already. Just sit there and look pretty, and when I'm done, I'll show you how much I appreciate your patience."

He quirked an eyebrow, settled back on the bed, and folded his arms behind his head, his biceps bulging. "I'll be the most patient man in the world if that's my reward."

Reese and Low arrived on Friday morning after driving through the night with a car full of wedding paraphernalia. Ryker and I were running lights into all the trees that surrounded the top paddock and around the outer walls of the barn. The wedding would be held right here, tomorrow night, under a full sky of stars. It was going to be beautiful.

Low's ute crunched over the grass, and before it had even come to a complete stop, Reese barrelled out of the passenger-side door and pounced on me, giving me a hug that could crack a rib.

She released me and hugged Ryker as well, much to his surprise if his startled face was anything to go by. She squealed as she looked around the yard, which was a little alarming for me, as I don't think I'd ever heard her squeal. Planning a wedding had changed her.

"You two are amazing! I can't believe how much work you've done! And Mum has already told me she's got all the candles and flowers sorted out. Did you even leave anything for me and Low to do today?"

I scoffed. "I'm pretty sure we'll manage to find you something. How was the drive?"

Reese launched into excited chatter about her drive here, explaining how she'd had to cradle her wedding dress the entire way, and I'd laughed, because she wasn't exactly a stickler for precision any other time.

"But what have you two been up to anyway?" she asked, wriggling her eyebrows.

I hadn't confessed to her yet that I'd been sleeping with Ryker, but it was probably written all over my face.

Ryker swooped in to relieve me from my embarrassment. "Gemma's building a website."

"For your photography?"

I nodded.

"About time! Make sure you include a store. You should be selling your images as prints."

I hadn't considered that. I'd thought the website would be more or less a portfolio, or a place where people could contact me. I hadn't actually considered selling anything directly.

We all turned to watch when a procession of cars—a battered-looking jeep, a family-style SUV, and a sleek red convertible sports car—wound around the house and came to a stop behind Low's ute.

"Wedding party's here!" Reese yelled at the top of her lungs, sounding slightly shrill, and ran over.

Low glanced over at me, and I gave him a *what the hell* look.

He chuckled. "Your sister is a little overexcited if you hadn't noticed."

"Oh, I noticed. Pretty sure people on the moon would have noticed. She's bouncing off the walls."

"You should have been in the car with her for the past twelve hours. She didn't sleep. She's had more coffee than the fuel the ute used to get here."

That explained things.

We watched Reese run to meet the cars with smiles on our faces as she flitted from one to the other, already calling out to them before they'd even had a chance to turn the engines off. Her entire face was lit up like a Christmas tree, and her enthusiasm was infectious. She deserved a perfect weekend and a perfect wedding.

"I'm really glad you decided to propose," I said to Low.

He ruffled my hair, like he always did. "Me, too, kid. I would have done it a long time ago if I'd known it would make her this happy. She always said she didn't care about a piece of paper."

"It's not really just a piece of paper, though, is it? It's you two announcing to everyone that you're a family. Forever." A lump rose in my throat, but it was happy tears pricking at my eyes. Tomorrow was going to be special.

"Come on," Low said to Ryker and me. "Come meet everyone."

Long legs appeared out the driver's side of the SUV, and I recognised the sandy-coloured hair and smiling face of Low's best friend, Jamison. He immediately ran to the passenger-side door and opened it, offering his hand to help a dark-haired woman out of the car. She moved stiffly, and when he closed the door I realised she was heavily pregnant. A lanky teenage boy emerged from the backseat with a curly, blonde toddler on his hip. Low strode over, making a beeline for the little girl who was already calling out to him and straining her chubby baby hands in his direction.

The teenager handed her over willingly, and Low covered her chubby cheeks in kisses as she laughed. "Gem, you remember Jamison, right?"

I nodded and waved to him.

"And this is his wife, Elodie, and their kids, Nathan and Sophie. Sophie is my goddaughter."

I smiled at Elodie and her heavy-looking stomach. She was pale and leaned heavily on Jamison, but her smile was brilliant.

"We've got you guys sleeping in the main house, in Reese's old room. Can't have pregnant women sleeping out in the tents," I said to them. We hadn't set them up yet, but most of the out-of-town guests would be camping in the paddock at the front of the house, closest to the road. There weren't any hotels in Erraville, and the couple of rooms above the two pubs had booked up quickly.

"Thank you," Elodie said gratefully.

Reese walked up beside her, taking her hand and squeezing it. "How are you feeling? I can't believe you came all this way after being so sick for this whole pregnancy."

Elodie shook her head and smiled. "I wouldn't have missed it for the world."

Jamison seemed worried, though, and so did Reese.

"Come on," she said, pulling her gently by the arm. "Let me show you to your room. Leave Sophie with Low, we'll watch her so you can rest."

Elodie followed her without complaint, and Jamison hovered after them. Nathan wandered over to the horse paddock while Sophie waved to her parents from the safety of Low's arms.

Well, that was Jamison and Elodie taken care of. Now to find somewhere for their other guests to—

Loud arguing from the back of the car convoy caught my attention, and Low sighed, rolling his eyes.

"Are you two serious?" Low called to the dark-haired, casually dressed man who had arrived in the jeep.

He and the stunning blonde woman in the convertible were staring each other down, their faces like thunder.

"You've been together for exactly thirty seconds and you're already arguing?" Low strode across the yard to them as if he may need to pull them apart at any minute.

"Hey," Ryker said to me quietly, leaning down so he could whisper in my ear. "Isn't she that actress? BB something?"

I nodded. "Yes, BB James. But to everyone here, she's just Bianca. She's my sister's best friend."

Ryker raised an eyebrow but didn't say anything else as he straightened, and Low called us over. "Gemma, Ryker, this is Riley. Gem, you already know Bianca."

Bianca pushed past Riley, who still looked irritated, and came to give me a hug. "Sorry, Gem. It's good to see you. It's been too long."

I hugged her back and agreed with her. Her gaze swept over Ryker, who was shaking hands with Riley, before returning to me. She winked and mouthed the word *nice*, then grabbed a tent bag from the passenger side of her convertible.

"Want to come show me where these are going?" she asked. "You can fill me in on all the gossip while I put it together."

Ryker had been pulled into a conversation with Low and Riley, so I nodded at Bianca and gestured towards the front paddock. "How was the drive here? I can't believe you drove yourself instead of just flying in."

A slight breeze blew while the two of us made our way to the front of the house, but it was mild for this time of year. I hoped it stayed like this for tomorrow night. Nobody wanted to be freezing at a wedding, especially if half your guests were sleeping in tents. Though Ryker had already chopped a large pile of firewood which sat waiting in a heap off to the side of the house. We figured the campers would probably like a bonfire to sit around once the wedding festivities died down.

Bianca huffed and rolled her pretty blue eyes. "That was your sister's not-so-fabulous idea. She thought it would be fun for the whole bridal party to drive down here in one big convoy. Jamison was driving anyway because Elodie can't fly in her third trimester. And apparently Riley was all for it. I didn't want to be the one who ruined her plans, but just between you and me, a flight would have been heaven in comparison."

"What happened?"

She threw her hands up in the air, and when she dropped them, the tent bag fell from her shoulder. "Riley happened! He's ridiculous!"

She unzipped her tent bag and yanked the synthetic material from its casing. Picking up a tent peg, she tried shoving it into the ground, without any luck because we hadn't had anywhere close to enough rain to make the ground soft. I picked up a hammer from over by the woodpile and passed it to her.

"You know what annoys me the most?" she asked, waving the hammer around to accentuate her words.

I quietly rolled back a little to avoid her flailing. She was obviously irritated, and I didn't want to be in the impact zone.

"He just can't let anything go. Every time we see each other, he brings up every horrible moment we've had over the past… what? Ten years?" She seemed to think about that for a moment. "Ten years, Gem. That's how long it's been since we've been together. Yet here we are, at yet another event, creating another scene. It's like he enjoys it."

"What happened with you guys?" I truly was curious. But I also wanted to be sure the two of them weren't going to do anything that might ruin Reese and Low's big day. Better to let Bianca talk it all out now than have her implode during her walk down the aisle as bridesmaid number one.

Her face turned red, and she looked down at the tent peg in her hand and began hammering again. She bashed the peg until it was so far down she was just hitting the dirt. "Too much to even get into. It's been a lifetime of one drama after another with the two of us. We'd be better off never being in the same room, but neither of us are willing to give up our friends, so sometimes, its unavoidable."

"Is that the story you're running with these days?" Riley's voice asked from behind me.

I cringed. I hadn't heard him approaching, what with Bianca's ranting and trying to avoid being smacked in the face with a hammer.

"It's just one drama after the other? Why don't you tell her the real truth?"

Bianca's spine went ramrod straight, and within a second she was on her feet and in his face. The tension between them was palpable, and both looked instantly ready to explode.

Well, this was awkward. Suddenly, putting tent poles together required all of my concentration. I clicked them in place, steadfastly ignoring the two of them facing off while I tried to work out how I could quietly leave. Obviously, more than just a chat with me was required for these two to sort out their differences. And from the heat practically radiating between them, their problems weren't something I could help with. I clipped the material of the tent to the poles as fast as possible.

"Really? You want to do this here and now? It's been ten years, Riley!" Bianca yelled.

Riley groaned. "This isn't one of your movies, Bianca! Quit acting like I'm the bad guy in this whole situation!"

"You are!"

Yep. Okay. Definitely time to get out of here. Riley swore under his breath as I abandoned my hammer and backed away. The tent was as up as I could get it— still missing the rain fly and a few hooks I couldn't reach. Close enough. I wasn't sticking around to get in the way of the tornado that was Riley and Bianca's relationship. It appeared ready to hit land and make a hell of a mess.

"Fine! Let's do this, then!" She took another step toward him, her shoulders shaking with anger.

He did the same, as if he were drawn to her like a magnet, looming over her. She didn't give him an inch, standing her ground until their chests were touching and she had to tilt her head back to look up at him. They both seemed to have forgotten I was even here.

"Fine!" he growled in her face.

The sexual tension between them was so electric it was practically crackling. He grabbed the back of her head, and for half a second I wasn't sure what he was going to do, but then he slammed his lips against hers. She didn't resist for a second, her arms coming around his neck, pulling him to her. His hands ran down her sides and over her hips before he dug his fingers in and lifted her off the ground. Wrapping her legs around his waist, she kissed him with the pent-up passion that only came from years of torturing each other. I knew all about that sort of kiss. Riley walked them to the half-assembled tent, and the two of them disappeared inside. Riley made short work of zipping it up, then in the next second, Bianca's moan floated out across the yard. My eyes widened, and I resumed my hasty retreat.

I met Low and Sophie on the way back to the barn. "Uh, where are you off to?" I asked, trying not to laugh.

Low frowned. "I was just going to go help Riley and Bianca with the tents. You can't leave the two of them alone or they'll just be at each other's throats."

I giggled. "I don't think that's a problem today."

Low tilted his head questioningly, and I wondered how I could put this delicately.

"You probably don't want to go out there just now. Maybe give them twenty minutes."

Realisation dawned on him. "For Christ sake. They're having hate sex, aren't they?"

I laughed. "Quite possibly. They were all over each other when I left."

He rolled his eyes. "They're hopeless. They do this all the time. I don't know when they're going to sort their shit out and realise they're made for each other. They always have been."

I shrugged. I couldn't talk. I knew all too well that these things would only happen when you were both willing to listen and forgive. I was just glad it hadn't taken Ryker and me another ten years.

19

GEMMA

The morning of the wedding, I woke up in Ryker's tiny bed with his mouth on my neck and his fingers deftly working my nipple. I moaned, rolling over to kiss him, letting my fingers trail over the ridges of his abs, and sneaking them into his PJ pants to palm his morning erection. He groaned, shifting his hips to thrust into my grip.

"What time is it?" he mumbled against my lips.

"Time for sex?" I asked hopefully.

He laughed, reaching over me for his phone on the bedside table.

"Yeah, maybe not." He turned the phone around to show me it was already seven a.m.

"Shit!" I sat up and fumbled around the bed, looking for the shirt I'd been wearing last night before Ryker had ripped it off me.

I pulled my chair over, transferred into it and raced for the door. In the doorway, though, I paused, remembering Ryker was still in bed. When I looked back, he had one hand behind his head, the other dipped below the waist-high sheets that gave me full view of his abs and arms. His hand moved up and down beneath the white sheet as he raised an eyebrow at me. My mouth dried, and I had to fight every urge in my body to get straight back into bed with him.

"Tonight," I said firmly.

"You got it."

With a groan, I left him to his morning wood. But I knew I'd still have the image of him touching himself in my head tonight when I'd take him in my mouth and—yeah. Best to stop that train of thought right now.

When I made it up to the main house, a kitchen full of wolf whistles greeted me. "Is it still called a walk of shame when you're in a wheelchair?" Reese shouted.

I rolled my eyes at her. "Could you be any less PC?"

Bianca and Elodie laughed from where they sat at the kitchen table, sipping coffee. A platter full of toast and eggs sat between them.

"So," Bianca said, picking up a fork. "Are you going to tell us all the details? We noticed you didn't come home last night."

I shrugged. "Pretty sure you know where I was."

Elodie smiled. "Yes, but that doesn't mean we don't want to hear every detail. I haven't had sex in so long because of this baby, I've probably forgotten how. Let me live vicariously through you."

"Hey, I wasn't the only one who got some last night," I said, staring at Bianca.

Elodie and Reese's jaws both hit the floor as they rounded on Bianca.

"You did not!" Elodie exclaimed.

"You and Riley? Again?"

Bianca blushed and shot me a dirty look. I smiled charmingly at her.

"Don't we have to start doing our hair or something?" she asked.

The shrill ringtone of Reese's phone pierced the air, and she shot Bianca a grin. "Saved by the bell, B." She frowned at the screen. "It's Lisa. She's doing the catering—hello?"

She pressed the phone to her ear and listened while Elodie and I went back to pressing Bianca for details about her escapades with Riley in a barely put-together tent.

"I'm surprised it didn't collapse on your head," I laughed, but the smile died on my face when Reese hung up the phone looking panicked.

The two other women fell quiet as well.

"What?" Bianca asked.

"Lisa. The caterer. Her son has just been taken to hospital in an ambulance. Severe asthma attack."

Elodie's hand covered her mouth. "Oh my gosh. Is he all right?"

Reese nodded. "I think so. But obviously, Lisa needs to be with him."

"So…she's sending someone else?" I asked, not understanding what the problem was.

Reese shook her head. "That's just it. There is no one else. She's a one-man band."

Bianca's mouth dropped open. "You're joking. So, there's not going to be any food?"

Reese's eyes were wide. "Her neighbour is driving the food over now. But none of it is prepared. What am I supposed to do with a van full of unprepared wedding food? I can't even make frozen pizza without burning it."

"You ask your family for help," Mum said from the doorway. She was still wrapped in her robe, slippers on her feet. But her face was determined. "I'm sure it's not as bad as you think. Some of it will already be prepared, I'm sure. And I'll handle anything that isn't. We have all day. You don't need to worry about it."

"It's too much for you to do alone, Mum." Reese dropped her head into her hands.

"This Lisa woman was going to do it alone."

"She's a professional. You're a good cook, Mum. But this is cooking for almost a hundred people," I said. "I'll ask Ryker to help you. He's a great cook."

Reese looked doubtful.

"Trust me. He's good. We'll make it work."

I called Ryker, and a few minutes later, he arrived in the kitchen wearing jeans and shirt, his hair still wet and slicked back from his shower. He tugged his shirt down over his abs as if he'd only thrown it on right before he'd walked in the door. The five of us were waiting for him when he arrived.

"Uh, hi?" he said, glancing from face to face before he settled on mine with a questioning expression.

"How do you feel about cooking for a hundred people today?" I asked bluntly.

To his credit, he immediately agreed to help, and as soon as the food had been delivered, he and Mum shooed us out of the kitchen, the two of them urgently discussing the meal plan.

Reese closed the door behind her and gave me a wobbly smile. "He's a good guy."

"He is. They've got this. Don't worry."

She nodded.

The next few hours were a blur of champagne, curling wands, and makeup instruments I didn't have names for. And a lot of laughs and smiles and nerves. The three of us in the bridal party took over the living room, along with Elodie, each taking turns with the hairdresser and makeup artist who had come in from Lorrington. Delicious smells wafted from the kitchen, and Mum forced food and water on us between alcoholic drinks, insisting that no one liked a drunk bride.

I'd thought starting at nine would mean we would all be ready and waiting by twelve. Apparently not. The ceremony started at four, and at three-thirty, Reese was still in a robe. I was beginning to panic. I hated being late. But Reese's smile was wide and relaxed as she stepped into her dress, and Bianca did up the zillion little buttons at the back.

A hush fell over the room, and Reese ran a hand down her torso, smoothing the fitted bodice which flared to a floor-length skirt with a long train. She looked at each of us in turn.

"Can someone say something?" she asked worriedly. "You're making me paranoid."

The rest of us burst into simultaneous reassurance that we were all just stunned by how beautiful she was. Mum, who had ditched her apron and gotten herself ready in record time, had tears running down her face which the makeup artist hurriedly fixed.

From the doorway, someone cleared their throat, and we all turned around to see Dad leaning on his cane, his eyes full of pride as he stared at my sister.

"You arrre..." he started, before he had to stop to swallow hard. His eyes glassed over, and she rushed into his arms. He wrapped his arm around her and kissed her cheek. "Tttime for you to get mmmarried," he said slowly.

Reese tucked her arm through his, and I took a deep breath while Elodie left to find her seat outside. And just like that, it was time for the ceremony. Bianca led the way to the back door and music began to play. I shot Reese a smile over my shoulder while Bianca descended the ramp, and she grinned at me. She was practically bouncing up and down with excitement, all thoughts of catering disasters obviously obliterated by the fact she was about to marry her best friend. Her enthusiasm was infectious. Everyone in the room could tell how impatient she was to get out there and marry the man she'd loved for the past ten years.

When Bianca was halfway across the paddock, I made my way down the ramp. Low and his friends had set up rows of white folding chairs, and I wheeled myself slowly through the middle of them, towards an arch that had been covered in fresh, pastel-coloured roses. I caught Ryker's eye when I passed, and he winked at me, which made me smile. He was wearing his thrift shop suit again, which still looked entirely too good on him, considering how little he'd paid for it. I was glad he'd managed to free himself from the kitchen long enough to see the ceremony.

Low and Jamison stood in front of the arch, wearing matching suits, and grinned as I moved toward them. Riley stood with them, too, but his eyes were glued to where Bianca stood on the other side of the celebrant. I almost laughed when I came to stop next to her. She dragged her gaze away from Riley to give me a questioning look. I shook my head slightly, fighting back a giggle. Those two had it bad.

The music changed to the traditional bridal march, and Reese, flanked by both our parents, descended the ramp while all the guests stood to watch. All three walked the aisle with grins from ear to ear, the crowd oohing and ahhing over how beautiful she looked. And she truly did. She'd always been a beautiful woman, but nothing could top how gorgeous she was today. Happiness radiated from her as she kissed our parents on the cheek and walked the rest of the way to her future husband alone. I sneaked a glance at Low, emotion welling up inside me as I took in the complete and utter adoration he had for my sister. His eyes were shiny, and I thought he might be battling to keep it together. He took two steps to meet her and dropped his mouth to hers. She kissed him back hard, and we all laughed when they pulled away, flushed.

"All right, all right, save it until I've gotten through the ceremony." The celebrant laughed.

Reese and Low positioned themselves in front of him, holding hands, and Low mouthed, *I love you*. I couldn't see my sister's face, but I'd be willing to bet she did the same thing right back.

The ceremony was simple and quick, but beautiful, the sun sinking behind them, splashing pinks and oranges across the sky. I wasn't the only one fighting back tears when Low grabbed my sister around the waist, dipped her slightly, and kissed her as the celebrant announced them to be man and wife. My mother was openly sobbing in the front row, as were Elodie and Low's grandmother. They didn't even get a chance to walk back down the aisle before the crowd swamped them with hugs and calls of congratulations. Sophie blew bubbles from a little white wand with a bit of help from Nathan.

I backed out of the crazy scrum of people, knowing I could wait a few minutes to say my congratulations when the crowd had dispersed. We had all night. Reese and Low were getting the beautiful, perfect day they deserved, and that filled me with both relief and happiness.

Ryker appeared at my side and spun my chair around, dropping his lips to mine. Surprised, but not at all adverse to the idea, I kissed him back, not caring that we'd effectively outed ourselves as a couple in front of everyone.

"You look beautiful," he whispered.

"Thank you." I smiled. "How's the cooking going?"

He nodded. "Surprisingly well. I thought we were screwed when you dumped me in it this morning."

I cringed. "I know. I'm sorry."

He shook his head. "You know I don't mind. I really wasn't sure we'd be able to pull it off. But your mum is kind of great. The two of us work really well together. Everything is prepared and ready to go. We decided just to do a big buffet and let people help themselves."

"That's a great idea. Then you'll both be able to enjoy the reception as well."

"Exactly. I didn't want your mum stuck in the kitchen when she should be having a good time."

"Thank you."

He kissed the top of my head. "You're welcome."

"Gem, we need you for photos!" Bianca called. I squeezed Ryker's fingers apologetically. He didn't know anyone here, and I felt a bit bad for abandoning him.

"Go. I've got to get back to the kitchen anyway. I have a surprise for you later, though."

I raised an eyebrow. "Tell me."

He kissed my cheek then straightened and walked away. "Later," he called over his shoulder. His words sounded enticingly like a promise.

20

RYKER

The Lawsons knew how to throw a party. Darkness had fallen as the bridal party returned from a few quick photos, then it had been straight into music, dancing, food, and laughter. A bare paddock had never looked so pretty. The thousands of lights Gemma and I had strung over the last few days twinkled against the dark backdrop of the night, candles providing an additional glow. Flowers covered every available surface. Large gas heaters had been set up amongst the tables, and a bonfire roared off to one side. Eighty or so people mingled in the various areas, some sitting chatting, some drinking around the bonfire, others cutting it up on the dance floor. And our buffet-style dinner went down without a hitch. Reese thanked me every time our paths crossed, and people went back for seconds.

I kept a low profile throughout the night, content to run a few plates back to the kitchen, then sit on the sidelines and just take in the atmosphere. Gemma, who had been talking with some family friends, came to sit beside me as Jamison, who was doubling as the Master of Ceremonies, announced that it was time for the first dance. Reese and Low glided out onto the dance floor like royalty, and he took her in his arms and they began to sway. Their dance was unchoreographed and sweet, the two of them moving with the familiarity that only came from years of slow dancing together.

After a minute or two, Jamison invited the rest of the wedding guests to join the couple on the dance floor, putting his microphone down and offering his hand to Elodie. Gemma and I watched as the dance floor filled with happy couples, and I found her fingers with my own, squeezing them gently.

"Dance with me?" I asked

She frowned at me, pulling her hand away. "That's not funny."

I took her hand back. "I wasn't trying to be. I'll carry you."

"And every person here will stare at us."

She had a point. I got to my feet. "Then this is the perfect time for my surprise."

Her eyes brightened. "What is it?"

I laughed and pushed her chair away from the light of the wedding reception. "I'm not sure you understand the concept of a surprise. It's where you don't ask what's happening and just go with it."

"I'm not good with surprises."

"You're not good with any situation you can't control."

"You noticed that, huh?"

"I did."

It grew darker the farther we went from the party, and the ground grew rockier as I headed for the thick grouping of trees that blocked their back paddocks from the view of the house. I fished my phone out and turned the flashlight on, passing it to Gemma to hold while I manoeuvred us through the trees.

"You're not taking me out here to kill me, are you?" she asked, rubbing her bare arms. It was colder out here away from the heat of people and the fire.

"Not tonight. Close your eyes, we're nearly there."

She obliged and covered her eyes with her hand. It suddenly

struck me how far we'd come in such a short space of time. She was trusting me again. She was completely vulnerable right now, and she was okay with it. I loved that.

I put the brake on her chair, parking her right beneath a large weeping willow, then found the switch I'd left dangling from it earlier in the day. I smiled at the fairy lights glowing in the space around us.

"You can open your eyes," I whispered.

She shivered when my lips skirted the shell of her ear, and she slowly lowered her hand. Her gasp of surprise as she looked around made me grin.

I'd laid thick blankets on the grass, with plenty of pillows scattered around. Earlier in the day I'd thought the music from the wedding would carry this far, but it didn't so I searched through my phone for an appropriate song.

As the notes floated over the still air, I held my hand out to Gemma. "Dance with me?" I asked again.

This time, she nodded, and I swooped her from her chair, holding her effortlessly to my chest. Her arms wrapped around my neck and she pulled me in for a kiss. We kissed soft and sweet, and all the unrequited feelings I'd had as a teenager mixed with all the new feelings I had for her as a man. We danced beneath fairy lights and kissed as though we were the only two people in the world. Out here, with no one around, shielded by the low-hanging branches of the tree, it felt like we were.

The song finished, and I laid her gently on the ground before covering her body with my own. I pulled a thick blanket over us and kissed her neck, finding the halter tie on her dress. She grasped the fly of my pants, palming my erection at the same time I found her bare breasts. She stroked over me, and I whispered in her ear all the things I wanted to do to her, knowing it turned her on. In the last few days, I'd realised how much of her sexual pleasure came from mental and visual stimulation. Talking dirty with her was just as effective as touching her. I'd had a feeling being out here, in the open air with the, admittedly, very small chance of being caught, would get her going, and I was pleased to see I was right. She worked my cock, and within moments of my mouth closing over hers, she was asking if I had a condom.

I rolled it over myself, running my fingers through her folds, testing that she was ready for me. We kissed hot and hard, the blankets slipping off my bare ass, and I pumped into her slowly, unable to look away from the depths of her deep-brown eyes. Her lips were like magnets for mine, and I kissed her, feeling the difference between this kiss and the heated one we'd first shared in the barn. Both kisses were hot, but things had changed between us. This kiss was full of emotion and feeling, and the depth of it hit me right in the gut.

"I'm falling for you," I whispered, the words from my heart, before my head realised what I was doing. My heartrate picked up when I heard what I'd said, and I prayed it wouldn't scare her away. Everything else in my life had been one disaster after another, but Gemma…she was the only good thing I had. If she didn't feel the same way…

Her fingers stroked the back of my neck, and she sighed, the sound happy as it floated away in the night air. "I'm falling for you, too."

It wasn't I love you's. We weren't there yet, but there was a promise in those words that touched a place in me I hadn't known existed before her. I'd had girlfriends, sure, but none that had ever evoked real feelings the way Gemma did. We kissed deep and slow, cementing the sentiment until a loud crack pierced the air and broke us apart.

We both twisted to look towards the party, though neither of us could see it through the thick trees.

"What was that?" Gemma asked sharply, her rapid breaths misting in the cold night.

"Was that a…"

"A gunshot," Gemma supplied.

My heartrate sped up. It had definitely sounded like one. Gemma's eyes were wide and panicked, and I scrambled off her, ripping the condom off while she tied her dress. I yanked up my pants and helped her into her chair before I took off running for the trees, pushing her in front of me. The ground was rocky, and she bounced around like a rag doll, fighting not to be tipped from the chair, but she didn't ask me to slow down or stop.

That crack of a gun had no place in the middle of people celebrating. Something was wrong. I could feel it in my bones, and the distant sounds of screaming only worsened the dread in my stomach.

"What is it?" Gemma asked in panic. "Can you see what's going on?"

I strained my eyes, but all I could see was the crowd of people, no one moving. I pulled up short, and Gemma whirled around on me.

"What are you doing?" she demanded. "Keep going!"

"And wheel you right into the middle of where someone is potentially off-loading bullets? No."

Her eyes narrowed. "Don't even think of telling me to wait here. I'll run over you with my chair again, so help me God."

Another gunshot rang out, and Gemma flinched as I ducked. Someone in the crowd screamed again, and the sound of a child crying went straight to my gut. What the hell was going on? The last thing I wanted to do was take Gemma closer to whatever the hell was going on over there, but I knew I wasn't going to be able to stop her. They were her family and friends; she wasn't the type to abandon them. And I wasn't going to abandon her.

I pushed her quietly to the back of the group with a finger over my lips in the hopes we wouldn't be noticed.

A sick laugh rang out across the open field, and my blood ran cold. "Sorry about that, folks. But my guys here get a little impatient when people don't answer our questions."

No.

"We're going to try this again, this time, without all the silence, and hopefully without the gunshots. Deal?"

Nobody said a word, but my heart threatened to thump right through my chest. This wasn't happening. I knew that voice.

Gerard laughed again. The flickering firelight cast shadows over his sharp features. "Fine. I'll take your silence as agreement. Adam Ryker. Where is he?"

Gemma looked up at me, a mixture of horror and confusion on her face.

Fuck. This was bad. Gerard was here for me, and I knew he wouldn't hesitate to shoot for real if he felt the need.

"I'm here," I said, the entire wedding turning to look at me.

A tiny sound escaped Gemma's mouth, and she grabbed my hand and yanked it to her. "No!" she whisper-shouted.

"It'll be all right," I promised, disentangling my fingers from hers when the crowd parted.

"Ah, there he is! The man of the moment," Gerard yelled, then turned to where Low stood with Reese behind him.

Low's expression was unreadable, but I could tell from his stance and clenched fists that he was ready for a showdown if it came to that.

"What an asshole this kid is, right? Stealing your thunder on your wedding day. Tsk, tsk."

Low said nothing, and Gerard shook his head. I walked slowly towards him and Gemma called my name, her voice breaking in the middle. Gerard peered around my shoulders, and I froze.

"Your pretty little girlfriend is here, too!" He laughed in mock delight.

I stepped to the side, blocking Gerard's view of her, a deep growl rising in my chest. "What do you want, Gerard? You've made your scene. You can go now."

Gerard wandered around the space like he didn't have a care in the world, his two towering chunks of man guard on high alert behind him. They'd tucked their guns into the waistbands of their jeans, but their fingers hovered inches above them.

"Oh, Ryker. I'd love to. Trust me. I didn't think there was a place more hick town than Lorrington, but this little hidey hole you found proved me wrong. Unfortunately, we have a problem, you and I."

I fought to keep control of my temper and didn't respond. He'd only tell me when he was done with his show.

"The money you owe me, of course."

My eye caught on Gemma's dad. Her mum had silent tears running down her face and looked absolutely terrified. But her dad just seemed disappointed.

"I don't owe you anything, Gerard. I gave you my car. We're even. You agreed."

"Did I, though?"

I racked my brain, running through the conversation we'd had in the parking garage of his fish and chip shop. I remembered telling him we were even, but for the life of me, I couldn't remember him agreeing. He'd just changed the subject. I cursed myself. I knew I didn't owe him a cent, but what the hell was I supposed to do now?

"Five thousand, kid. Interest."

"This is bullshit. We both know I owe you nothing."

"Five K, kid. Now."

I lost control of my temper. "I don't have one thousand, Gerard, let alone five!"

Gerard's gaze bore through me for a moment, before something in his eyes changed and he grinned, revealing a mouthful of teeth, in the exact same manner a shark would. He looked around him, spinning in a full circle then coming back to focus on me.

"This is a nice place, isn't it? Much nicer than that shitty little apartment you and your girlfriend in Lorrington were sharing." He glanced over at Gemma again. "This one is a bit of a step up for you, isn't it?" He winked at Gemma, and my skin crawled.

"Got yourself a nice little cash cow with all this land, and nice horses. Don't you? Does she know all about the money you owe me? Maybe she can pay your bills, like a regular lil' sugar momma."

He made a move to pass me, but I blocked him. No fucking way in Hell was he going anywhere near her.

"Enough." The words came out quiet and cold. I moved until I was inches from Gerard's face, nose to nose with him, staring him down. "I'm not giving you shit. Leave." I seethed as shame rolled through me. I'd brought all this to the Lawsons' doorstep, ruined the wedding and endangered lives in the process. I should have just stayed away. I'd never be able to look any of them in the eye again. My heart panged at the thought of losing Gemma. She couldn't be with me after all of this. I already knew that without even looking at her.

The cold steel of a gun barrel touched my temple, and the click of the safety being flicked off echoed in my ear. Gemma cried out, and I closed my eyes briefly, trying to calm myself. I was going to end up with a bullet in my brain if I didn't settle down and focus. I took a deep breath, ignoring the thug with the gun to my head.

"She's not my girlfriend. She has nothing to do with this."

He quirked an eyebrow. "She's not your girlfriend? You're not fooling anyone with that, son. Seems to me like you're in love with her. So, you can pay me my money. Or she can. I'm not fussy. But either way, someone here is paying up tonight."

"I'll pay," Gemma's dad said in a surprisingly clear voice from behind Gerard. He leant heavily on his cane, his face pale, but his voice determined. "Leah, go get the money from the safe."

Mrs Lawson turned to Gerard for permission, and he waved a hand dismissively at her. "Go on, then. I don't care who pays this money, as long as I get it."

She turned and ran for the house, her long dark hair, shot through with grey, billowing out behind her. The crowd stood in shocked silence, the only sound Gerard's rambling. Fury raged through me like an out-of-control fire. I wanted to kill him with my bare hands. I wanted to hurt him, the way he'd hurt me and these people who had done nothing wrong except to take in a no-hoper like me who made bad decision after bad decision. But there was nothing I could do. Nothing but stand and wait while I died inside. The gun never wavered from my temple as I internally berated myself.

After what felt like a lifetime, Gemma's mother finally reappeared with a small bag and handed it to her husband with trembling hands. He took it from her, limping across the grass before holding it out towards Gerard. I closed my eyes, disgust for myself rolling in like freezing mist. This wasn't right.

"Mr Lawson. Stop. You don't have to do this."

The gun at my temple pressed harder into my skin, hard enough to push my head to the side. I gritted my teeth.

Gerard opened the bag and studied the contents for a moment then clapped Gemma's dad on the back. "Very good of you, mate." He glanced around at the frightened crowd. "Is there any dessert?"

When no one replied, he laughed and motioned to his guards. The gun at my head disappeared.

"No? Never mind. I never was much one for sweets. Congrats again to the happy couple," he said, tipping an imaginary hat in Low's direction before he turned back to me. "See you around, Ryker."

"No, you won't. We're done, Gerard. This is it. We're even."

He glared at me for a long moment until he broke into a grin and laughed. "Of course we are. I'm a fair man, Ryker. I only want what I'm owed."

I almost laughed in his face. Fair and Gerard didn't belong in the same sentence.

"Pleasure doing business with you, kid."

He and his men disappeared around the front of the house,

and a moment later an engine started up, gravel pinging off other cars as they took off onto the road.

For a long time, no one said anything. Every eye was on me, no doubt waiting for me to explain myself. But I had nothing left to give.

"Adam," Gemma called, her voice breaking.

There was nothing to say, nothing to do. All my skeletons had just been laid on the table for the whole world to see, and it had left me empty. Any self-respect I might have scraped together over the years was pulverised under the hammer that was Gerard. I had no excuses, no explanations.

I shook my head quietly and walked away, leaving the stunned crowd of people without a word. No one tried to stop me, and for that, I was grateful.

21

GEMMA

The police swarmed our property not long after Ryker had left. They questioned everyone, quickly releasing most people who hightailed it to their cars or the tents on the front lawn, ready for this nightmare of a day to be over. They took longer with my family, since we'd been in the thick of it. A policewoman sat on a chair in my office in the barn, shooting questions at me.

"And where were you when the gun was allegedly held to Mr Ryker's head?" the policewoman asked.

I didn't like the way she said 'allegedly'. Like she didn't believe my story. But getting shirty about it wouldn't get me anywhere, so I answered calmly, "I was behind him."

And wasn't that ironic. I'd been behind him but only in the physical sense. I certainly hadn't had his back, had I? I'd been terrified I was about to witness him get a bullet in his brain, but then I'd let him go like I didn't even care. What was I supposed to do? I'd had my mother in hysterics, my sister devastated, and Low and my father looked like they wanted to murder someone. I didn't want that someone to be Ryker.

I stifled a yawn of sheer exhaustion, and the policewoman,

whose name tag read Constable A. Hayle looked at her watch. "It's late, and we have enough for now. You'll need to come down to the station on Monday morning."

I nodded dumbly. Her partner was waiting for her when we walked to the barn door, then the two of them climbed into their police cruiser. I lifted my arm to shield my eyes from the headlights, blinking in the glare as they turned around and bounced down the long driveway before disappearing into the inky blackness of the road.

Someone cleared their throat from my left. My parents, Reese, and Low were seated around a table, the only light a couple of barely flickering candles that were still holding on to the last of their fuel. Reese's head rested on folded arms as she watched me from the corner of her eye. Mum and Low wore blank expressions as if they were lost to their thoughts. It was Dad who had caught my attention.

I wheeled over to them slowly, putting on the brakes, and waiting. Because I knew I had it coming.

"What the hell, Gemma?" Reese asked without any preamble. "What was all that?"

Mum snapped out of her trance. "Did you know Ryker was mixed up with a bad crowd?"

Low kept staring into the thicket of trees at the edge of the property, but tension held his shoulders rigid.

"Yes," I admitted. "I knew."

"Ddddon't you think you should have told us?" Dad asked. His face was like thunder, and Mum nodded her agreement.

"It's not what it seems," I said in a rush. "He borrowed the money to buy his business, but then there was a fire, and he lost it..."

Reese squinted at me like I wasn't making any sense.

I sighed. "He was trying to do the right thing. He thought that loan was paid. He thought it was all over and done with. He couldn't have known Gerard would show up here tonight. He went to the police."

"You ssshhould have ttold us," my father said again.

He was right.

"I know. You just had a lot on with your recovery and all. I dealt with it myself." Because that was the truth. I had. I turned to Reese. "I'm sorry. I didn't know any of this would happen. Neither of us did."

She sat back in her chair, an unhappy sigh ripping from her chest. "I'm not angry at you, Gem. What happened wasn't your fault. But I'm worried about you. I was terrified when that creep looked at you like he might eat you for dinner. Those guys don't seem like they're messing around. What if they try to hurt you in order to get at Ryker?"

"They won't. It's over. The police will have to take this seriously now."

"Sounds like Ryker thought it was over once before as well," Low said, speaking for the first time.

I glanced from him to Reese to my parents. They all stared at me with the same sort of intensity, and I frowned.

"What are you getting at?" A sinking feeling of suspicion made my skin crawl. "Is this some sort of intervention? Is that why you were all out here waiting for me?"

"We don't think you should see Ryker anymore," Mum said quietly, ignoring my questions.

"What?"

Reese looked at me with pleading eyes. "He's dangerous, Gem. He could have gotten you killed tonight. Or me. Or Elodie and the baby. There were one hundred people here who could have been injured. Or worse."

"You've got to be kidding me. Of all the people, I can't believe *you* are telling me to stay away from him. Would you have stayed away from Low if I'd told you to? If I'd said he was dangerous?

Ryker made a mistake that he's been trying to rectify ever since. He's not a bad guy."

"We're not saying he is. But there was all the bullying when you were in high school. Now this. He makes poor choices."

Blood rose in my cheeks. "Like me? Am I one of his poor choices?" It was an irrational statement. Deep down, I knew that. But couldn't they see I had feelings for him? Their words hurt as much as if they'd been criticising me personally. Because essentially, they were. They were criticising my choice to be with him. I pushed back from the table. "You do all realise I'm an adult, don't you? You can't force me not to see him."

My dad nodded. "Wwwee know."

Mum squeezed his hand. "But we hope you'll consider our point of view. Someone could have been hurt or even killed tonight. We don't want that person to be you. He can't be around here anymore. We have children here. It's not safe."

My mouth dropped open. "He lives here!"

"Not anymore. He can come pick up his stuff whenever he's ready."

"You're firing him?" Tears pricked at the backs of my eyes. I knew he wouldn't go back to living with his father. So where would that leave him? Would he go back to Lorrington? Panic set in. I didn't want to lose him. Not when he hadn't even done anything wrong.

"This isn't right," I said, backing away from the table.

Mum's expression was sad. "When you have children of your own one day, you'll understand."

I had to bite my lip in order to stop the sharp words burning on my tongue. And this was what it all boiled down to. They still saw me as a child who needed taking care of.

That hadn't been true for a long time.

RYKER'S ROOM seemed cold and unfriendly without him in it, but I pulled his sheets up around my chin anyway, wondering where he was. I wanted to give him space but as I laid there in the darkness, sleep refused to shut down my brain. So instead, I stared with unseeing eyes at the rough log walls of the barn and waited. It was close to dawn when the door finally creaked open. I whipped around, my heart thumping as he stood silently in the doorway.

"I'm so sorry," I babbled, wishing I could jump out of the bed and throw my arms around him. My relief at having him home outweighed all other emotions. "My parents are firing you. I'll talk them out of it, though. You just need to give them some time..."

I stopped my mouth when he shrugged out of his jacket, dropping it on the floor before making short work of the buttons on his shirt. He kicked off his shoes as he crossed the room, and my mouth dried when his shirt slid off his shoulders, revealing the abs and chest I hadn't had long enough to touch.

A lifetime of touching him wouldn't have been enough.

The button on his fly was next, and he pushed his pants to the floor, taking his boxer briefs with him so he stood naked in front of me. He leant in and kissed me gently, pushing me onto my back as he slid beneath the blankets. Our fingers found each other in the dark, his mouth covering mine again and again. He peeled off the t-shirt I'd found in his top drawer, and within moments he was kissing his way down my neck.

"Ryker. Wait. Let's talk."

"Don't want to talk," he mumbled.

I pulled his head away, cradling it between both my hands so I could look into his eyes. Then almost wished I hadn't. The depth of pain and shame I saw there made me want to weep. Instead of forcing him to talk things out the way I wanted to, I let him slowly lower his mouth to mine again. Talking wasn't what he needed right now, and I could respect that. There were other ways I could make him feel better.

I pushed him off me, rolling us so he was on the bed before kissing my way across his jaw and down his neck. I bypassed his collarbone because I'd learnt he didn't like being kissed there and instead let my lips trail down his abs, using my core and upper body strength to shift my body. I licked and kissed and nipped at his skin, spurred on by the way he watched with a lustful gaze. His fingers threaded through my hair, and he gathered the long lengths up in his fist, the slight tug on my scalp turning me on.

I found his erection, hard and wanting, and mine for the taking.

Our eyes locked as I shot my tongue out to lick at his tip then I closed my mouth over him. He was warm and hard, and I so desperately wanted to erase every bad thing that had happened tonight from his memory. So I ran my hand up and down his length and sucked him deep into my mouth, over and over until all I saw in his eyes was pure, unadulterated desire. His head tipped back, and he groaned, the raw, primal noise flushing heat over my skin. He let my hair fall, gripping both sides of my face and sitting up to brand my lips with his kiss. He flipped me to my back, but I wasn't done with him. I'd never be done with him.

I reached for his cock, but he caught my hands, pinning them above my head with one hand while the other found my breast. His mouth worked one side, while his fingers worked the other, and within moments he had me begging for more. He sucked on his fingers and then they were inside me, searching for the spots where I had the most feeling.

"Ryker..." I moaned. He ripped the top off a condom, rolling it on before pushing inside me. He buried his face in my neck, kissing and sucking as his hips moved in slow thrusts.

"Look at me," I whispered. He lifted his head to stare into my eyes. His shoulders shook with the effort of holding himself above me, and I pulled him down and kissed him softly. "I love you. I don't care what's happened in the past, or what anyone says. I love you."

He stilled, something unrecognisable flashing in his eyes. My breath caught, and panic set in that I'd said too much too soon. But then his mouth crushed down on mine, hot and hard and demanding, and I felt in that kiss everything he hadn't said. I felt his love in the tender way he held me. In the way he'd protected me from Gerard. In the way he'd never given up fighting for me, even when I'd hated him to my very core. He didn't need to say it, because I knew without words that this thing between us was special and right.

So why did this feel like goodbye? Tears pricked at the backs of my eyes, and I dug my fingernails into his back as if marring his skin would keep him mine.

If only it were that simple.

I closed my eyes, and he rolled his hips one last time, finding that spot within me that lit my soul on fire. We came together, quiet and intense, and different to every other time. Then he gathered me in his arms, my back pressed against his chest, his lips resting on my shoulder. I threaded my fingers through his, locking his arm around my waist, wanting to stay in the protective cocoon of his arms forever.

"Gemma, I..." he murmured after a long time.

"Yes?"

He paused. "I'm sorry."

Something told me that wasn't what he'd wanted to say. "I know. It'll be okay."

But in the morning, when I woke up alone, I wondered if it ever would be again.

22

RYKER

With no ride and nowhere else to go, I walked the few kilometres back to my dad's house like a dog with its tail between its legs. Shame rained down on me, swirling around until it was all I could think and see and hear.

I opened the squeaky screen door of the clapboard house, so familiar, even though I hadn't lived here in years. Unsurprisingly, silence greeted me on the other side. It was barely six a.m. on a Sunday, and my father would be in bed for hours yet, sleeping off the effects of whichever bottled friend he'd met the night before. The living room was dim in the early morning light, and my hand was on the knob to my bedroom door before I realised my father was even in the room.

"So. The prodigal son returns."

I sighed and answered him without turning around. "What's that supposed to mean?"

"It means maybe it'd be nice if you didn't only come home when you ain't got nowhere else to go."

I scoffed, in no mood for his bullshit. "That's rich coming from you. You're probably only here right now because Jerry kicked you out of the pub."

"Don't take that tone with me, boy." It was meant to sound like a threatening growl, but his words were slurred. He was still drunk.

I whirled around, zeroing in on his slumped form in the armchair. His keys, wallet, and an empty bottle of vodka sat on the low side table one of my brothers had built in woodwork class. Ring marks stained the surface. Pathetic. "Whose fault is it that I never come home? That *none* of us ever come home?"

"You're all grown men. You do what you like."

Of course. He never took responsibility for anything, did he? I huffed out a breath. I didn't want to stand there, waiting for his next barb, watching him wallow in his pitiable state. It was all too easy to wonder if I was really just looking into a mirror.

I closed the door, fell back onto the bed, and slung an arm over my eyes. But Gemma's "I love you" and the memory of the way she'd held me was still all I could see. I'd been falling for her ever since she'd come back into my life. Hell, I'd fallen for her years ago, back before I even really knew what love was. I'd wanted to tell her I loved her. But how could I do that? Her family were the most important to her, and after tonight, I wasn't welcome in their home.

I wouldn't make her choose me over them.

I had no home, no car, not a cent to my name, and I'd brought a thug like Gerard to their home where he'd robbed her parents of their savings. That was all on me. I wasn't good enough for their daughter. They were right about that. In the state I was in, I wasn't good enough for anyone.

The door swung open so hard it crashed into the wall behind it, scaring the shit out of me.

"What the fuck?" I yelled, instantly on guard in case my father had decided to pick a fight instead of just sleeping it off. But it was my brother, Jared, or Red as he was more commonly known, who blocked the doorway.

He threw a pair of boxing gloves at me. "Get up."

"Where the hell did you come from?"

He'd moved to Sydney years ago to train and came home even less often than I did.

"I got in last night. Heard your showdown with the old man, but I didn't want to get involved. You know how I get with him."

Yeah, I knew. He had no patience for the man who had made our teenage years miserable. It took all of his self-control not to lay him flat every time he came home. And my father knew it. He avoided Red like the plague.

"Thanks for the backup."

He rolled his eyes. "You didn't need it. Now, get up."

"Fuck off."

"I need to train. And you're getting fat without me around to kick your ass."

"You're a dick. I am not."

"Prove it then."

A workout didn't sound like the worst idea in the world. I already had two messages on my phone from Gemma that I had no idea how to respond to.

"I'll be there in five."

Red cracked his knuckles. "Hope you've been practicing. I haven't had sex in weeks, so everything is going into my training. You're in for a world of hurt if you aren't up to speed." He grinned.

Crazy fucker. We both knew that even if I had been training night and day, I still wouldn't be able to keep up with him. He had a natural talent for boxing that I didn't. I was in for a world of hurt, all right. But I'd welcome it.

Red was already running sprints across the home paddock when I made it out there. Despite the cool morning, he'd lost his shirt, and muscles rippled beneath his tan skin. He dropped to touch the ground at each end before popping back up, his arms pumping, determination on his face. I strapped the gloves on and followed suit. I took it easy at first, but after Red threw an elbow into my side, I picked up the pace, and soon we were running full speed in an effort to beat each other across the yard.

Sweat rolled down my spine, and my chest heaved as I stopped short, holding up a hand in defeat. I sucked in the air my lungs were starving for, while Red slowly jogged in circles around me, barely puffing.

"Told you you were out of shape."

"I'm not," I grumbled. "You're just a machine. How is it possible that you're even fitter than the last time I saw you?"

He shrugged, shifting his weight from side to side, warming up his joints. "I've got a big fight coming up. I'm training more."

I wasn't sure how that was even possible. He'd already been training three hours a day when I'd seen him a few months back. Not long before Gemma had come back into my life.

Shit. I straightened up and motioned that I was ready to spar. Ready to take my beating. We danced around each other for a few moments, each of us testing the other and refamiliarizing ourselves with the way the other moved. We'd often sparred together as teenagers. And by sparred, I meant he beat the shit out of me, despite being a year younger. But I was still pissed off from arguing with our old man, and angry with myself over the mess with Gerard, so I moved with a bit more spark than usual.

I threw out a right hook, and it connected. Red barely flinched, but his eyebrows shot sky high, as if he was surprised I'd managed to land one. There was something to be said for pent-up rage and adrenaline.

He swung back, and I ducked, but I had no hope of avoiding the punch he followed up with. His glove hit my ribcage with a thud.

"You're going easy on me. Stop it."

He danced back, eyeing me warily. "Of course I am. I'm not going to beat the shit out of you. We both know I could."

"You're a cocky bastard. You know that, right?"

"If you got it..." He roundhouse kicked me, and it landed, but I barely felt it.

"Come on. You wouldn't have half-assed it when we were kids."

Jared stopped, concern replacing the humour in his eyes. "Why do you suddenly have a death wish?"

"I don't. I just don't want my younger brother babying me."

"You're letting him get to you."

Frustration tightened the muscles across my shoulders. "Who?"

"Dad."

"Fuck off."

"What then?"

I sighed, dropping my guard. "Do you think I'm like him?"

"What? You're nothing like him."

I shook my head. Red didn't know half the stuff that had been going on. "I got involved with some bad shit. Put a lot of people in danger. People I...cared about."

Red pulled off his gloves and ran his fingers through his shoulder-length hair, scraping it back into a ponytail at the nape of his neck. "Did you beat up a kid?"

I screwed my face up. "No."

"Then you aren't like him."

It wasn't that black or white, though, was it? "Do you remember all the times we'd go into town and people would avoid us because of him? People were scared of making eye contact with us, in case he was drunk and ready to make a scene. He always did that. Made piss-poor life decisions, without any consideration of how it would affect us or Mum. Mum left because she couldn't handle the way he acted."

"Where are you going with this?"

A cool, early morning wind stirred the dried grass of the paddock. "I don't want to be like him. I don't want people to avoid me in the street, or for the ones I love to live a half-life because I'm only half a man. But I just keep doing it. Making one bad decision after another, same as him. And I can't even blame my mistakes on an alcohol addiction. I've been stone cold sober every time."

Jared raised an eyebrow. "Is that honestly how little you think of yourself? You aren't half a man. You're twice the man he is, because you actually *care* when you fuck up. He never did. You don't want to be like him and hurt the people around you? Then don't. Don't give up. Don't take the coward's way out and run away with your tail between your legs. Go back. Make it right. Show her you're the man she thinks you are."

I dropped my gloves on the ground. "How did you know there's a girl?"

"Isn't there always?"

I punched him in the arm. "She's special, though. And I don't know how to make this right."

"That isn't really the point. The point is, are you willing to try?"

23

GEMMA

It took me a long time to drag myself out of Ryker's bed. The longer I laid there, the longer I could pretend last night's disaster had never happened. I could pretend that my boyfriend's loan shark hadn't shown up, fired a gun, ruined my sister's wedding, and robbed my parents of their savings. I felt safe wrapped in sheets that smelled of him, with the memories of the slow, sweet sex we'd had between them. We'd woken up together every morning since Melbourne, and I already missed him. He hadn't answered either of my texts, and I wasn't surprised. I'd felt something change with us last night, and not in a good way.

My phone buzzed from somewhere on the floorboards, and I leant over the side of the bed and rummaged around until I found it, hoping it was a message from Ryker. But it was just an email notification.

The preview caught my eye, though, and I opened it, my heart stopping as I took in who it was from.

Inside Photography magazine.

In all the craziness of yesterday, I'd completely forgotten that our exhibition at the gallery had closed and the winner had been announced last night. The email title gave nothing away, and the nerves that erupted in my stomach swirled, making me nauseous. I don't know how I'd ever convinced myself I hadn't wanted to win this competition. That magical night at the gallery had been like a wake-up call. If I didn't pursue my photography now, when would I? This was the break I needed to be truly independent. This job could be the beginning of a whole new life for me. I needed to win.

With trembling fingers, I stabbed at the email.

Dear Miss Lawson,

I skimmed the opening paragraph until my gaze tracked over the words I'd been looking for.

Congratulations!

My breath caught in my throat and excitement raced through me. My hand shook so much it was hard to focus on the screen.

Inside Photography magazine is pleased to inform you that you have won third place in our first ever sports photography internship program. As one of our winners, you have won a free one-year subscription to the magazine that will be delivered to you monthly. We thank you for your participation and wish you all the best with your future endeavours.

I closed my eyes, letting my head drop back on my shoulders and disappointment crush in on me. Well, that was that. No Melbourne. No internship. No experience of a lifetime.

I sighed as I focussed back on the email, a link at the bottom catching my eye. I followed it to the magazine's home page where photos of the gallery opening were displayed. The very first photo was of the two young guys from Sydney, the one's who'd belittled my work. They stood in front of their photos, with huge grins on their faces. The caption below read: *First and second place getters, Miles Henry and Tobin MacIntosh, with their entries. Miles wins a year-long internship with our sports photography team. Tobin wins a week-long sports photography course, run by our industry professionals.*

It was like salt in the wound. So much for their worries that poor little white boys would be beaten out by the girl in the wheelchair. I tried to fight back the bitterness that turned my mouth to acid. I stared at their photo for a long time. Their work was good, I'd give them that, but so was mine. Did they know how lucky they were? Did they appreciate the opportunity they were being handed? Had they wanted it, even half as much as I had? I felt like crying, but my eyes were dry. And then I felt like a jerk for being a sore loser. I'd wanted it so bad, though. But it had been ridiculous to get carried away in dreams of a life in Melbourne. Dad might be doing better, but maybe this was a sign I needed to stay.

I flopped back onto Ryker's bed and wondered if I could have a do-over of the last twelve hours.

24

RYKER

It took me a week of getting my ass kicked by Jared to come up with a plan. Gemma hadn't tried to contact me beyond the two messages she'd sent the morning after the wedding. I hadn't expected her to. I'd sent her a message, saying I just needed some time to get my head together, but I missed her voice. I missed sleeping next to her with my arms wrapped around her and the fresh citrus smell of her. I missed catching her eye across the yard and knowing the tiny smile that tilted her lips was for me.

I waited until I knew she'd be occupied by her little kids' riding lesson before I rode my old bike over to her house and knocked on the door. From the road, I'd seen her in the middle of the ring, but I hoped she hadn't noticed I was there. I wanted to talk to her parents first. I needed to make this right, not just with her, but with them, too.

I sucked in a breath, knocked on the door, and squared my shoulders, trying to look more confident that I felt. Mrs Lawson opened the door, her eyebrows shooting up in surprise when she realised it was me.

"Ryker!"

"Can I have a few minutes of your time, Mrs Lawson?" I was so nervous, it felt like going for the most important job interview of my life.

"Of course. Come in."

Mr Lawson sat in an overstuffed armchair in the living room, a half-eaten sandwich resting on a plate on his lap. "Hhhavent ssseen much of you lately," he said, brushing crumbs from his hands.

"I know, sir." I wiped my sweaty palms on my jeans. "I thought it best if I gave everyone some space. But I wanted to come and apologise. And to let you know I'm going to pay you back every cent you lost."

Mr Lawson nodded. "I knew you would. Thhhhat was the reason I gave thhhhat thug the money in the first place. Gemmmmmma says you bought a business when the owner's wife was sick?"

"Yes, sir."

"Thhhhat's admirable. You might have gone about it the wrong way, but I can see your heart was in the riiiight place. And you went to the police when you realised you were in over your head. They told us that."

I shook my head and tried to interject, but he held up a hand, silencing me.

"Everyone makes mistakes, son. It's how you go about fiiiixing them that shows what kind of man you are. You're a gooooood kid, Adam. You always were, even if you've lost your way a few times. You caaaan come back from this."

You could have bowled me over with a feather. "Thank you."

The Lawsons exchanged a glance.

"Is what he said that night true?" Mrs Lawson asked quietly.

My brow furrowed in confusion as I tried to recall Gerard's rant. "Is what true?"

"That you're in love with Gemma."

I nodded without hesitation. "Yes."

Mrs Lawson looked down at her hands. "I thought so. I have a confession to make."

I waited patiently. This conversation had gone down a path I hadn't been expecting. I still hadn't even gotten to my reason for being there.

"The night of the wedding, we told Gemma we didn't want her seeing you. We were upset and scared and we had no right to say that to her." She paused before meeting my gaze. "I'll make sure she knows we have no problem with her dating you. She wouldn't have listened anyway, but I don't want us to be any sort of barrier between the two of you. If she loves you, too, then that's good enough for us. But I think you might have some making up to do for disappearing on her."

I could barely digest their words, but still, a broad smile spread across my face. "I do. And even though you're being incredibly kind right now, I want to make it up to you, too." I met both their gazes with as much confidence as I could muster. "That's what I wanted to talk to you about. I have an idea I want to run by you."

25

GEMMA

I watched Ryker enter my house, yet I couldn't bring myself to follow, as if the sight of him had me frozen to the spot. Hope soared within me, and Meghan had to call me three times from her saddle before I heard her. I hadn't heard from Ryker all week, beyond a text message that said he needed time.

I'd been content to mourn the loss of my Melbourne dream alone, not wanting to bring anyone else down with my sombre mood. I'd been giving him space, knowing we both needed it to come to terms with everything that had happened. But as the days ticked by and he didn't call or drop by, I'd begun to question if he was ever coming back.

I didn't even know where he was staying. I'd wondered if he'd gone back to Lorrington to stay with Danni. Despite knowing they were only friends, my stomach churned at the thought of him living with her again, when he should have been living here with me.

When he rode away from my parents' house without a word to me, it felt like the morning he'd left all over again. A heavy weight pushed down on my chest as I tried to concentrate on the kids and their lesson, but my heart wasn't in it. My heart wasn't here at all. Part of it was with him. The other part was in Melbourne.

Shit. I was being pathetic and I hated it. I'd always prided myself on being strong, but this moping was anything but. When the lesson finally finished, I wheeled myself into my office and sat at my desk, clicking the top of a pen absently while I thought about what I was doing with my life. The last few weeks had shown me that this farm and the business—they just weren't enough anymore.

There wasn't much I could do about the Ryker situation—if he didn't want me anymore then nothing I said was going to change his mind. Though the thought of never resolving this, never being with him again, caused something deep inside me to tear apart. Something I was scared may never heal. So instead of focussing on a hurt that might consume me whole, I decided to focus on myself. I browsed through the website I'd abandoned when I'd missed out on the internship. It was only half finished, but I'd already uploaded all my favourite photos. Most of them were the kids with the horses. There were a few other shots interspersed throughout, but again and again it was the kids and the horses that drew my eye. They were what I knew. I got kids. I got horses. I didn't want to give either of them up, I just wanted to shift focus. Literally.

The idea crept up on me slowly, but by the time it was fully fledged in my brain, I wondered how I hadn't thought of it sooner. I opened my internet browser and typed in Riding for the Disabled. The smiling faces of kids upon the backs of their ponies and horses made me smile. I'd never been associated with the company before, having had my father to teach me to ride again after my accident. But I'd heard about them and always thought the work they did was admirable. If we'd had any need for that sort of service out here, I would have trained as one of their coaches a long time ago. But teaching wasn't what I wanted, and if what I did want was photography, then I needed to make it happen for myself. There wasn't going to be a flashing sign at the top of their website advertising the perfect position. I was going to have to take matters into my own hands. Dreams don't work unless you do.

I found the contact details for the head office, shot off an email with half a dozen of my favourite photos attached, and crossed my fingers. As the email sent with a whooshing noise, a weight lifted off my shoulders. Maybe nothing would come of this, but I'd keep researching, keep sending out my work, and eventually I'd find something. I had a destination and a plan to get there, and that was all I really needed.

I trailed my way through the barn and paused in Ryker's doorway for a while before gathering up the few items of mine I'd left down here. My toothbrush, a phone charger, a couple of photography magazines. I piled them onto my lap, then returned them to my bedroom in the main house. I wasn't going to stay down in his room without him anymore. It was too pathetic, and I was done with pathetic.

For the next week, every moment I wasn't teaching, I was shooting. I shot roll after roll of film, and when I ran out, I switched to digital. When the sun set in the afternoons, I spent hours in my darkroom or laid on my bed with Photoshop open on my laptop. I was determined to shoot all new, better work for my website. I didn't hear from Riding for the Disabled, but I refused to let it get me down. Getting discouraged wasn't part of the plan. I scoured the job sites for photography work, and though the jobs were few and far between, I applied for everything I found. Any job would get my foot in the door, so if I was even remotely qualified, I applied.

I'd quizzed my parents about what Ryker had been doing here that day, and all they said was he'd come to apologise. I was glad he'd done that, but it hurt he hadn't made the same effort with me. Two weeks after the wedding, without a word from him, I assumed our relationship was over. I'd tried ringing him, more times than I could count, but every call had gone to voice mail. Each day I grew more and more upset that I'd meant so little to him that he could just leave without a word.

Friday night rolled around, and I sat at the tiny desk in my bedroom, cursing my laptop for running so slowly, though it probably had something to do with the uncountable number of layers I'd added to a photo I'd shot that afternoon. The days were getting longer as we edged closer and closer to spring and the sunsets got prettier and prettier. I'd gone out to one of the paddocks where the horses we didn't use for classes hung out during the day and shot over two hundred photos of them with the sun sinking behind their backs. They were great photos straight out of the camera, but I'd been learning new Photoshop tricks. I'd spent my night alternating between YouTube tutorials and swearing at my computer when it didn't do exactly what I wanted.

The house was quiet around me. Mum and Dad had gone out for dinner and a movie in Lorrington to celebrate their wedding anniversary, so I didn't expect them home until sometime after midnight. It was nice having the house to myself for once.

Something clanged against the cement floor outside, the noise ricocheting around the still yard, and I jumped. I whipped around to look out the window into the darkness. The moon and stars were out in full force tonight, so I could see the yard quite clearly, even if the shadows deepened the darkness in spots. I peered through the window, straining my eyes, not seeing anything odd, before I reluctantly turned back to the computer. I tried to focus, but my gaze kept straying to the window, adrenaline still coursing through me. It was a little breezy outside, so I convinced myself it had just been the wind knocking over a bucket, and closed my laptop.

I was headed for bed when movement outside my window caught my eye. My heart seemed to leap into my throat as a human-shaped form moved silently through the paddock, heading towards the thicket of trees at the back of the property.

My mouth dried. There was someone out there. Panic coursed through my veins, settling in my stomach. What if it was Gerard? Or one of his thugs? My pulse pounded, and for the first time in my life, I wished I owned a gun. I fumbled on the desk for my phone, surprised when my fingers plucked out Ryker's phone number instead of the police. But it made sense. If he was staying next door at his father's, he'd get over here a lot faster than the police from town. I'd been working hard at being the strong, independent woman I wanted to be, but I wasn't stupid enough to think I could take on an intruder, especially if it was one of Gerard's guys. They'd already proved they didn't have a problem with shooting.

I hit the call button and pressed the phone to my ear, keeping my eye on the shadowy figure. The call connected, and I waited impatiently for Ryker to answer the phone, hoping he wouldn't ignore me this time. I prayed that he somehow knew this one was different.

My fingers trembled when the figure at the back of the yard stopped in his tracks and fished something out of his pocket. It flashed in his hand, lighting up his face. I slowly lowered the phone as he looked up at me. My heart felt like it was going to burst out of my chest, but it wasn't from fear anymore. I knew he could see me. Our eyes locked, and just like all the other times—in the barn, in Melbourne, while we made love in his bed—I couldn't turn away. He shoved his phone back in his pocket and picked up the shovel and hoe he'd been carrying and disappeared into the trees.

Was he stealing our equipment now? Why couldn't he answer the phone? I forced myself not to care. It was just one more rejection in a long list of them.

26

RYKER

The hum of the generator muffled the thud of the shovel hitting the dirt. I stomped down on the edge, lifted it, and flipped the dirt off. Over and over I repeated the motion, taking pleasure in the monotonous, mind-numbing work. It never quite dulled the thoughts of Gemma. Her face as she'd stared at me through her bedroom window was hard to forget. She'd been scared at first, but that had quickly changed to surprise, then hurt, then anger. And I'd turned away because it ripped my heart in two to see her like that and know it was me, causing her pain all over again.

My phone rang, and I pulled it out of my back pocket, checking the caller ID. Jared.

"Hey," I answered, sticking the shovel in the dirt so I could lean on the handle. "What's up? I'm kind of in the middle of something."

"Are you out digging in the dark again?"

"I was. Until you rang."

"It's Friday night. Why aren't you at work?"

"Mike made me take a night off. Said I looked like rat shit."

My brother chuckled. "You probably do. When was the last time you slept? Between pulling double shifts at the bar, the mechanics, then spending all night digging up that paddock, I don't know how you're still standing."

"It's better than sitting at home, getting into fights with Dad on my night off."

"Fair call. Did you talk to her yet?"

I kicked at a lump of dirt with my foot. "I can't. Not yet."

"Why?"

"Not until the garden is ready and I've paid her dad back."

His sigh was loud through the speaker. "You're still doing it."

"Doing what?"

"Trying to make up for something you haven't even done wrong. Punishing yourself. I'll bet if you just talk to her, she'd understand. You never lied to her. What happened sucked, but it wasn't your fault."

"I just want to get it finished. I need to prove I can do something right." More than anything, I wanted to run up to Gemma's room, break the damn door down, and pull her into my arms. I wanted to tell her that I was sorry and that I loved her. But I had to prove to myself first that I could be good for her. I refused to turn her into my mother, spending all her time hiding at home because her husband was an embarrassment. Then have her run off to the city because she couldn't stand the sight of me anymore.

"Take it from someone who knows—you wait too long and you'll miss out entirely."

I nodded, even though he couldn't see it. I knew he was right. I knew she'd move on. Hell, maybe she already had. It'd been weeks since we'd laid together in that tiny, rickety bed when she'd told me she loved me. My love for her had only grown stronger, but the look on her face tonight hadn't been one of longing.

I surveyed the large plot I'd spent weeks digging out, mostly by hand because the physical work felt almost like a punishment. I'd lugged bags of chicken shit down here from my family's stash, using it as fertiliser, and I'd done most of it in the very early hours of the morning by the light of a generator.

Shit. Red was right. It had been weeks' worth of soil preparation, and the tiny seedlings I had growing in our greenhouse were ready to go. I was stalling down here, scared of the plan all coming together and actually having to face her.

I hung up on Red without even saying goodbye. The hurt in Gemma's eyes stabbed me over and over like a knife, and I suddenly knew it had to be tonight. I had to finish this garden and get her back. I was going to lose her for good if I didn't do it now. There was still five hours until sunrise. If I worked all night, I could get it finished.

I left the tools where they were and rode through the darkness towards our house, a tiny headlamp lighting my way. I'd had to invest in one when I'd started sneaking through the fence to the Lawsons'. The first time I'd tried to ride over here in the dark, I'd crashed and burned into a hole the size of Texas.

I headed straight for the greenhouse, but as I surveyed the trays and trays of vegetable seedlings, I realised they weren't going anywhere with only a bike for transport. I needed the ute. I jogged up to the main house, not bothering to open the door quietly. Dad would likely be passed out by now, and I didn't really care if I woke him anyway. Lord knew he'd woken all of us up enough times over the years when he'd stumbled in drunk.

I swiped the car keys from the kitchen bench and slipped outside again. I was tired. But the thought of seeing Gemma in a few hours and finally making this right kept me going even when my body wanted to stop. I yanked the handle of the car door and jumped backward as something tumbled out and landed in the dirt at my feet.

"Fuck!" we both yelled.

I instinctively went into fight mode, crouching, ready for a confrontation until I recognised the lump on the ground.

"What the hell are you doing out here, Dad?"

"Fuckin' sleepin'." He sat up slowly from the dirt, rubbing his back, and groaned. "What'd you want?"

He reeked of alcohol, and my irritation rose.

"Did you drive home from the pub?"

He clambered to his feet. "Yeah."

Un-fucking-believable. "You're completely wasted, and you drove home. Do you have a death wish? Don't you even care about how many people you could have hurt tonight?"

He shouldered past me, and I stumbled back. We were similar heights, but he had at least fifteen kilos on me, most of it stored in a beer gut.

"I didn't though, did I?" he slurred.

He stumbled towards the door, and my anger turned to rage. I'd seen Gemma's parents leave the house earlier—what if it had been them he'd crashed into? What if Logan, or Red or Dallas had unexpectedly decided to come home for a visit and it had been them he'd collided with? Fury slammed through me at the pure selfishness of his actions. I strode across the lawn and yanked his shoulder, turning him around.

"Why don't you care?" I yelled, getting in his face.

His booze breath was enough to get me drunk just on the fumes, and it angered me further that he probably wouldn't even remember any of this in the morning. It must be nice to be so blissfully unaware of every fuck-up you made. Shame about those of us around him who weren't so lucky.

"About what?"

"About anything! About the fact you could have killed someone, or yourself tonight? Or how your shitty behaviour kept Mum a prisoner in this house until she got up the guts to leave it?

Or how about the fact you've never given a shit about any of your sons?"

His eyes cleared a little as he shoved me out of his face. I clenched my fingers into fists but let him move me back.

"You don't know nothing, boy," he growled.

"Don't I? Enlighten me then, oh wise one! Because from where I'm standing, you're just a mean old drunk that liked to take his anger out on his kids."

"You got no idea how hard times were when you boys were little. You got no idea how many hours of work I did, and all for nothing when the drought killed everything in sight. You were damn lucky I could even keep a roof over your head."

"Maybe we would have had extra money if you hadn't been drinking it all at the bar."

"You're an ungrateful shit, Adam. I did everything for you. And then you went and sold the damn car."

"What?"

He stabbed a meaty finger into my chest. "You thought I didn't notice? You sold the car. The car I gave you. Like it meant nothin'."

I narrowed my eyes. "I did what I had to do to make things right. Because that's what a man does, Dad. He makes shit right, even when it's hard. He doesn't go hide in a sticky-floored pub and drown his sorrows like a coward. Yeah, times were tough, but you were weak." The words hurt to say, even after all the years of hostility between us. He was still my father. "I sold the car to pay for a mistake I made. And I'd do it again. It's not that the car meant nothing, but the people I love mean more."

He stared at me for a long time, looking more sober than I'd originally given him credit for. Then he turned and stumbled back to the house. This time I let him go. There was nothing more to say. Nothing was going to erase the years of abuse he'd put us through.

Instead, I slid into the driver's seat of the rusted old ute and put it into first. From the greenhouse, I loaded trays and trays of seedlings into the back. It was time to stop looking behind me. Those relationships and the bad choices I'd made were in the past. It was time to look towards my future and the woman I wanted to spend it with.

27

GEMMA

I couldn't sleep. It had been one thing to not hear from Ryker for a few weeks, but it was another to look him in the eye and see nothing there. He hadn't stopped. He hadn't tried to give me any sort of indication that there was still something between us. He'd hadn't even waved as he would have if we'd been friends. That had hurt.

I was still lying in bed thinking about it when I heard the front door open and close. "Mum?" I called.

Her dark-brown head poked around the dim corner.

"Hi, sweetheart. What are you still doing awake? It's really late. Or rather, early."

I shifted onto my side and propped an elbow beneath my head. "Can't sleep."

"Something on your mind?" she asked, coming to sit on the edge of my bed. Dad appeared in the doorway behind her and leaned on the scratched wood, his cane resting lightly in his palm.

I'd thought I wanted to whine about Ryker, so it was a surprise even to me when something entirely different came out of my mouth. "I think I need to move away."

Mum's eyebrows shot sky high. "Why?" She didn't sound

defensive or negative. Just curious and surprised. "Because of what happened with Ryker?"

I shook my head. It was partially that, but it was more about me. "I need more than this." Then I realised how horrible that sounded and rushed to clarify. "It's not that this life is bad. Please don't think that's what I meant. I know you both love it here and I'm not in any way dismissing the lifestyle you've chosen. But I don't think it's right for me. Not entirely anyway."

I glanced over at my dad, not knowing how he'd react, but now that I'd started, I may as well lay everything on the table. "I love teaching, and the kids, and working in the family business. I do. But there are no opportunities here for me. And I want more. I've been applying for photography positions."

"In Sydney?"

"Sydney, Melbourne. Pretty much anywhere. I haven't had any interest yet, but I'm not going to stop trying until I do."

I fiddled with a loose thread on my flannelette sheets, picking at it until the seam began to unravel. "I feel awful about this. I know how much you guys need me and I owe you for everything you've done for me over the years. I know how much you've sacrificed and that I sound like an ungrateful brat—"

"Stop." My father held up his hand. "Yyyyou owe us nothing."

My mother was nodding in agreement. "You don't. You had an accident. It was our *job* as your parents to look after you, no matter what."

"But you've given up more for me than the average parent—"

"Do you thhhhhink I owe your mother because she tooook care of me after my stroke?"

"No, of course not." I could already see where he was going with this.

"My point is, if this liiife isn't making you happppy anymore, then you need to find one that does."

"But the business..."

"Will be just fine without you," my mother interrupted. "We

already have some ideas and plans for the future. Even without the stroke, your father couldn't have worked forever. This sort of work is tiring and taxing, and we've been looking into other avenues. The last few months have made us realise we're too reliant on the horse-riding lessons. We need to diversify."

"How, though?"

My father shook his head. "Thhhat's not a conversation for thhhree in the morning."

"Is it seriously three? What were you two doing in Lorrington anyway?"

Mum laughed. "Having fun. You should try it sometime, Gem. It'd be good for you."

I FELL ASLEEP EASILY after my parents left to climb the stairs to their room. But it couldn't have been much later when a tapping noise woke me up. I blinked blearily around the room that was only just beginning to lighten with the first streaks of predawn sunlight. The tapping noise came again, and I whipped around to stare at the window. I could have sworn it came from there. I got myself over to the window, practically jumping out of my skin as a head appeared on the other side. "Jesus Christ, Ryker!" I yelled. Then lowered my voice as I yanked open the window a few inches. "What the hell are you doing? You scared the shit out of me!"

"Sorry! Sorry." He held his hands up in a calming gesture. "I need you to come with me."

My eyes narrowed. "You haven't spoken to me in weeks, and now suddenly I'm supposed to just drop everything and follow you around like a lost puppy?"

He shook his head. "Not like a puppy. But I really need to show you something. It will help explain everything, I promise."

I was tempted to slam the window in his face, but at the same time, I wanted to lean through it and plant my lips against his. Finally, he'd come. "Fine. Can I at least have five minutes to get dressed and brush my teeth?"

He gave me that damn winning smile that made my stomach flip and nodded. I took ten minutes to get ready, just because I could, then rolled myself down the ramp at the back of the house to where Ryker waited, his hands shoved deep in his pockets.

"Hey. I wanted to show you something."

I raised an eyebrow and waited.

"Is it still all right if I push your chair?"

I squinted at him. "Depends on where you're taking me."

"Not far. Promise. But it's a surprise, and I want you to close your eyes." He shifted his weight from foot to foot, his entire attention laser-beamed on me. Nerves or impatience, I couldn't tell which, had him vibrating on the spot.

"Fine." I covered my eyes with my hands. With my sight gone, my sense of smell increased, and as we bounced over the dirt and grass lumps, I realised all I could smell was him. "Ryker, what the hell have you been doing all night? You reek. And not of anything good." My nose crinkled with the foul smell. "You smell like chicken shit and sweat."

He chuckled, and the sound went right through me. I'd missed his laugh.

"Yeah, I know. I'm sorry. I should have gone home for a shower first, but I just couldn't wait another minute to show you."

"Can I open my eyes yet?"

"Soon."

I held on to my chair with one hand, while the other covered my eyes. I had a pretty good idea by the direction and the rough terrain where we were headed. "Why are we going out to the junk paddock?"

We stopped moving. "Open your eyes," he said close to my ear.

I took a second to enjoy the feel of him so close to me before I opened my eyes and gasped.

Backlit by the rising sun was a full-sized paddock of freshly planted seedlings, all in impossibly neat rows. "Did you do this?" I looked up at him with wide eyes. It was beautiful in its simplicity. "Why? How?"

"I'm starting a business."

"A seed-planting business?"

He laughed. "No. I'm going into business with your parents."

"You're what?" I frowned, confused. "You need to start supplying information. Because this isn't computing."

"Your parents and I talked. I knew they had vacant land down here, and when we were down here the night of the wedding, I realised it was the perfect spot for vegetables. The soil was already not too bad, and we can use the dam water."

"So, you're going to grow veggies down here to sell at the farmers' market?"

He shook his head. "No, no. Well, not just that alone. That wouldn't make much money. Do you remember how beautiful the yard looked during the wedding?"

"Yeah, it was amazing."

"I thought so, too. And people liked the food, don't you think?"

"They loved it."

"Well, so did I. That whole night was a rush for me. Until…"

Neither of us had to say what had happened next. "Anyway. I want to do it again. I asked your mum if she'd consider letting me run a pop-up restaurant here once a month."

"And she agreed?"

He grinned. "Not only did she agree, she wanted to be involved. We worked really well in the kitchen together. And they're wanting to bring in some income from sources that don't rely on the riding lessons."

"Why would you want her in on your business idea, though?"

His eyebrows pulled together as he frowned at me. "They're good people who needed help, and for once in my life, I had something I could offer. They helped me out when I needed it, no questions asked, and I wanted to do the same for them. I'll still pay them back the money, of course—I already gave your dad a thousand, but he gave it back to me and told me to invest it in the garden. So, there's a drip irrigation system now, which means these plants will pretty much take care of themselves."

"Even though they fired you and kicked you out?"

"I had a loan shark with a gun follow me to their daughter's wedding. They bailed me out when I had no other options. I understood why they had to kick me out. Your parents are amazing people, Gemma. I'm honoured they even want anything to do with me after everything that happened."

"I can't believe all this." A smile pulled at my lips but on the inside, it was bittersweet. He'd be back in my life, but only as my parents' business partner?

"Believe it. Here's the business plans I drew up."

He handed me a folder with clear plastic sleeves that contained pages of neat spreadsheets and drawings and even logo design options. I leafed through it, amazed at the amount of work he'd put in.

He pointed to a page of information. "See here, we'll get organic certification. Then we'll use the veggies as the basis of all our dishes. We'll base dishes on whatever's in season, and we'll source fresh meat from one of the other local farms. There's a mock-up of a menu in the back if you skip ahead."

I flicked through and drooled over his proposed menu. Three set courses each month. Homemade pasta, meat, and vegetables, the star of each meal. My mouth watered at the thought of Ryker and my mother cooking together on a regular basis. "Ryker, this is amazing." I couldn't help studying his face, reminding myself of all the little features I'd fallen in love with.

"Thanks. Your mum got so excited about it that she started

talking about putting a little cabin down the back here and promoting the property as a farm-stay destination. People would stay in the cabin, help with the garden and the horses, or take some lessons. Then we'd feed them under the moonlight, while surrounded by fairy lights and flowers."

I reached over and took his hand and squeezed it, trying to tamp down on the way my skin sparked when it touched his, and how much I'd missed the feel of his hand engulfing mine. "I can't believe you've come up with all of this in just a few weeks. There's a lot of work to be done, but I know you. And I know my mother. The two of you will have it all up and running in no time. People are going to love it."

I surveyed the rows of tiny plants that would one day be served on the plates of guests to our farm-stay. One by one, the knots that had twisted my stomach ever since the wedding unravelled, and relief seeped in.

Like a lightbulb going off in my head, I suddenly understood now what Dad had meant earlier when he'd said he was in talks with someone about diversifying. "Why didn't anyone tell me?"

"I asked your parents not to. I wasn't sure if I could pull it off and I didn't want it to be yet another failure in my long list of them. I didn't want to disappoint you again."

"You didn't disappoint me, though."

He sighed. "I wanted to prove to you I could get something right. I don't want to ever be a burden or an embarrassment to you. Or to your family. I've got no home, no car, no money. I had to have something, Gem. I couldn't come asking for forgiveness with nothing."

A flicker of hope sparked in my chest. "Does that mean you're apologising?"

He leant down in front of me, resting his hands on the armrests of my chair. "I am. I'm so fucking sorry, Gem. Not for the stuff with Gerard. I made a mistake that bit me in the ass hard, but I never lied about any of it. But I am sorry for leaving the way I did. I just got scared I was turning into my father."

"You're nothing like your father."

"I don't want to be," he said, dropping his gaze.

Without thinking, I placed my palms on either side of his face, and his gaze lifted to meet mine again. "You've already proved you aren't."

"I hurt you. I saw the look on your face last night."

It was true. He had. Neither of us needed me to confirm it.

He knelt in the dirt in front of me, pulling me as close as he could get, and I went willingly. "I won't ever do that again. That night when you told me you loved me, all I wanted to do was say it back. But I was so weighed down by everything I'd done, I didn't want to drag you down with me."

His gaze dropped to my lips before meeting mine again. "I made a mistake. It won't be the last one, because as you might have noticed, I make a lot of them." His fingers snaked through mine and squeezed them tightly. "But I don't make the same mistakes twice."

Tears pricked the backs of my eyes as my heart raced.

He closed in and brushed his lips across mine. "I love you, Gemma. You're beautiful and smart, and I've loved you in one way or another since we were kids. But nothing can top the way I love you now." His voice cracked, and I thought my heart might break. "I want this. I want you. I want *us*."

A tear dripped down my face, and he kissed it away. My bottom lip trembled, and I opened my mouth to speak, but emotion clogged my throat. Confusion flickered in Ryker's eyes, and he pulled away an inch, looking suddenly uncertain. I tried clearing my throat, but the lump there was like a tennis ball, refusing to budge, and another tear slipped from my eye.

He sat back on his heels. "Don't cry. If I'm too late and your feelings have changed, I'll understand." He went quiet while I battled to find the right words, my heart and my head a jumbled mess. He dropped his gaze. "If you're going to break my heart, Gem, just break it. I get it."

I shook my head and grabbed his hand, pulling it to my chest. "I love you, too, you idiot. Girls cry sometimes when they're happy, you know." I half laughed, half sobbed the words. I'd missed him so much. I wanted us just as much as he did. Screw-ups and all, I still loved him. Nothing he did was ever going to change that.

His worried brow smoothed out and he smiled his million-dollar grin. His fingers found the back of my neck, and he guided me to him. I closed my eyes, expecting his kiss, but he hovered over my lips.

"I am an idiot. But you love me. So, I'll take it."

I rolled my eyes and kissed him hard, fisting my fingers in his shirt. We kissed with all the pent-up passion I'd missed the past few weeks. It was like the first time, yet old and familiar. I was breathless and aching for his touch by the time I roughly pushed him away, unable to go on any longer, even though every cell in my body demanded it. His eyes fluttered open as he groaned.

"What's wrong?"

I wrinkled my nose at him. "I love you. I really do. But you still smell like chicken shit."

28

GEMMA - TWO MONTHS LATER

Ryker kissed a path up my spine, over my shoulder, and along my neck, leaving a trail of goosebumps in the wake of his warm mouth. I closed my eyes for a brief moment while his tongue circled my ear. Then I elbowed him sharply in the chest.

"Unf," he grunted, flopping back on the bed behind me.

I laughed as I glanced over my shoulder at his overstated hurt impression. "I'm trying to work, Adam."

"So was I. It's my job to turn you on. Especially when you're lying naked in my bed."

We were back in the squeaky, wire-framed bed in the shearers' quarters. Mum and Dad had let Ryker move back in as soon as they saw how much work he'd done with the garden. And anyway, it wasn't like they could use the excuse he couldn't be around their business anymore. Considering he was their business partner.

Things had gone quiet on the Gerard front. The police said he'd disappeared from all known premises, but they continued their search for him. We refused to let the niggling worry he might return rule our lives, though. Mum and Ryker had had two pop-up restaurants so far, just for local folk. The first one had been quiet. But I'd sat at a table with my father, sister, and Low and devoured the food Ryker and Mum had made in the kitchen. Mum's pasta fell apart in your mouth, and the rabbit stew Ryker had made, despite my hesitations about eating poor, defenceless bunnies, was to die for—perfectly seasoned, in a thick sauce that made me want to lick my plate. The customers at the tables around us seemed to agree, and the next month the pop-up restaurant had been sold out. Word spread, and we were already booked out for the next one, which was a shame for me and Dad, because it meant we'd be roped into helping in the kitchen rather than sitting at one of the tables drinking wine. Nothing had happened yet with the idea to build cabins, but Reese and Low had liked the idea when we'd pitched it to them and were considering investing in the project. I had full confidence that one way or the other, Ryker and my mother would get one built. They were an unconventional team, but they got stuff done. Dad and I had been shocked at the speed with which they'd pulled the pop-up restaurant together.

With Ryker suitably chastised for interrupting me, I went back to scrolling through the photos I'd taken yesterday. I'd picked up some local work with the junior cricket league and had taken all their team photos before their matches on the weekend. It had been good to spend the day away from the farm and to be behind the lens, though not particularly challenging. Each kid had been posed the same way for their individuals, which really only left me clicking a button. Their group photos were a little more interesting, but still, lining kids up under the shade of a tree and yelling to make sure I had their attention wasn't exactly showing my work in a hot, Melbourne gallery.

It didn't matter, though, and I was grateful. I scrolled through the photos, culling out any that had closed eyes or weird facial expressions, while Ryker grabbed a notepad and scribbled new menu ideas.

It was only a few moments before his fingers were trailing over my bare skin again, though. "I'm really happy, you know?" he said quietly.

I gave up working and rolled over to face him. "Are you?"

He kissed me softly. "I really am. My life is pretty damn perfect right now. The restaurant is going great, the cabins are practically a sure thing, and organic certification won't be too far behind that. Meeting you again and setting things right between us... I don't know, Gem. I feel like the universe and I are at one with each other again. I feel like I've been forgiven."

"I already forgave you months ago."

"I know, but karma and all that..."

"Since when do you even believe in karma? You aren't going all hippy on me, are you? What kind of country kid does that make you? We don't believe in such rubbish out here," I joked.

"Shut up," he huffed, then smiled. "You need to get those photos edited today?"

I nodded. "And you're doing kitchen prep for tomorrow night?"

"Yeah. So I guess I'll see you later?"

I nodded.

"I love you." He brushed a strand of hair out of my face and tucked it behind my ear. "You're the best damn thing that ever happened to me."

I grinned. "Ditto."

He rolled his eyes. "You're such a romantic."

I tugged his mouth down to mine. "Want to see exactly how romantic I can be?"

He groaned when I found his cock beneath the blankets. "Yes. But I have to go work. And so do you, Miss Official Photographer for the Lorrington Cricket Association!"

I laughed and pushed him out of bed. "Shut up."

"You shut up. I'm proud of you. You did a great job with those kids yesterday."

His praise was nice. I had done a good job. Did it really matter that the subject didn't exactly set my soul on fire? I was shooting for money, and that was one big step up from where I'd been six months ago. Ryker had been so happy and excited for me, and his enthusiasm was infectious. He was right. I'd edit these photos like a complete pro, the club would love them and ask me to come back next year, and they'd spread the word to all the other local clubs. That was the plan.

I grinned while he picked himself up off the floor, then walked naked to his bathroom. The shower turned on, and Ryker's off-key singing filtered back to me, making me smile. He was still working two jobs to pay my parents back, and so far he hadn't taken a cent of the pop-up restaurant money. He was lucky to get five hours of sleep per night, but something had changed about him. He talked more than he ever had. He smiled. He laughed. He was driven and motivated and never complained about how much work he did. His mum had even come to one of the pop-up restaurants with his brothers who had all flown in for it as a surprise, and I knew that had made his day. He'd told me all about the showdown with his father, and finishing that chapter in his life seemed to have lifted a weight from his shoulders. And his happiness made me happy, too. I loved him so damn much, more than I'd thought humanly possible. We were practically living together—I hadn't slept in the big house a single night since we'd gotten back together, and things just felt right. I knew we were young, and there was still a lot that life could throw at us, but this thing between us felt like forever.

Ryker switched to a Katy Perry song when he left the bathroom, waving as he headed for the main house, and I went back to flicking through photos. I scrolled through slowly, deleting, sorting, and doing basic lighting adjustments as I went. I laughed at the faces some of the little kids had pulled. So cute.

At the end of the posed photos, I paused. There'd been a men's cricket match starting right at the time I'd finished the last set of team photos. Ryker had wanted to watch for a bit, so we'd joined the players' families and friends on the sidelines. It had been a surprisingly good match. The teams were fairly even in terms of skill, and the family on the sidelines were really into it, creating an exciting atmosphere.

We'd ended up staying for over an hour. Even though I was only contracted to shoot the posed photos, I'd picked up my camera and started snapping candid action shots. I looked through them now, my heartbeat picking up. I was so pleased with how they'd turned out. The light was great, they showed movement, and the facial expressions on some of the players' faces was perfect. I added them all to the 'to keep' folder, figuring the club might like to give copies of them to the players. Or maybe they could use them on their social media. Either way, I didn't want them to go to waste.

Ryker's life was good, and so was mine.

My email pinged, and I minimised Photoshop to read it. My eyes widened as I took in the sender, and I scrabbled to open the email with my pulse pounding. I read it all the way to the end, skimming as fast as I could to get all the information.

Then, in a state of shock, I read it over twice more, slowly and carefully, poring over every word as if there may be some sort of hidden meaning. There wasn't.

All I had was a job offer for a full-time photography position at Riding for the Disabled.

In Sydney. Twelve hours away from the man I loved.

I ROLLED SLOWLY into the kitchen of the main house where Ryker sat chopping what seemed to be a mountain of carrots.

He looked up when I came in. "Hey. You done already?"

I went to sit next to him, but my body moved in slow motion. My mind whirred a hundred miles a minute, yet my arms seemed to have lost all strength to spin the wheels. I folded my hands on my lap as Ryker peered at me with a curious expression.

"You look like you've seen a ghost."

I shook my head. "No, no. Nothing like that. Where are Mum and Dad?"

"Your dad had physio, remember?"

"Oh, right. Yeah. Damn."

"What's going on?"

"Nothing, it's probably better that I talk to you first anyway."

He sat back in his chair and focussed his attention on me.

"I got the job at Riding for the Disabled."

His knife clattered to the table, startling both of us. "The one you applied for months ago and never heard back from?"

I nodded. "Apparently they loved the idea of having a photographer on staff. But to create a position, there were a lot of hoops and red tape. They didn't want to offer it to me before they were sure they could."

"But it's a sure thing now?"

"Yeah. Sounds like it."

His lips morphed into a slow grin. He stood and pushed his chair back so hard it clattered to the floor behind him. Then he threw his arms around me, lifting me straight out of my chair. "Yes!" he yelled, loud enough to deafen me.

"Omg, Ryker! Don't drop me."

He ignored my protests, swinging me in a circle. Holy shit, the kitchen was not big enough for this. "You got it! You got the dream job!". His grin stretched ear to ear as he put me back in my chair and sat down again, grabbing my hand and kissing my palm.

"Do you even know how proud I am? They didn't even have a photography position and they created one. Just for you. I knew you were that amazing, and now the whole world will know it, too."

He shook his head and laughed, and the depth of pride and happiness in his eyes shot straight to my heart. Oh, how I loved this man. This man and his huge heart. I didn't know how I'd spent so many years hating him and ignoring him when I could have been holding him and loving him.

Ryker ran his hand through his hair. "Shit. So when do you start? How long do we have to find a place in Sydney? We'll have to fly down since neither of us has a car right now… So I guess we should look for a place that's already furnished, too?"

I coughed on my surprise. "Wait, what?"

But Ryker had gone into full organisation mode and was listing off all the things we'd need to do. I didn't think he even heard me.

"We'll have to organise someone to take over my jobs here at the farm, though your dad has been stealing a lot of them from me anyway and—"

I grabbed his hand and squeezed it to get his attention. "Ryker, stop. You don't have to do all this, I'm not going to—"

His eyes darkened, and he leant forward. His fingers found the back of my neck, and he pulled me to him roughly, kissing me hard. His kiss was bruising and branding, and for half a second, I tried to talk through it, but he wasn't having it. And I gave in and kissed him back until I was breathless.

"Don't you even think about saying you aren't taking it. You are. End of story. And I'm coming, too."

I shook my head. "And do what?"

"Sydney's a big place. I'll get a job in a kitchen. Or I'll go back to mechanics. Whatever."

I was still shaking my head, and he frowned at me, tugging my chair closer so my legs rested in the gap made by his. "You're it for me, Gemma. When I say I love you, it's not just words. I love every damn thing about you. The way you look. The way you care so much for other people. The internal strength you have. But most of all, I love the way you make me feel. I don't ever want to be without that. And your happiness means everything to me. You're taking that job, and I'm going with you."

"But you hate the city." I laughed.

"I liked Melbourne."

"You liked the hotel room in Melbourne."

He chuckled. "True." His fingers found the sides of my face, and he brushed his thumbs over my cheeks as he stared deep into my eyes. "You're going. And I'll learn to love it."

I shook my head, the fog of shock finally lifting away, only to be replaced by an overwhelming love. For him to offer to give up everything he had here made tears prick the backs of my eyes. He was such a good man.

"You know how you feel about me giving up this job? That's how I feel about you giving up yours. You and Mum have a good thing going here, Ryker. You said it yourself this morning, that you're the happiest you've ever been, and your life is perfect. That isn't all about me. And I won't drag you to Sydney and make you miserable. That would make *me* miserable, then we'd both be miserable, and that would be a huge buzzkill."

I smiled, trying to lighten the mood, because he suddenly looked very serious.

"So, what are you trying to say? I'll stay here, and you'll go there? You want to break up?" His voice cracked, and my stomach rolled.

The pure pain in his expression made me fist his shirt and drag him against me. He didn't move, and I kissed him hard, every feeling and emotion I had swirling through my body trying to seep from me and into him, to take away that expression on his face that cut deep to the bone. When we pulled away, I ran my fingers through his hair, and he closed his eyes, leaning into my touch.

"I don't want to break up, Adam. I love you, you stupid man.

You're it for me, too. I'd marry you tomorrow if you wanted me to."

"I do. Marry me."

I laughed and shoved him in the chest. "Settle down."

He smiled. And threaded his fingers through mine. "So, what are we going to do? How am I going to do that thing you like with my tongue if you're all the way in Sydney and I'm here?" He traced a path up my neck before placing a kiss on the delicate skin. I trembled beneath his lips.

"I already called the RDA. The job is based in Sydney, though I'll be doing some travelling around to their various chapters, too. But I organised it so I'll only do three days a week. They were fine with that. They were pretty much willing to give me anything I wanted, actually. They think I'm a good role model for the kids and an ambassador for the company."

His shoulders relaxed a touch. "And you're good with that? I know you weren't keen on the idea when you thought the magazine was trying to use you for publicity."

"This feels different. It doesn't feel like a bid for attention. It just feels…natural. I get what some of these kids are going through, because I've been there myself. I don't just want to be the photographer, you know? This job will combine everything I love. Horses, kids, and photography. I'll have a purpose there. I won't just be a talking point."

"So where does that leave us?"

"That leaves you living here, running the restaurant and helping Mum start up the farm-stay. And me in Sydney three days a week with Low and Reese. I know they won't take rent money from me, so I'll use that money to fly home for the rest of the week. I'm sure you can live without me three days a week."

He gave me a wicked grin. "Think of all the phone sex we can have."

I rolled my eyes, and he sobered, tipping my chin up to stare into my eyes. "I love you. I'm going to miss you like hell when you aren't here, but as long as I know we're good, I'll be okay."

"We're good. We're really damn good."

Then he kissed me so long and with such emotion, I knew without a doubt we'd be just fine.

EPILOGUE

RYKER

Heatwaves rose from the black tarmac of the airport runway, heating the soles of my feet, despite my shoes providing some resistance. It wasn't quite summer yet, but even spring had some scorching days, and today was one of them. I tapped my foot, searching the cloudless blue sky for any sign of Gemma's plane. Nothing.

It had been a long three days since I'd kissed her goodbye and watched while her plane had taken off for Sydney. We'd talked every night on the phone, FaceTiming each other so I'd seen the pure excitement that had radiated as she'd talked a million miles an hour about her first week at her new job. I hated her being gone, but her happiness had doubled the size of my heart. She was in her element.

I patted my pocket, checking to make sure the small, square box was still safely tucked inside, and tried to calm my growing nerves. Where the hell was this plane? I checked my watch, then felt foolish. The plane wasn't even due in for another three minutes. Another three agonising minutes. And that was if it was even on time. I took my sunglasses off to clean them, despite them being speck-free.

The low buzz of a far-off engine caught my attention, and I squinted up into the sun, raising a hand to shield my eyes from the bright light. I spotted the tiny eight-seater that ran between the major airport and the little one here in Erraville. The noise grew louder as the plane approached and touched down at the end of the runway with smooth precision. After a couple of little bunny hops, it cruised along on its wheels, gradually slowing until it came to a stop a few hundred meters from where I stood.

My stomach flipped. I couldn't wait to see her, though I was nervous about the box in my pocket. But even if she shot me down, I had to ask. It had been all I'd thought about for the past three days.

Airport officials in fluoro orange safety vests rolled a ramp to the plane's door before opening it so the passengers could disembark. I walked across the runway so I could stand at the bottom of it. My fingers twitched. I wanted her back in my arms. I wanted to kiss her and hold her and tell her how much I loved her. I'd managed to fill my days with work, but I'd missed lying in bed with her at night with my lips pressed to her neck.

Two middle-aged men and a woman exited, one by one, talking and laughing as they walked down the ramp and unhurriedly made their way to the cargo hold of the plane where they'd collect their belongings. No need for a fancy baggage claim at an airport that was little more than a single runway. They chatted cheerfully with the luggage handler while I bounced on the soles of my feet, waiting for the baggage guy to get Gemma's wheelchair so she could leave the plane. I rolled my head to ease some of the tension building across my shoulders.

"Fuck it," I muttered, striding up the short ramp and into the cabin of the plane. There was no one there to stop me.

The interior was darker than outside, and it took me a second for my eyes to adjust, bright blotches blurring out my vision.

"Ryker?"

Blinking rapidly, I headed towards her voice and found her staring up at me in astonishment from a seat at the back.

"What are you do—"

"Fuck I've missed you." I leant down and cupped her face, crushing her lips to mine.

She gasped, as if I'd taken her by surprise, but in the next moment, her arms came around my neck, and she was kissing me back just as hard. Our lips parted, our tongues moving together as I tried to refamiliarize myself with her. Had she changed? Had she fallen in love with the city? Was she upset to be home?

But there in her kiss, all I found was the same hungry wanting I felt for her. I knew her. And this thing between us was right. Three days apart, or three years, it wouldn't matter. What we felt wouldn't change. She could go and chase her dreams, and I'd chase mine, but we'd always come back to each other, time and time again.

I dropped to my knees, pressing my forehead against hers, closing my eyes while we both caught our breath. When she opened hers, I was holding the ring.

"Holy shit," she stuttered, her lips pink from our kiss, her hair slightly messed up from the plane trip or my fingers, I didn't know. But in that moment, she'd never looked more beautiful.

"We don't have to do this right away. Or not ever if you don't want. But three days apart from you showed me I can't live without you. We don't have to be tied at the hip, but I want to know you're always coming home to me. And I want you to know I'm always going to be here for you. If that means one day moving to the city, then I'll do it. Even though it stinks and there are too many people." She chuckled, but I kept going. "Or we can live here, and you can commute. Or we'll do something entirely different. I don't know, we can do whatever we want. I just want to do it all with you by my side."

Her bottom lip trembled, and her eyes went glossy with emotion. "I—"

"Wait, I haven't finished. Let me do this properly." I pulled the ring from the cushions it was nestled between and held it towards her. "I thought I loved you back when we were kids, but that's nothing compared to the way I love you now. I want to make you happy, every damn day for the rest of our lives. I'll fuck up along the way, you know I will. But no one will ever love you more than I do. It isn't humanly possible."

She grinned and I grabbed her hand.

"Marry me, Gem. Be my wife. We'll get a house and a dog and raise a few kids." I took a deep breath, trying to rein my swirling thoughts into some sort of coherent sense. "I want it all. I want you."

A tear dripped down her cheek, and she brushed it away, nodding.

"Is that a yes?" I asked hopefully, my hand hovering in the air, fingers twitching to slide the ring over hers.

Her smile spread from ear to ear. "It's a yes."

A heady combination of relief, joy, and excitement swept through me like a tidal wave, but one I'd be happy to drown in. I bundled her into my arms, burying my face in her neck and breathing in the familiar citrus smell of her shampoo. She hugged me back just as hard, her tiny body trembling in my arms. Eventually, I pulled back to find her hand and slipped the diamond and sapphire ring I'd bought at an Op shop.

"It's not much," I whispered.

"It's everything. You're everything," she whispered back before claiming my mouth as hers again.

Because I was hers. And she was mine. And there wasn't a single negative that could ruin that.

THE END

You've waited a long time for Bianca and Riley's romance. Grab it here or keep reading for a sneak peek!

Want a free book? Get Only the Lies for free when you join Elle's reader family newsletter. Join here for free!
www.ellethorpe.com/newsletter

ONLY THE BEGINNING SNEAK PEEK

CHAPTER 1

BIANCA

"Fuck, you have great tits."

I checked my watch. Wow. What a compliment, and not even ten minutes into the date. I fought to keep from rolling my eyes, and instead, smiled tightly at the dickhead sitting across the table from me.

He was a handsome dickhead, with his dirty-blond hair and chiselled jaw. His collared white shirt clung to a muscular frame, tanned skin on display where he'd left several buttons undone. Not just several. Half his shirt, really. I could see the tops of his abs. He obviously thought it was sexy, and maybe his shit comeon lines, if that was what that had been, worked on some people. Maybe he just flashed that fake white smile, told women their tits were great, and they threw their underwear at him.

Vomit.

"You wanna get outta here?" he asked, voice smooth as silk.

"What?" I stuttered. Was he serious? Our waiter had barely had time to take our entree order. "What about dinner?"

He shrugged, and then one eye kind of half closed, and he went back to smirking at me.

I stifled a laugh. Was that supposed to be a sexy wink? It

looked more like an eye twitch. Suddenly, I regretted every single one of my life choices that had led to this moment.

"Sure, we can eat. If you really want."

What I really wanted was a drink. And to yell at my best friend for making me come on a ridiculous Tinder date anyway. I should have known better than to take advice from someone who had been with her husband for ten years and had probably never even downloaded a hookup app.

"Excuse me for a moment." I picked up my bag and carried it to the bathrooms, pulling out my phone while I locked the stall door behind me. At least it was nice in here. The tiles were black marble, or at least imitation marble, and the fittings glinted silver under chrome lights. Sitting on the closed lid of the toilet, I called Reese.

"I hate you," I moaned when she answered.

"What did I do?"

"You made me come on this stupid date! The guy's opening line was to tell me my tits were great, and he's already giving me the come-on. He's probably going to ask me for anal before we even get to dessert at this rate."

Reese snorted on her laugh. But I was serious, so it didn't seem all that funny. "I should have never come."

That sobered her. "Why not? You keep telling me there's nothing between you and Ri—"

"Don't say his name!" I cut her off, imagining one hand on her hip and a frown creasing the space between her eyebrows.

She sighed. "B, he's one of our best friends. His name is going to come up."

"No, he's one of your best friends."

"Come on, you know that's not true. He cares about you, and you care about him, in some weird, demented sort of way. Not that anyone else would know it with the way you two go at each other like pit bulls in a dogfight."

I sighed. She was right. But I wished she'd stop. She was only making things worse. Every time his name was said out loud, all it did was make me think about the last time we'd been together. And all the times before that.

"You're thinking about him, aren't you? B, you gotta stop this. You and Riley—"

"Aaaah!"

She was rolling her eyes for sure.

"Fine. You and the man who shall not be named, you can't keep doing whatever the hell you've been doing for the past ten years. Just tell him you love him and live happily ever after already."

Jeez, she was over the top. And I was supposed to be the actress. Maybe I should get her a job on my show. "You said it yourself, Reese. All we do is fight."

"And fuck."

My cheeks heated at the thought. Yes. We fucked. A lot.

"We don't work. We can barely be in the same room as each other without a screaming match breaking out. Yeah, there's chemistry there. There always has been. We scratch an itch for each other from time to time. But chemistry isn't the grounds for a relationship."

There was a moment of silence, then, "I know."

"Are you pouting?" I asked with a laugh. I knew our friends wanted Riley and me to get our shit together, but it was never going to happen. There was nothing between us. Nothing but history. And history should stay in the past. "Look, I'm ditching this date."

"No, wait. Stop. You know I'm Team Riley but I'm also Team Bianca. Tell me, once and for all, there's really nothing there between you two, and I will never mention it again."

Ugh, the woman was exasperating sometimes. "There's nothing between us," I said truthfully. "I mean it, Reese. I need you to have my back. You know I have no willpower around him. I need a boyfriend. I wouldn't still be having casual sex with him if I had someone else. That's why you made me come here, remember?"

"Right. No more sleeping with Riley. I shall never speak of the two of you again. Now get back out there and give that guy a proper chance. Maybe he was just nervous."

I doubted the dickhead had ever been nervous. And I also doubted Reese would never speak of Riley and me again. I'd told her just last week that I was done giving in to my basic urges, which was why I'd agreed to come on a Tinder date. Riley and I hadn't dated in ten years. It was time to put whatever we were to each other to bed. To start acting like grown adults. Not horny twenty-somethings who hated each other but couldn't keep their hands to themselves.

But goddammit. Was the dickhead waiting for me in the restaurant really the answer? Riley and I might have spent years arguing, but he'd never leered at me the way Dickhead had.

"Okay, I'm going back to deal with Prince Not So Charming." I laughed, though it sounded fake even to my own ears.

I said goodbye to Reese and pushed open the bathroom door. I'd been in there for ages and I semi hoped my date might have given up and gone home. I slid my bag strap up on my shoulder, flicked my hair back off my face, and lifted my head.

And froze. My gaze collided with familiar brown eyes, and heat swept through my body like a wildfire. I swore quietly under my breath.

Riley.

This was exactly why he was the man who should not be named. Because everything about him, his name, his beautiful face, his smouldering gaze—everything about him scrambled my senses. I'd never been able to think straight around him. There had always been something between us. Something so damn strong it had a force of its own. Something strong enough that it had withstood ten years.

I faltered. Images of the last time we'd been together flashed in front of my eyes. His lips on my neck. My legs wrapped around his back. His cock buried deep inside me and my orgasm roaring through my core.

Fuck.

I had to stop this. My date was waiting for me. And, with a start, I noticed Riley was on a date of his own. The realisation hit me like a punch to the stomach. The woman across from him chatted happily, not seeming to notice that he'd been staring at me since I'd walked out of the bathroom. Jealousy flared in my chest. It wasn't like we kept each other updated on our lives, but surely Reese would have told me if he was seeing someone. Her husband was his best friend after all. She had to have known…

I couldn't stop staring, his eyes holding me to the spot. The air between us crackled with an energy so tangible I could practically see it. I shook my head slightly. *Get a grip*. He wasn't mine. He hadn't been mine in so long, I had no right to be jealous. Dragging my gaze away from him, I pulled back my shoulders and made my way to my table.

I knew he was watching me. And despite knowing I shouldn't, I liked it.

CHAPTER 2

RILEY

"Do you know her?"

I whipped my head back to focus on my date. Cora. The woman from the office of the construction company I worked for. I didn't go in there much, just a few times a month to drop off paperwork. But she always flirted with me, and she was gorgeous, with long auburn hair and big green eyes. She'd lined them in black tonight, and her lips were plump and red. She was a flat-out siren, really. Just…not the siren I wanted.

"Uh. No," I lied. "Sorry. She just looks like someone I know."

"Isn't it funny when that happens? When I was in high school…"

Her voice faded into the noise of the restaurant, and I smiled, nodded and occasionally made encouraging sounds when she paused for breath. She was a talker. But that was fine, because I wasn't.

Cora filled me in on her entire high school experience while I fought every muscle in my body. Every instinct screamed that Bianca was close by. I curled my fingers around the tabletop, digging my fingers into the hard wood, struggling to keep myself out of her magnetic pull. It was an almost painful feeling by now.

Being in the same room as her but not touching her. It was the same physical ache that hadn't let up for even a minute since she'd broken my heart ten years ago. Fuck.

Cora excused herself to go to the bathroom, a welcome relief, and I reached for my phone, listening to the voicemail message Low had sent me earlier in the week.

"Listen, bro. Reese would kill me if she knew I was telling you this. But Bianca was over here last night, and, well...she told Reese she doesn't want to do the fighting hate-sex thing you two have been doing anymore. She said it's holding her back, and I'm sorry, man, but I think she's right. She's holding you back, too. Have you even dated at all in the past decade? You're going to end up one of those old men who sits on his porch and yells at the neighbourhood kids if you keep this up. Just...I don't know. Branch out. Leave B alone. You guys have been there, done that. It didn't work. I know it's not my business, but maybe it's time to accept that. See you at football on Saturday."

I stabbed the cancel button. I'd listened to the message probably fifty times the day he'd sent it. At first, I'd been pissed off and ready to storm over there and tell him exactly where to shove his shit advice. What did he know about Bianca and me? We were...complicated.

But the more I'd listened, the more my anger had dissipated. Nothing he'd said was a lie. Every time I saw her, we somehow ended up in an argument, or we ended up not talking at all and just started ripping clothes off. There was no middle ground. Nothing solid to build on. Just the glimmering memory of something magical that had turned sour.

A loud scrape of a chair caught my attention, and I took the opportunity to swivel backwards, my gaze landing on Bianca's lithe frame. She was shaking her head at her date, her expression full of irritation. I picked up my wine glass, forcing myself to take a sip and remain seated. I didn't like the way he was leering at her. He said something back to her, then she threw her hands in the air and stormed away from him.

I frowned, though pleased she was ending her date. The guy was a complete tool. Who did he think he was anyway? He looked like an over-tanned, washed-up Hollywood wannabe who was past his prime. But I didn't like that she was upset. I followed her with my eyes until she disappeared around a corner into the depths of the restaurant and I lost sight of her. My gaze narrowed on the over-buffed jerk she'd been out with. He didn't try to go after her. Just pulled her plate of food across the table and started eating. I let out a long breath, trying to calm the protective urge to go after her and make sure she was okay. If Low's message was true, and I had no reason to doubt him, Bianca didn't want me around. I'd half-heartedly tried this before. Avoiding her. I'd tried it many times, actually. But she was like a drug I couldn't quit. And she seemed to feel the same about me. Every time I'd managed to leave her alone, inevitably, she'd turn up somewhere I was, and we'd fall back into our same old routine. We weren't together. We hadn't been since we were barely older than teenagers. And yet we couldn't seem to get out of each other's bubbles.

Cora leant in and raked her fingernails gently across my forearm. I hadn't even noticed her return. She had her breasts pushed so high they practically spilled from her dress. What the fuck was wrong with me? Sitting here, pining away over a woman I'd never been able to have. A woman who clearly didn't want me, not for anything more than to argue or have sex with, when there was a perfectly viable alternative right in front of me. One who was giving me every signal in the book that she was a green light.

"Listen, Riley," Cora said, her voice sultry. She looked up at me through lowered lashes and licked her tongue over her lips. It was supposed to be a seductive move but did nothing for me. "I'm not going to beat around the bush. I don't need this to be some epic romance."

I paused. "Okay."

"You understand what I'm saying?"

Oh, I understood. I just wasn't sure I wanted to do anything about it.

But then I heard Low's voice in my ear. *"Leave B alone. You're holding her back."* Tension threaded through my back. That was the last thing I'd ever wanted. I never wanted to be someone who held her back. She was a star in an inky-black sky. If she wasn't allowed to shine, the nights would be dark.

I nodded to Cora. "I understand." *Fucking hell. Grow a pair, Riley.* I was single. Cora was single. She wanted this. And maybe it was what I needed. I hadn't slept with anyone but Bianca for most of my adult life. I'd put her on a pedestal. Staying faithful to a woman I wasn't even in a relationship with. It was fucking ridiculous.

I held my hand out to Cora, and she gave me a million-dollar smile. Then I led her to the door, like I took women home every day. Other single men in their thirties did this? Didn't they? Screw it. I was doing it. I could do a night of casual sex with someone other than Bianca. Pussy was pussy. A tight wet hole to get off in.

Even as I thought it, I knew I was full of shit. I couldn't pull that sort of attitude off. But I continued the internal pep talk anyway. *Change is as good as a holiday. You have to move on with someone else eventually. Get back in the saddle.* All the clichéd metaphors I could think of.

I held open the restaurant door, then put my hand on the small of Cora's back as I walked her to her car.

"My place?" she purred, pushing herself against my chest in the dimly lit car park.

She was warm and soft where I was hard, and it was on the tip of my tongue to say yes, when a shiny red convertible parked in the next row over caught my eye.

Bianca's convertible.

I stepped back, running my fingers through my hair. Hadn't she left? But if her car was still here, then maybe she was, too.

And so was that jerk she'd been on a date with. Unease settled over me. She hadn't wanted to be near that guy. *I* didn't want her near that guy.

All thoughts of going home to have meaningless sex with Cora disintegrated. I had to find Bianca. Just to make sure she was okay. Even though we fought all the time, she was still my friend. Sort of. At the least, Low and Reese would have my head if I told them I'd just left when she could have been in a dangerous situation.

I opened the door for Cora, and she got in. "Follow me home?"

I shook my head. "Maybe next time." I was an asshole. I knew I was giving her mixed signals. I expected her to spit fire at me, but to my surprise she just shrugged.

"You know how to reach me if you change your mind." She drove away with a small wave.

"You're a fucking idiot," I muttered to myself as I watched her headlights disappear into the darkness. And I was. Cora was amazing. And maybe I'd really regret letting her go when I woke up with a raging case of blue balls tomorrow morning.

But there was no denying that if Bianca needed me, I was going to drop everything for her and run.

I always had. And I always would.

Keep reading here!

ALSO BY ELLE THORPE

The Only You series (complete)

*Only the Positive (Only You, #1) - Reese and Low.
*Only the Perfect (Only You, #2) - Jamison.
*Only the Truth - (Only You, bonus novella) - Bree.
*Only the Lies - (FREE Only You, bonus novella) - Cleo.
*Only the Negatives (Only You, #3) - Gemma.
*Only the Beginning (Only You, #4) - Bianca and Riley.
*Only You boxset

Dirty Cowboy series (complete)

*Talk Dirty, Cowboy (Dirty Cowboy, #1)
*Ride Dirty, Cowboy (Dirty Cowboy, #2)
*Sexy Dirty Cowboy (Dirty Cowboy, #3)

*25 Reasons to Hate Christmas and Cowboys (a Dirty Cowboy bonus novella, set before Talk Dirty, Cowboy but can be read as a standalone, holiday romance)

Buck Cowboys series (Spin off from the Dirty Cowboy series)

*Buck Cowboys (Buck Cowboys, #1)
*Buck You! (Buck Cowboys, #2)

Saint View High series (Reverse Harem, Bully Romance)

*Devious Little Liars (Saint View High, #1)

*Dangerous Little Secrets (Saint View High, #2)

*Twisted Little Truths (Saint View High, #3)

Saint View Prison - (Reverse Harem, Romantic Suspense)

Book 1: Locked Up Liars (Saint View Prison, #1)

Book 2: Solitary Sinners (Saint View Prison, #2)

Book 3: Fatal Felons (Saint View Prison, #3)

Add your email address here to be the first to know when new books are available!

www.ellethorpe.com/newsletter

Join Elle Thorpe's readers group on Facebook!

www.facebook.com/groups/ellethorpesdramallamas

ACKNOWLEDGMENTS

I'm going to admit something here. Only the Negatives was a very difficult book to write. When I tell people about how I struggled with this story, they automatically assume it was hard to write because Gemma is in a wheelchair. That's not it at all. You can write almost anything if you do a lot of research. And I'm no stranger to research.

It was just a difficult book to get right. It took more rounds of editing than ever before to get the story I knew was in me. I wanted to throw my laptop through the window more than once.

The only reason I didn't, was because of these amazing people.

To my editor, Emmy, from www.studioenp.com . Thank you for all your hard work and for always being a complete pro. To all the instagrammers, bookbloggers and reviewers that make up my promo team. I'm so incredibly grateful for you all. Your support means everything.

To my amazing critique partners. To Jolie Vines for getting where I was going with this book and for loving Ryker like I did. And to Zoe Ashwood, for kicking my ass and telling me to cut most of the first act. That hurt, but you were 100% right. That piece of advice really turned this book around.

To my beta readers Shellie Maddison, Ally Murphy, Alisa Cavanaugh, Tamara McCall, Shannan Percival, Elizabeth Gonzalez Valiente, and Karen Crompton. Thank you for all your advice. Not one of you sugar coated anything with this book and that was exactly what I needed to get it right. You're an integral part of the process and I could not do this without your feedback. Please don't ever leave me!

And last, but never least, to my family. To Jira for always supporting my dreams. To Thomas and Felicity for proudly telling anyone who'll listen that their mum is a writer. To Heidi for putting up with me writing when we could have been doing more fun things. Bet you can't wait to go to school full time this year and not be so bored, huh?

And to my extended family. To Michela, Luke and Merinda for always reading my books. To Joel for selling my books while on camping trips. To Lauren, Holly, Melanie and Ellen, for buying them even though you aren't really readers. To Chris and Ben for always asking how the writing is going. And to Mum, for finally reading Only the Positive, even though I know the sex scenes killed you. I did tell you not to read it!

ABOUT THE AUTHOR

Elle Thorpe lives on the sunny east coast of Australia. When she's not writing stories full of kissing, she's a wife and mummy to three tiny humans. She's also official ball thrower to one slobbery dog named Rollo. Yes, she named a female dog after a dirty hot character on Vikings. Don't judge her. Elle is a complete and utter fangirl at heart, obsessing over The Walking Dead and Outlander to an unhealthy degree. But she wouldn't change a thing.

You can find her on Facebook or Instagram(@ellethorpebooks or hit the links below!) or at her website www.ellethorpe.com. If you love Elle's work, please consider joining her Facebook fan group, Elle Thorpe's Drama Llamas

- facebook.com/ellethorpebooks
- twitter.com/ellethorpebooks
- instagram.com/ellethorpebooks
- goodreads.com/ellethorpe
- pinterest.com/ellethorpebooks

www.ingramcontent.com/pod-product-compliance
Ingram Content Group UK Ltd.
Pitfield, Milton Keynes, MK11 3LW, UK
UKHW041414180426
11947UKWH00007B/121